T0095440

GENESIS DÉJÀ VU

The Beginning

DEXTER JAMES

GENESIS DÉJÀ VU
THE BEGINNING

This is a work of fiction. All of the characters, names, incidents, organizations, and dialogue in this novel are either the products of the author's imagination or are used fictitiously.

iUniverse books may be ordered through booksellers or by contacting:

iUniverse
1663 Liberty Drive
Bloomington, IN 47403
www.iuniverse.com
1-800-Authors (1-800-288-4677)

Because of the dynamic nature of the Internet, any web addresses or links contained in this book may have changed since publication and may no longer be valid. The views expressed in this work are solely those of the author and do not necessarily reflect the views of the publisher, and the publisher hereby disclaims any responsibility for them.

Any people depicted in stock imagery provided by Thinkstock are models, and such images are being used for illustrative purposes only. Certain stock imagery © Thinkstock.

ISBN: 978-1-4917-7377-2 (sc)
ISBN: 978-1-4917-7376-5 (e)

Library of Congress Control Number: 2015912230

Print information available on the last page.

iUniverse rev. date: 08/24/2015

To Jean

CONTENTS

Chapter 1

IN THE BEGINNING

The Arctic North Pole

Unbeknown to most of the earth's approximate six billion inhabitants a large, solid, piece of matter was hurtling towards their planet at an unprecedented speed. As with all asteroids and comets, only a few informed astronomers were monitoring its path with any great scientific interest. Its size and trajectory were no cause for concern, either to the professional or amateur star-gazer. Unbeknown to them, this innocent piece of rock rapidly approaching the earth's atmosphere was unique and was about to introduce a new chapter in the earth's history. During the millions of years since the earth's existence countless meteors of this type have entered the atmosphere and merely burnt to insignificance before reaching the earth's surface. One such exception occurred sixty-five million years ago. On that occasion, the result was not only the extinction of every species of dinosaur but also almost every air breathing being on earth.

Unbeknown to all the present inhabitants on earth, history was about to be repeated but in a very different way.

After travelling through the earth's atmosphere and disintegrating to almost nothing, the remnants of the small meteorite crashed into the ice and snow of the Arctic with so little force that observatories throughout the northern hemisphere registered an insignificant spike on the Richter scale, certainly not enough for further investigation. Fragments of the projectile were scattered over a widespread area around the steaming core of the meteorite that lay cracked open like a broken egg. To the naked eye, all that could be seen were the jagged edges of rocks, hundreds of millions of years old, that a few minutes ago had been hurtling randomly around the universe until the beckoning pull of earth's gravity provided it with a final resting place.

But these shards of stone once belonged to a planet that had disintegrated long ago, in a time from a by-gone age. The small planet had supported life forms similar to the simple single cell protozoa found on earth. Amongst this array of creatures existed a strain of microbes that flourished in an air enriched environment. These microbes survived because of a flexible trait in their genes that enabled them to adapt to their ever-changing environment, similar to many species on earth. The gobi is an example of a fish that can actually change sex as and when necessary; the wolf, which only breeds when enough elk is available to sustain the extra mouths to be fed. The characteristic of these microbes was the capability of shutting down its entire life support functions in inclement conditions, for an indefinite period of time. Now, the cold, pure, air of the Arctic began to penetrate the fissures of these alien rocks, enveloping the microscopic organisms with a life giving essential. The microbes that had laid dormant for millions of years, harboring in their ancient tomb were silently beginning to stir.

The cold was not a factor, compared to the extreme temperatures encountered during its journey though the millenniums -50c in the Arctic appeared positively balmy; their activated body structure contained a high percentage of glycerol which enabled them to withstand the cold. Slowly, they began to rise into the atmosphere, like an invisible army gingerly forming ranks after a long march and a short rest. Almost immediately they began to reproduce, the single cells splitting and creating more cells which split and created more cells - ad infinitum. The air provided them with an elixir, an elixir for life as they began reproducing with full abandon and as they did so the swirling winds at the top of the world began to cast the harbingers of death to the four corners of the earth.

Their first victim was an old male polar bear that had ventured too far north, probably in an attempt to quietly find a place to die. Ironically, its wishes were granted but not in a manner of its own choosing. The microbes invaded every orifice of the unsuspecting animal and those lucky enough to travel through the mouth and penetrate the respiratory system found themselves in Utopia. The high oxygen content found in the warm, wet, atmosphere of the lungs resulted in reproduction at such a rate that in a matter of seconds the bronchial tracts of the bear were clogged, causing an agonising, yet mercifully quick, death.

As the migration of the deadly microbes rapidly expanded across the top of the globe, all animal life fell victim, seals, polar bears, surfacing whales, birds and of course, humans.

An invisible, living fog had begun to drape a killing curtain of death over the earth and any air breathing creature was doomed to an agonising death.

The first humans to be stricken were five men stationed at a small meteorological observatory in the northern tip of the Canadian Arctic. They were innocently going about their business in the dark cold north unaware of the deadly peril that was silently approaching them.

Chapter 2

THE DEVASTATION BEGINS

The Arctic North Pole

Dave Simons, a happy go lucky type was a seismologist from the University of County Durham U.K. and he had just completed calculating the epicentre of the meteor impact that had occurred only thirty minutes ago. He estimated that their small enclave of buildings had escaped destruction by a mere 149 miles.

"We just had a close shave Chalkey," he shouted out to the cook who was his usual grumpy 'who gives a shit?' self. A retired sergeant from the catering corp. of Her Majesty's army Chalkey White had never gotten used to civilian life. A balding, pot-bellied bachelor, his lot in life was to cook for those who couldn't, in the most God-forsaken reaches of the world. Then, on his return to civilisation with plenty of hard cash he would booze and whore it up until he was broke and then repeat the whole process again. Apart from his ornery attitude he was indeed a great cook and in an emergency he was known to be unflappable as his years of army training would kick in, which would prove invaluable. But he was powerless to repel the enemy that was about to invade the sanctuary of their heated living quarters. The first indicator came when a representative from a Chilean research team, Miguel Santes began to choke and reach for his throat. He had been sitting next to Dave reviewing some statistics, suddenly, with no warning he stood and kicked away his chair. This caught the attention of both Chalky and Dave but before they could react they were simultaneously displaying the same afflictions. Eyes bulging, mouth wide open in a desperate attempt to reach for a breath that wasn't there. Their faces turning first red, then scarlet before finally turning a deathly blue as their bodies fought in vain for a whiff of life giving air. With flailing arms and bodies bouncing together in a macabre dance of death, they died. During the commotion, hot soup and food that was being prepared on the stove had been overturned and was now seeping towards dislodged electrical equipment. Grease from the cooker caught fire and in a matter of seconds the small hut was ablaze, propane gas tanks began to heat and explode and within minutes the observatory station was no more. The other two inhabitants of the station had been outside dressed to the nines in the latest technologically correct cold weather clothing, feeding their packs of dogs. Neither they nor the dogs were in a position to care if the place burnt down.

With a frightening speed the murderous microbes were breeding exponentially and continued southwards with their deeds of death. Even the worst chemical or biological weapons ever conceived by the super powers could never have had such a devastating effect as was being concocted by these silent, invisible invaders. Ironically, the purpose of such weapons was to enable enemy forces to occupy territory with minimum resistance and destruction - a feat that was being perfected by these invisible warriors. It appeared that history was indeed about to repeat itself, as they did 65 million years ago, the microbes were on the verge of killing every air-breathing being on earth. The theories that had abounded over the years. A cloud of dust obliterating the sun, the change in temperature that resulted in all the same sex being born which in turn led to extinction of the dinosaurs. Regardless of what the theories were, the reality was that the whole life-cycle of the earth was about to turn another revolution as the microbes travelled south.

Chapter 3

NORTHERNMOST SURVIVORS

The Arctic North Pole

Underneath the frozen ice-packs between Canada and Greenland in the Lincoln Sea the nuclear submarine USS Augusta was patrolling the ocean depths. Its official mission was to gather scientific data for a secret government project. So secret that Admiral John Stanford had no idea of the specific objectives of the mission. The 'need to know' principle was in full force and the civilian scientists on board were keeping 'mum' about the whole thing. Admiral Stanford was a wizened old veteran and his take was that the cold war was over and the necessity for nuclear submarines supporting long range inter-continental ballistic missiles was about as much use as tits on a bull. Especially in the Arctic, who is going to attack? Canada? Greenland? Hardly, in his opinion this was just a make work project for a friend of a senator. Nevertheless, orders were orders, and he had been in the navy too long to question his lot in life. A third generation matelot, he was a navy man right through to the cockles of his heart. He was of medium height but the once muscular body was now best described as portly. However, he was still active and made sure he participated in cardio exercise every day, even on board the submarine. A regime he insisted must be extended to all personnel serving on any submarine he commanded. His eyes were a startling blue and were the highlight of his ruggedly handsome face, hardened by his many years at sea. His career in fact had involved him in just about every theatre of war the U.S. had ever participated in during his tenure in the navy. From the Vietnam War right up to the Gulf War with a few other sorties in between that the media was never privy to. A widower, he transferred to submarines just after his wife died, fifteen years ago. He had two children a daughter, Lucille, living in Charlestown NC with her husband and two daughters. A son, a Navy Seal killed leading a team during an undercover mission during the Gulf war, leaving a widow and an 18 month old son living in Wilmington NC. For some reason visiting his children had never been the same since his wife died possibly they reminded him too much of her. Consequently, he had never seen his grandchildren although photos were regularly sent to him. As a result, his life was the navy and as with all career channeled individuals it was sometimes difficult to understand that his charges had lives outside this tin fish. As for civilians, that was even worse, he had no real authority over them, sure, he could pull the *'I'm the captain of this vessel'* routine but after a while that wears a bit thin, especially with the pair of female scientists that were now approaching him. Janet Delaney, the self-installed leader of the team was a Biogeographer studying the geographical distribution of living creatures and Mary Briggs was a Marine Biologist assisting Janet in her research. During the next two years they hoped to cover all the oceans, using the resources of the U.S. Navy, studying the effect of climate change on marine species and their survival expectancies in a Darwinian like research project. But some events had occurred during the last few hours creating a disruption to their research. Janet stopped in front of the Admiral and arms akimbo she delivered with her usual abruptness.

"Admiral, we believe there is a serious problem on the surface!" Janet said with some authority.

"Really Miss Delaney - and what is that?" The Admiral replied, trying to stay composed, still looking nonchalantly at the papers in front of him on his desk. He had arrived at that juncture of his career where he just wanted the simple life, give orders, see them obeyed and carry on. But this civilian was making the twilight of his career a living hell, this trip had forced his decision, on his return to base he would retire.

"Numerous carcasses of polar bear, arctic fox, walrus and seal have been sighted floating in the sea." Janet said as if this should be a startling revelation to the Admiral. It had already been reported to him that an unusual amount of dead animals had been sighted but until now it hadn't given him cause for alarm.

"So? That's where a lot of these animals die. We see them all the time." He replied, continuing his matter of fact poise.

"Not in this magnitude Admiral, there are hundreds maybe even thousands of carcasses floating out there. We would like a detachment of your men to select some samples so we can run some tests." Janet demanded. So there it was, the latest demand in a long string of demands that had continually tested his patience. Stanford paused momentarily before he answered. Here in front of him were two very beautiful women, in fact too good looking to be shut up in a submarine with 130 sex starved seamen. Janet was short with short dark hair and dark blue eyes that were covered by thick rimmed glasses. She generally wore 'frumpy' old fashioned clothes that belied a great figure. No nonsense, all business, she was too focused on her job to have any interest in the seamen on the submarine. Unlike Mary who would have loved to fraternize with the personnel but was kept too busy by her demanding boss. Mary was a few inches taller than Janet with short mouse brown hair and big 'take me to bed' brown eyes. These women were far different from the Admiral's poor late wife. She too had been beautiful but she never questioned the man's right to make the final decision. It was like a switch had been hit sometime in the beginning of the nineties he mused. One day we had men and women living and working as we had done for thousands of years, suddenly the switch was thrown and the whole world turned around. Now there were female senior officers and you had to think twice before issuing any orders in case they could be considered as sexual harassment. He was cognisant of this before answering, as calmly as he could.

"My orders are quite clear Miss Delaney. We are to continue on this course."

"Can't you call headquarters or whoever you have to contact and inform them that we have a potential ecological catastrophe here? I'm sure they would understand." Janet was insistent.

"As you are aware Miss Delaney, until midday tomorrow we are maintaining radio silence and -"

"May I remind you Admiral that your orders are to extend to us full co-operation and all the facilities you have at your disposal." Janet interrupted unceremoniously.

"And may I remind you Miss Delaney that your requirements do not include jeopardising the safety of my ship, my men or disobeying my orders." The Admiral replied, raising his voice an octave and not with a little hint of frustration.

Mary Briggs had been quietly witnessing this jockeying for one-upmanship. In fact, she had been witnessing this clash between the modern opinionated woman against the old-fashioned conservative, chauvinistic, male since they arrived on the submarine almost a week ago. At first she had been mildly amused but the incessant badgering the seamen received from Janet had gotten tedious to the point that she had alienated the two women from the crew. Much to Mary's displeasure. She was a work-hard, play-hard character who had been hoping for a month on board a submarine with her pick of flirtatious seamen at the same time as enjoying a once in a lifetime opportunity to study the flora and fauna of the Arctic first-hand. Miss Goody-two-shoes had put paid to that, shooing away any male that so much as looked at the women. Mary had met Jane at university and during those years of study Janet came across completely different, she appeared humorous and genuinely seemed to care about her work, traits she had in common with Mary. They quickly learnt that the Delaney family originally came from the same part of Ireland as Mary's grandmother, a further bond. So when Jane was offered the project on the submarine she was told she would need the services of an assistant with the appropriate experience, Mary jumped at the opportunity to work with her. She was beginning to regret that now as the Irish in her was beginning to boil. Up until this point she had, as usual, stayed in the background saying very little, it was time to say something.

"Admiral that activity recorded on the seismic monitor a few hours ago? It could have been a nuclear explosion, the Russians could be testing."

"Absolutely not. First of all, the readings do not support a nuclear bomb. Secondly, the Russians are not in a position to carry out testing without our knowledge and thirdly there is a treaty that prevents nations from testing in the Arctic." Stanford said.

"Treaties have never stopped countries before and after all, something did happen up there and an extraordinary large section of wildlife has been affected. Now, you have all the facilities here to test for radio activity and if it isn't that, we have the expertise to establish the cause of death. At the most, you will lose half a day. What do you say Admiral?" Mary asked. Well, here was a compromise. It wasn't a demand from a spoiled brat but a reasonable synopsis of what had occurred with a perfectly good solution. Admiral Stanford reluctantly agreed to order a detail of men to retrieve a carcass to carry out the necessary tests. He called in his number two, Lieutenant Hargreaves to carry out the orders.

Oblivious to the carnage that was occurring on the surface a detachment of divers were subsequently detailed to obtain the carcass of a dead polar bear. Meanwhile, the microbe invasion was spreading southwards at an alarming speed. Any air-breathing creature was being invaded by a multitude of minute microbes until they bred themselves to death in their host's lungs. A few of the off-spring at the top of the tracheal tubes were able to return to the atmosphere to begin their prolific reproduction cycle. The others remained in the bodies where their normal short life-cycles were played to the end, at the expense of their victims.

Their journey continued rapidly southwards over the continental shelf of North America, Russia and Asia killing everyone and everything in their wake. The further south the horde traveled towards the warmer climes reproduction began to increase to unprecedented rates.

Chapter 4

SAVED BY AN ACCIDENT

Maine U.S.A.

In Maine, an elderly couple was being admitted to the emergency ward of Portland General Hospital. They were still alive thanks to the skill and training of a pair of paramedics and an alert paper boy. Little Robbie Peterson had been delivering papers on this particular route for two years. During that time old John Hamax would be waiting at his white picket fence for his morning paper, weather permitting, accompanied by his old mutt, Pippa. On those really bad days, John would wait inside looking expectantly from the front window for his daily rag. On these days rather than toss the paper over the fence Robbie would make the extra effort to walk to the front door where John Hamax III would gratefully meet him and take his paper. This was a gesture not forgotten at Christmas time when a hefty tip was always proffered.

On this particular morning John was nowhere to be seen. It was cold, a light frost had blanketed anything that was exposed to the elements but it was a pleasant morning, one that would typically find John standing outside. Even so, Robbie would have expected to see John at the window. Concerned, Robbie lifted the latch to the neatly painted white gate and walked slowly up the narrow path leading to the Cape Cod style home. He peered through the window. Pippa could be seen wagging his tail, pleased to see him, but he appeared agitated. At the edge of the carpet was a small mound of the dog's excrement. Robbie realised something was wrong, neither John nor his wife would leave the dog like this. Robbie immediately dropped his heavy bag of papers, jumped the fence separating the Hamax's house from next door and ran up the path to the neighbour's house and began banging on the door. Dave Morelli was an out of work commercial fisherman, someone who for years had been up with the crack of dawn but during recent times had nothing to get up for. It was a few minutes before Dave finally answered the door but on seeing the concern on the paper boy's face and learning the circumstances he leapt into action. Running back upstairs to don some clothes he quickly reiterated the problem to his wife. Knowing the Lomaxs habits she didn't hesitate, she called 911 while Dave was dressing. Dave ran back down the stairs where a flustered Robbie was still standing and retraced his steps by jumping the fence. He went round to the back of the house and tried the rear door. It was locked but he knew if either of them were up they would be seen in the kitchen. There was no one to be seen. Banging on the door and shouting at the top of his voice brought no response, except the excited yelps of Pippa. Without wasting any more time he broke the glass on the door, reached in and unlocked the mortise lock and opened the door. Quickly he ran up the stairs with Pippa close at his heels. Modesty prevented him from bursting into their bedroom so he tapped lightly on the door.

"Mr. Hamax are you O.K.? Mrs. Hamax are you there?" Dave asked but receiving no reply he gingerly opened the door and saw two comatose bodies lying in the bed. He knew they had installed a gas fire in the bedroom and although he couldn't smell any gas in the air a sixth sense told him a lack of oxygen was the problem. He ran to the windows and fully opened them. It was at that time he heard the siren of the ambulance approaching the house. Quickly, he ran hell for leather downstairs to unlock the front door as the paramedics came bursting through. Following a brief exchange of words one of the paramedics returned to the ambulance to obtain some oxygen bottles while his partner was led to the bedroom by Dave. It was established the Hamaxs were still alive but barely. Then Dave noticed the cause of their predicament. Being an old-fashioned house there was a fireplace in the bedroom. Although fully modernized, they had opted to have the natural gas fire installed in the grate rather than block off the whole fireplace. Up until the early hours of the morning a brisk north wind had been blowing. It had apparently snuffed out the flames in the fire but the gas was still continuing to waft into the room. With both the door and windows closed the room had turned into a death-trap. Dave knelt down to turn off the small gas tap.

Now armed with this knowledge the two paramedics began to move into top gear. Oxygen was immediately administered and drips were inserted into their arms to provide the necessary life support via intravenous liquids. By now the commotion had alerted other neighbours and they provided assistance with the stretchers allowing more time for the paramedics to care for their patients. One of the rescuers had unwittingly stepped into the present previously left by Pippa and had subsequently trodden the mess up the stairs and into the bedroom. From the time of the initial call to their arrival in the emergency room turned out to be less than forty minutes. It was this speed and efficiency that saved the lives of Mr. and Mrs. Hamax. It was this accident that would also save the lives of Mr. and Mrs. Hamax while everyone else around them would be losing theirs.

Chapter 5

A GRISLY
REALISATION

St. Santia - Caribbean

The clear blue waters of the Caribbean offered some of the best scuba-diving in the world. The colours, marine life and aquatic vegetation were a far cry from the icy landscapes of a North American winter. Bob Grayling was one of four divers in a group chartering a small boat from their island resort. He was a handsome blue eyed man with a shock of unkempt blonde hair and a tanned well-built muscular torso almost void of body fat. He could easily pass for a Californian beach bum. His diving buddy for this dive was Maria Desouza a legal secretary from Toronto. She was an attractive slim, short red-head with dark brown eyes. She was generally shy and withdrawn due mainly to a history of being sexually abused by foster parents but Bob managed to bring the best out of her from their very first meeting. They had met at the International airport in St Maarten as they waited for a local flight to the small island of St. Santia where it was claimed was the best diving conditions in the Caribbean. Bob and his roommate, Tony Dilenti, found themselves waiting in line next to Maria and her friend, Marlene LeCroix. Fins and snorkels bulging from nylon nets carried by all four of them were a dead giveaway as to their intentions. Usually travelers on diving packages will rent the heavy equipment but when it comes to mask, snorkel and fins, no self-respecting diver could enjoy a dive using rented personal equipment. So naturally, with common interests apparent, a conversation began and they soon discovered they were all traveling to the same destination. When their flight was called, or rather their pilot, cum baggage-handler, cum navigator, cum tour guide, approached them they discovered they were the only passengers on the twin-prop to the island. Bob sat in the rear of the plane with Maria, he had found her accent both friendly and sensual, but then coming from Boston almost any female would have an interesting accent, well almost anyone, unless of course they came from New York. Tony sat quietly next to Marlene LeCroix, originally from Quebec but now a Systems Analyst at a large bank in Toronto. She was not a slim girl but nonetheless had a good, well, proportioned figure. Her eyes were a vivid green set in rosy red cheeks framed by long sandy coloured hair. She was a bubbly character; always smiling revealing a set of pearly whites that would have made her a poster girl for any dentist. Tony, an architect from Boston was of medium height but prone to weight gain and as a result, he always seemed to retain chubby cheeks and with it a low self-esteem. His brown eyes were always alert, looking, observing. His brown hair was fashioned in a college cut that never appeared to need combing. This unlikely pairing probably contributed to the cordial but nevertheless perfunctory conversation that was had during the short flight. The flight was bumpy and uncomfortable but not enough to dispel the expectation of a great holiday. Little did they know that this was to be the last flight of their lives.

The foursome was on only their second dive of the vacation and they were taking it easy. A relaxing forty minute dive at between 40 and 60 feet would not be too taxing on the system, no decompression times to worry about, yet the full beauty of the clear waters could still be appreciated. Bob signaled to Maria that it was time to return to the boat, she acknowledged with the globally known O.K. sign, forefinger and thumb forming an 'O' with the other fingers extended. They began a slow ascent to the surface. Even though it was a short, shallow dive risk of the 'bends' is ever present if ascents are made too quickly. They were now within visual range of the boat at a depth of 5 metres and approximately 20 metres distant, Tony and Marlene were finning languidly towards them. As they approached the surface Bob stretched out his arm above his head and slowly turned full circle looking above them for errant boats. The fact that a motionless boat surrounded by buoys and flying the 'international divers' flag, red with white diagonal stripes, was no guarantee an ignorant tourist in a high powered boat was not going to plough over some divers as they reached the surface.

Bob's hand broke the surface a few yards away from their chartered boat and he began swimming towards the ladder on the stern. A few seconds later Maria surfaced and instantly blew out her mouthpiece and shouted a large 'whoop' of pleasure. Bob returned the call and then called out to Dexter, the owner of the chartered boat. Normally, Dexter would have been on his feet watching the ever present bubbles in expectation of his charge's return, while barking out orders to his two sons as they assisted the divers back onto the boat. But this morning, much to Bob's displeasure, no-one could be seen. Grabbing the top rung of the ladder with one hand he bent his legs and reached down with his other hand to remove his fins. Lifting them out of the water momentarily to let the warm sea water drain off before he tossed them over the stern and onto the deck of the boat. Now he was able to step onto the bottom rung of the ladder without the awkward obstructions of the fins. As his head and shoulders rose above the stern he shouted out some good-natured ribbing to Dexter and his sons for not assisting him but his voice trailed to silence at the sight of three bodies lying in grotesque positions on the deck of the boat. For a few seconds he gazed hypnotically, unable to grasp the reality that was before him until he felt the bile in the pit of his stomach rapidly rising to his mouth. Instinctively he leapt sideways and backwards into the water where he retched uncontrollably. At first, Maria thought he was being his usual zany self but the sound and visual reaction of his discomfort wiped the smile from her face. She quickly removed her fins and tossed them into the boat and began to scale the ladder.

'No - don't go up there'. It was a desperate cry from Bob as he tried to reach for her arm to prevent her from seeing the ghastly sight. Bob was only a few metres from her but he was still wearing his air-tank and weight-belt and without the fins his movements were quite cumbersome. But with an effort he managed to reach out and snare Maria's weigh-belt to prevent her from peering over the top.

"Bob stop it. I don't like it - what the hell is wrong with you?" Maria was suddenly quite concerned. Admittedly, she had only met Bob a few days ago and how well can you really know someone in that short space of time? But this strange behavior was quite out of character compared to the Bob she had begun to know.

"You can't go up there Maria." Bob shouted at her. She turned to look at him.

"What do you mean I can't go up there? How the hell do you think we are going to get back to shore?" Maria replied, she looked away and tried unsuccessfully to continue to climb the ladder but again Bob's vice-like grip on her belt made it impossible. However, she was too uncomfortable with the situation to let go of the ladder and slip back into the water with a man who was beginning to act a little too crazy for her liking. The impasse was broken by the sound of Tony and Marlene simultaneously breaking the surface of the water only a few metres away. Not fully understanding the pose of their two fellow divers Tony swam towards them and began to tread water while removing his mouthpiece.

"What's up guys? You two look as though you've seen a ghost." At Tony's question Maria looked at Bob for an explanation. He waited for a few seconds while Marlene joined the trio at the back of the boat and then he told them what he had seen. At first they didn't believe him, it was too incredulous. They had seen no other boats during their dive and it was unlikely that food poisoning could have killed all three men at once and so suddenly. Tony motioned with his head for Maria to get down so he could look for himself.

As she climbed down Bob released the grip on her belt and she immediately swam ungainly, without her fins, over to Marlene, still uncertain about Bob's state of mind. Tony didn't look as long at the bodies as Bob had and the fact that he was expecting a grisly sight his reaction was far more controlled. He slowly slipped back into the water and the look on his face was all the confirmation the girls needed.

"So what do we do now? We have to get back to the island in the boat. I can't swim that far," Maria asked, her voice beginning to crack with emotion. They all considered this for a few seconds then Bob took control.

"Tony and I will have to get into the boat and we will move the bodies. We've all done enough diving trips on boats to know how to get this baby back."

"I can't go up there with three bodies lying there, can't you throw them overboard?" It was Maria who was now moving towards being hysterical.

"Be reasonable Maria we can't just dispose of the bodies, the authorities are going to want to know what happened. We'll find something to cover them up, don't worry." Bob said soothingly, he was trying to console her and he gave her arm an affectionate squeeze and as he did so he felt the goose bumps that had emerged all over her body. Without further hesitation Bob climbed the ladder, closely followed by Tony. On boarding the *death-boat* they rid themselves of all their equipment and stowed it safely away. Immediately, they began to look in the many cupboards that were located all over the deck of the boat. In one of the cupboards they found a large canvas awning that looked as though it was used for covering the exposed part of the deck either from the sun or rain. Then they positioned the three dead men together, as best as they could and covered them with the canvas. Once this was accomplished they went to the rear of the boat and helped the two girls onto the deck. Marlene had calmed down but Maria was still bordering on the hysterical. They all walked gingerly past the canvas never taking their eyes off it as if they were expecting something ghoulish to happen unexpectedly. At that second Maria in her nervousness stood on one of the ropes trailing from the canvas and with her other foot she tripped on the same piece of rope which flung her head long onto the covered bodies, dislodging the canvas and leaving her face to face with the grisly, contorted death mask of the youngest of Dexter's sons. Her scream was loud enough for her to have been heard on the island, had there have been anyone alive to hear it. Bob turned and picked her up and was ready to slap her face in the time honoured fashion for breaking a woman out of their hysterical fits but it was not necessary, she fell into a merciful faint. Just as quickly Tony had reached down and covered up the body before Marlene could see anything, her view had been obstructed by Bob and Maria. Tony carried Maria's limp form down the wooden steps into the cabin and laid her down on a bunk. Marlene followed him down and stayed beside her friend. Topside Bob proceeded to start the engines, Tony came back up the steps and began hauling in the anchors. Once the anchors were on board and secured he retrieved the diving flag. Within minutes they were headed for shore, leaving the marker buoys that Dexter had secured where they were in case they needed to return to the spot after reporting to the authorities.

As they approached the marina everything appeared to be normal, they could see the sun worshippers lying on the beach and a few swimmers basking in the sea. The first hint that something terrible was wrong occurred when Tony, who was standing on the prow, sighted a wayward snorkeler directly in their path. He yelled to the man to get out of the way even though he knew it was futile. If he couldn't hear or feel the boat approaching there was no way he would hear anything else. He signaled to Bob who slowed the engines and gently steered the boat towards the swimmer.

"Hey bud, you're a long way from shore." Tony shouted, but there was no response. Then he noticed the body was lifeless, stretched out in classic snorkeling form but absolutely motionless except for the bobbing of the waves. He unhitched a boat-hook and gently turned the swimmer over.

"Oh my god!" Tony squealed and immediately dropped the boat-hook as though an electric current had been transmitted right through it from the thing in the sea. The body had the same macabre look as Dexter and his sons that he had seen when he first looked into the back of the boat. Bob came running towards him retrieving the boat-hook. He quickly glanced down at the mutated form in the water, he didn't need to look twice to understand that whatever killed this poor sod had killed Dexter and his sons.

"Tony get the binoculars, they're hanging next to the wheel." Bob shouted at Tony who was still gazing down at the body that had now returned face down in the water. At Bob's words he snapped out of his trance and proceeded to fetch the binoculars. He passed them to Bob and as he did their eyes met. It was as if they knew what was going to be discovered on the beach but they had to look, they had to know. The binoculars were high powered U.S. army issue, who knows how Dexter had gotten hold of them. Tony brought them to his eyes, made a few adjustments to the focus and set his sights on the beaches along from the marina. There was no movement. He began to scan further along the beach. To the naked eye the view was just like an advertising feature in a travel brochure, the greens and blues of the sea lapping over the sun-drenched, white, beaches populated by scantily clad tourists languishing on lounges beneath the shade of palm trees. The reality of the view, revealed with the assistance of the binoculars, was like viewing a giant photograph, except the waves and the fronds of the trees were providing some movement to the vista. Homing in on one of the bathers lying on a lounger his worst fears were realised. Requiring further confirmation he turned his attention to the furthest point on the beach, a small bar that provided snacks and refreshments. By this time of the day the place would be humming but the bartenders and patrons were lifeless. One of the servers was lying prostrate on the floor and the few customers were strewn in various ungainly positions around the tables and floor of the bar.

Slowly he brought the binoculars down from his eyes and let them hang from its lanyard round his neck. He nervously wiped his hand across his mouth and looked down to the cabin at the two girls. Maria had recovered and was being comforted by Marlene but all eyes now turned to Bob.

"There's no easy way to say this, but while we were diving something has killed everybody in sight." Bob stated to nobody in particular. Involuntarily, both girls brought their hands to their mouths and Tony slouched down on the deck in silent shock. Continuing, Bob added, "what's more, I can't see a living thing out there, no birds, dogs, cats, nothing. Every living creature appears to be dead."

"This is too incredible, what the hell could cause this?" Tony asked.

"Whatever it is couldn't we still get it?" Maria shouted up from below but before anyone could offer any conjecture Maria broke into more hysterics. This time Bob did not hesitate, he jumped down to the cabin, bypassing the steps and slapped her hard across the cheek. She was silenced immediately but if looks could kill he would have been as dead as the bodies littering the shore. He took a deep breath and attempted to get some order back amongst them.

"In view of the circumstances I think we should dispose of the three bodies into the sea. Then we will head to the marina and attempt to get some sort of help from there. By phone, CB, radio, whatever. While Tony and I are topside maybe the two of you can make a start by trying various channels on the radio." Bob suggested, but he didn't hold out much hope that the girls would contact anybody although it would keep them busy and more importantly, it would keep their eyes averted from the grisly task Tony and him were about to perform. He looked at each of them and on receiving no response he climbed back on deck, cut the engines and began to move away the tarps covering the three bodies. They found two pairs of work gloves in a work box on the starboard side of the boat and began moving the bodies to the side of the boat. In case their cause of death was something contagious they made sure not to let any of their own exposed skin touch the bodies as they tossed them overboard. None of the four survivors were particularly religious but each had their own silent prayers as every splash accepted another soul into the sea. Meanwhile, Maria and Marlene tried unsuccessfully to tune into any voice communication surfing the wavebands on either the ship's radio or the local CB bands. In addition to the main radio there were a couple of hand held radios that the girls brought topside after they heard the third and final splash. The two men were sitting down regaining their breath, it had been quite exerting tossing three fully grown men overboard, especially immediately after a good dive. As they all sat topside with the boat bobbing gently in rhythm with the gentle waves there was a realization of an eerie silence that they all seemed to notice for the first time. With the engine off there were no sounds of gulls squawking, no jet-skis or speedboats powering through the waves, no hawkers shouting their wares and no calypso steel drum band supplying background music. Just the rhythmic sound of the water lapping against the side of the boat and the surf breaking over the beach. In other circumstances it may have been idyllic but it sent shivers down their spines. Bob broke the silence.

"Let's go. The quicker we get to shore the sooner we can reach help."

Bob started the engine, pushed the throttle to almost full and they began to speed along the smooth blue sea. Nobody spoke during the trip back to the marina. Bob searched the horizon as he operated the helm and Tony searched in vain with the binoculars for any sign of life. Maria systematically tried raising a response on every band on the CB while Marlene tried the same thing on the ship's radio. All that was heard was the familiar cackle and the usual frequency noises, but no sound of any people. They found Dexter's cell phone and tried dialing various contacts from his list, to no avail. Bob slowed the engine as they went through the entrance of the marina, the girls came topside and all four of them searched fruitlessly for signs of life. Bob had the boat just above idle speed as he approached the dock, he had never had to dock a boat of this size before and he knew from experience that docking can be an adventure even for the most experienced boaters. But with little wind and a 'straight-in' parallel dock any onlookers, had there have been any, other than those on the boat, would never have known he hadn't accomplished this many times before. Tony went forward and dropped the tethered fenders over the docking side of the boat. He then prepared to jump onto the old, rickety, wooden dock to secure the boat. As the fenders touched he jumped athletically from the boat and tied the bow and stern lines. So now with the boat secured Bob turned off the engine, climbed off the boat and walked with Tony towards the small bamboo hut that represented the boat charter's office. The girls remained on the boat, watching them walk towards the office while maintaining their vigil on the radios. As the men went towards the hut bodies could be seen floating in the sea beneath the very planks they were walking on. As they approached the hut they could see even further carnage in the cool shade of the trees. Inside the hut, Theresa, the young girl who had booked their charter lay against the back of her chair, her arms hanging limply beside her, head reaching backwards gazing open-eyed at the ceiling. The once beautiful local girl with her low cut blouses and short miniskirts that brought in more repeat customers than any medium of advertising could ever do was just another fatality.

Bob walked through the makeshift door and picked up the telephone receiver and waited for the dialing tone. On a cork notice board on the wall was a list of emergency numbers including the coast guard, police and emergency services in the main town of St. Johns. One by one he dialed them all, each call proving fruitless. He began to think that because of the disaster the phone lines were not performing correctly. To test them he dialed the long distance number of the Hurricane Centre in Bermuda, he knew it wasn't hurricane season but at least there should be someone manning the phones. He received a recorded message referring him to another number which he dialed and waited. As he waited a chilling, tingling fear began to run through his entire body. After two minutes with no reply he hung-up. He looked at the board again and dialed the Miami Hurricane Centre where there was sure to be someone but that yielded the same result. Finally he dialed the Massachusetts coast guard whose number was etched in his memory from all his diving expeditions off the eastern sea-board. To his astonishment, this 24 hours a day, seven days a week, 365 days a year establishment was not replying to his emergency call.

"Tony, this is unreal," Bob's voice was barely audible, "I can't reach anybody. It's like we are the only people left alive in the whole world."

Chapter 6

MUDDLING
IN MAINE

Portland General Hospital – Maine U.S.A.

John Hamax felt sluggish as he slowly came out of a deep, deep sleep. His eyelids felt like lead but he knew he was awake so he forced his eyes open. The light was intense, this wasn't his bedroom something was wrong, he must still be dreaming. He reached over to touch Joan, his wife of 42 years but his arm thrashed in thin air. Again he opened his eyes fighting the light until he could focus on his surroundings. He felt the mask around his mouth and a slight panic began to grow in the pit of his stomach. His hand reached up and removed the mask, sitting up he looked around at his surroundings. He was in a hospital room, beside him was another bed and as he looked across he couldn't be sure whether it was his wife or not. Another wave of panic began to envelop him. The last thing he could remember was going to bed and falling asleep now here he was in what appeared to be a hospital room. He looked behind him and he saw the emergency buzzer that communicated with the nurse's room. He reached for the button and pressed. In the distance he could hear the sound of a bell ringing and in the corridor he saw the reflection of a red light flashing above the mantle of his door. He released the grip on the buzzer and gently laid back against the pillows, his whole body relaxing in the knowledge that help was only seconds away. As the seconds went by the panic began to return. Something wasn't right, if he was in the hospital why hadn't anyone responded and come to attend to him? In fact, except for the sound of the emergency bell, that he had invoked, the place was void of all the normal sounds you would expect to hear in a hospital.

It was like a living nightmare, regardless of the consequences, it was time to take action. He swung his legs off the bed and attempted to stand up. A momentary spell of dizziness overcame him but when it passed he walked tentatively to the end of the bed keeping both hands flat on the sheets for support. For his age he was a spritely, slim man with a full mane of grey hair. Soft spoken and gentle with it, he was a kind good natured man always upbeat. At the end of his bed was his chart. He reached for the chart with his long arms and fingers and lifted it off its hook. He tried to focus his ice blue eyes as he sifted through the pages trying to decipher the medical 'gobidlygook'. This was no small task without the aid of his reading glasses. In fact, there was very little he could make out, except for an entry handwritten in block capitals on the very last page 'GAS INHALATION - SUSPECTED GAS FIRE LEAK'. His face cringed, the skin, like tanned leather as a result of years of exposure in open water during all seasons wrinkled like a Shar Pei. John couldn't know that the author of the entry was one of the paramedics attending the scene nor could he read where it stated how close to death both he and his wife had been. At least now all the tumblers had fallen into place and he began piecing together what had happened. Joan had always been leery of that damn gas fire in the bedroom, he thought, 'it will be the death of us', she would mutter every time he turned it on. Thinking of her triggered an immediate reaction. 'Oh my God, Joan!' Dropping the chart it clattered on the linoleum floor as he staggered over to the only other bed in the room. There was Joan, ashen faced but breathing steadily. He held her hand in one of his and brushed the hair from her forehead with his other hand. The tears began to well in his eyes as he called her name. As usual she was right, that damn gas fire was almost the death of them and it still might be the end of Joan.

As if it was a signal, Joan slowly opened her eyes and called his name. It was almost unintelligible, distorted by the oxygen mask and the hoarseness of her voice but it was the most beautiful sound John had ever heard.

"'Joan. Joan. You're O.K. I'm here. Can you hear me?" He asked with a slight tremor in his voice. He was looking at her beautiful face. The once long black hair was now a cropped grey, her face was much older than it once was but it still retained the beauty John had fell in love with all those years ago. Where he was tall and slim, she was short and had gained a little weight over the years. Not that John was noticing that right now, his only concern was for Joan's wellbeing.

"I can hear you, what's wrong? Where are we?" She replied hoarsely.

"We're in the hospital, dear. It was that damn gas-fire but we're O.K." He replied with obvious relief and gently, he reached up and removed the mask from her face.

"Humph - we'll discuss that later." She said with great effort. "I'm so dry. Can you get me a drink of water and something for my headache?"

"I'll go and find someone, I need a drink myself. Surprisingly, nobody has come by. You would have been marched in front of the nurse parole board if you had left patients like this," he bemoaned.

"Oh, quit complaining and go find someone," she admonished him.

Gingerly, John took short baby steps to the door. The red light above him was still flashing as he held onto the doorjamb and peeked into the corridor. The sight that befell him made him return his head to the room with his eyes tightly closed and beads of perspiration beginning to form on his head. He thought perhaps that because of the gas and the oxygen he was a little light-headed. Combined with the blinking red light this had created a 'flashback' to his days as a paratrooper during the war. Admittedly, he had never truly been affected the same as some war vets had been but what else could explain all those bodies that he had just seen in the corridor? Slowly he opened his eyes and looked across at Joan who was still lying peacefully on her back, unaware of the panic that had just gripped him. Never one to shirk his duty, John took a deep breath and stepped into the corridor.

The bodies were not a figment of his imagination. They were real. Strewn all over chairs, beds, trolleys, gurneys, bodies of all shapes and sizes. The only common denominator was the bulging eyes, the white mucus looking gel omitting from every facial orifice and the ghastly look of terror transfixed on their death masks.

John's legs felt weak, he had witnessed death before but he had never gotten used to it. Even with nothing in his stomach but bile, he began to retch uncontrollably. After a few deep breaths he tried to ignore the carnage and headed for the nurse's station where the emergency bell was still ringing. No solace was found there, the nurses in their crisp, white uniforms were lying, sitting in various undignified positions but still at their posts. "Well that explains the lack of response," he said to himself. John picked up the nearest phone and dialed 911. No reply. He looked up at the clock, it was 2:30 p.m. there was something else that was bothering him, the sound of traffic, there wasn't any. He sidled over to the window and looked outside. He was obviously in the emergency ward, which was on the ground floor so his vision of the main road was limited. But he could see enough to determine that the traffic wasn't moving and the sudden demise of the drivers had created countless accidents along the highway. Over to his right he could see a TV. Slowly he walked over to the set and turned it on. One by one he changed the channels. Each of the stations he turned to were airing out of focus scenes or emitting a high humming sound which you normally receive from those channels that terminate transmissions at night. He checked at the back of the set to ensure the set was on cable. It was, which meant that these stations were from all over the country. Finally, some live action appeared on one of the stations, his heart skipped a beat with the hope that there was someone he could contact, until he realised it was a recorded review of last night's NBA games. He gave the dial one more flick, there; reporting even in death was the CNN announcer lying prostrate on the news desk. No sound was emanating from the television, no life appeared on the screen. This was CNN, this was Atlanta. He was in Maine and there didn't appear to be another living soul in between, except him and his wife. Not for the first time to-day he remembered his wife. Oblivious to the bodies he fumbled around and turned off the annoying bell before filling a jug with water from a water-cooler. He then took two cardboard pyramid shaped cups from the holder and returned to his wife.

By now his wife was sitting up in bed propped up by her pillows as if waiting for her first coffee of the day, which he brought up to her every morning. As he walked towards her she could see he was physically shaken but his wife put his appearance and shaking hands down to the effects of the gas.

"John, come and lay down. You shouldn't be doing this; the nurses should have fetched the water. You've just been through a terrible ordeal," she whispered sympathetically.

"You've never said a truer word Joan," he paused as he poured some water and passed a cup to his wife, "Joan, I don't know how to tell you this. We're the only people alive in the hospital. In fact, as much as I can make out, we're the only people alive in the whole country." Joan just stared at him. He had always been a practical joker and in all of their forty-two years of marriage she had never mastered the art of knowing when he was being serious or otherwise. Under the present circumstances she just didn't appreciate his timing.

"Oh John, this isn't the time for your jokes. That gas must have affected you more than you think." She told him as she thumped her hand on the bed and shook her head in exasperation. "What did the doctor say? When can we go home?" John just looked at her sadly, the tears were beginning to well in his eyes as he saw the frustration of trying to convince someone that he couldn't find another living soul and what's more, he was scared. Scared because he had no idea as to what had happened. "Joan, I'm serious. There are bodies out there in the corridor. Bodies on the streets, the TV. Stations are dead, go-ahead try the radio for a real voice, you won't find one. I called telephone numbers, no reply. Something has happened, it looks as though everyone has been asphyxiated, except us. I guess we survived because we had on the oxygen masks. Joan please believe me, a major catastrophe has occurred, there appears to be just you and me left." What he was telling her was incredible, too unbelievable for words but the sincerity in his voice, the tears flowing down his cheeks; this was the serious John talking. She turned round to the radio built into the wall and turned it on. She fiddled with the tuner and picked up a station playing music, she looked at her husband as if to say, 'there, so much for your tales'. But he merely po-pooed it as piped music. She tuned into another station where people were debating some political issue. Again, she offered the same smug look but John pointed out that they were discussing a vote that was going to occur in the senate, which in fact happened last week, so it was a recorded program. All the other stations were either static or playing piped music, there was no live voices. It was slowly beginning to dawn on her that John was indeed telling the truth and there was no one else alive – until they heard the unmistakable, shrill sound of a phone began to ring, first one, then another.

Chapter 7

VACATION CUT
SHORT IN THE
ISLANDS

St. Santia - Caribbean

A feeling of pure helplessness was overpowering the four vacationers. The girls had joined the men in the hut and they had tried all the local emergency numbers. They had dialed long distance to their respective families, places of work, newspaper offices and television stations. They had tried all wavebands on all the radios in the hut, both commercial and personal sets. All attempts were unsuccessful, there appeared to be nobody else left alive - anywhere. Nobody spoke as a hollow, numbness seemed to envelope them. They were unsure of their next move that is until Maria declared she was dying of thirst which was when they realised, they had not eaten or had a drink since well before their dive. That was when the questions began to arise.

"Will we be able to drink the tap water? Whatever has caused this could have contaminated the water, couldn't it?" Marlene asked as Maria nodded her head in agreement. They all contemplated that for a while until Bob replied,

"I don't think so. We were in the water and we're fine as are the fishes. I believe that what caused this was in the air and affected air breathing creatures and whatever it was now appears to be either dormant or dead, otherwise we would have also fallen victims by now." He said it with a conviction that was not totally convincing.

"If it was in the air it could be like a dust just lying around contaminating anything it touches. In which case what is it?" Tony said and then answering his own question, "I think it could be one of those chemical warfare toxins that some terrorists have let loose."

"If that's what has happened, somewhere, someone is alive." Bob replied. "But I doubt it. No, I think this is some kind of natural phenomenon. Don't ask me why I think that, I don't know. And if it was some fanatic we certainly don't want to let him know we're alive."

"What makes you think it's a him?" Marlene asked quite indignantly.

"My apologies, Marlene, yes this particular nutter could be a woman," Bob was rolling his eyes and shaking his head as he retorted, "although I hardly think this is the right time to open a debate on sexual equality."

"That's the trouble with men, it's never the right time to discuss equality." Marlene stated categorically but before anymore could be said Maria, knowing her friend's views stepped between the two, her arms extended in an effort to keep them apart as if she was a boxing referee. "This is not doing anything for my thirst guys. What are we going to do?"

"'I think we should go to the store and drink bottled water and only eat canned or sealed food until we can get a handle on exactly what has happened. Who's game?" Bob asked. Everyone nodded their agreement and they left the hut. They retrieved their personal belongings from the boat and carried them to the car park that serviced the marina. Outside was a really old Mini-Moke that had certainly seen better days. Bob and Tony had driven one of these on a previous diving trip. It had been explained to them that it is a type of Mini made well before BMW brought out the modern version. Built in Britain during the sixties the Moke was like a baby Jeep built on a mini chassis. It was open topped, had a low fuel consumption and was an excellent vehicle for driving round the island, almost like a gas golf cart. They 'commandeered' the vehicle and set off for the small group of stores located about a mile away. Bob was elected driver and as he pulled away he instinctively reached to turn on the radio. The absence of any sound was depressing but he kept it on anyway, just in case. They left the beach area and drove along a road bordered by palm trees and hibiscus plants. With the wind blowing gently by them and the sun shining in a flawless blue sky the tranquil setting reminded them that this is what they were here for. Unfortunately, as they turned into the small car park servicing the collection of stores the full reality of the recent devastation came flooding back. Bodies littered the streets and in one of the supermarkets they had actually piled on top of each other while they had lined up at the cash registers. The girls couldn't look; they just sat in the back and held each other. Bob headed for a small convenience store at the end of the line of stores. His reasoning was that there would be fewer bodies there. He stopped the car as close as possible to the door and put on the hand brake. Leaving the car running Bob and Tony climbed out of the car.

"Any special orders ladies?" Tony asked but there was no reply from the girls so he quickly turned to catch up with Bob who was already entering the store. There was only one body in the store, which they assumed was the owner and he had died next to the cash register in the corner of the store. As a result, the entire store was clear of any obstructions and they went freely about their looting. They piled some items into a wire hand-basket, bottled water, canned drinks, cheese and cracker lunches, packaged meat, canned fruit, a can-opener and some flashlights and batteries. There was plenty of fresh fruit but still unsure of the cause of the devastation they were reluctant to handle it, with the exception of the bananas as the thick skins would have protected the actual fruit.

Within a minute, they were back in the car and as quickly as they came they were back on the road to the beach. They stopped at a small empty car park close to the beach. There were some picnic tables and benches which overlooked a part of the beach that was devoid of bodies. Just before they began to eat their purloined lunch another fact of life came to their attention. With all the excitement they had failed to notice the demands of their bodies and the need to relieve their bladders was becoming desperate. Surrounded by bushes and trees the men went to the left, women to the right and in somewhat discreet locations but not exactly dignified they did what they had to do. Fortunately, there was a stand pipe with a tap by the picnic tables where they all washed their hands and after using some face wipes that the girls had in their bags they were ready to eat their lunch. Except for the requests to pass around various food items nobody spoke during their lunch; the silence was only punctuated by the waves cascading against the beach and the slight breeze sighing through the fronds of the palm trees and the lush green vegetation. Tony was the first to finish his lunch; he guzzled down one of the bottles of water and banged the empty plastic container on the table. This had the desired effect of attracting everyone's attention.

"Without anyone to man the hydro plant I expect we will be without electricity within 48 hours. Without electricity the phones may kick into their own back-up system, which could probably last an additional 24 hours. The police station back there, it must be the best place on the island for communications. It must be full of personal computers, telephones and fax machines. I think we should spend the afternoon there phoning and sending faxes to try and get in touch with someone who can tell us what the hell is going on. What do you guys think?" Nobody replied at first then Maria, always the practical one provided her thoughts, "I agree, splitting up would not be practical and there certainly doesn't look like there's any help in the immediate vicinity. It is early in the afternoon right now but we have to consider where we are going to sleep tonight. The hotel will be full of bodies so we will need somewhere else to sleep and we need to stock up on food and emergency goods before it gets dark."

"Why not get some sleeping bags and mattresses and sleep in the police station. I bet they have some emergency rations in the building and if there were someone trying to reach the island that would be the place they would call. Meanwhile, we could continue calling round the clock." Bob offered his thoughts and everyone nodded their approval. The decision made, they collected their garbage and threw it in the large painted oil drum that doubled as a garbage bin. This was an act ingrained in their upbringing; it didn't occur to them that there was no longer anyone around to empty the bin.

The police station was a large, old, grey building built at the turn of the 19th century. Built by the occupying British, its Victorian style was accentuated by statues and cameos of Queen Victoria. On the short drive over Bob and Tony had come up with a game plan. They had decided to reconnoiter the building, clear the bodies and locate the communications room. When they arrived and entered the building they were surprised to find the inside was cool, maintained by well-placed ceiling fans. Even so, after two hours of moving 23 bodies from the various four floors to the basement they were sweating profusely. They had located the Communications centre on the main floor and dressed in protective overalls, masks and gloves found in one of the cupboards, they had cleared that level with the help of the two elevators. Bob dragged the bodies to one elevator and sent it down to the basement where Tony emptied it, sending the other back up to Bob. Once the room was cleared of bodies the girls were called in, as pre-arranged, to begin the arduous task of calling as many numbers as they could using whatever emergency numbers they could find in the station. Meanwhile Bob and Tony would continue to clear the building and search for suitable emergency rations and a place to sleep. Once their tasks were finished, they would help out making the telephone calls.

Bob and Tony returned to the communications centre with the good news that they had found the emergency rations. There were enough, flashlights, batteries, food, bottled water, sleeping bags and emergency medical supplies to last a regiment a week. Unfortunately, they were in the basement where all the bodies were. So, first thing in the morning they would use the elevator system to bring all the supplies to the main floor, for now they had brought more than enough to last them through the night. During the time it took for the men to clear the bodies the women had dialed approximately 100 numbers between them, with no success. Maria and Marlene explained the difficulties they were experiencing while Bob and Tony thirstily downed the remaining bottled water they had brought from the store.

"What we need," said Bob "is one of those automatic dialing machines that calls and starts talking all by itself." Not for the first time that day Tony banged an empty water bottle down as he finished drinking and headed for an adjoining door. Bursting through the door he began to look at the back of all eleven personal computers that were scattered throughout what was the island's Customs and Excise division. As he had hoped, they all had internet connections, for the purpose of looking up criminal activities on various databases across the world, including Interpol, the CIA and Scotland Yard. He looked up to see the other three looking at him like a crazed man as he was walking, stooped over between the back of the desks. He stood up arms outstretched smiling even more like a crazy man.

"Eureka," he shouted, "all these machines are connected to the internet. All we have to do is download the necessary telephony software, load it on to all these machines and 'voila' we have ourselves eleven operators." It was Bob who was skeptic, "but back at the office we have a whole team of telemarketers that are hooked into a big computer that calls the numbers."

"Yes but that's using a predictive dialer which is a tailor made system that dials the numbers and prompts a telemarketing agent when someone answers the call. That's much more sophisticated than we need. All we need is to call a number, if after a few rings, say four; it doesn't get a reply, hang-up and dial the next number. If we do get a reply a message will be played leaving a number to call. We can also set it up so that an alarm goes off for a successful call. O.K. this will take me a couple of hours to set-up. Why don't you all continue calling and faxing while I do what I have to do? Once it's rolling we will relieve you girls to cook dinner and set up our new home." Marlene was about to say something about the sexist categorisation, but again Maria cut in, "alright, we don't have much choice. You're the only one out of us who can do this. So for now we will oblige." She grabbed Marlene's arm and pulled her through the door into the other room, but her glaring eyes never left Tony who was already connecting to his repository of software.

Tony had developed various computer skills while he was studying architecture at university. He had learnt to surf the Internet and various other bulletin boards to obtain information on new techniques and Computer Assisted Diagrams. Like most career paths in the modern age, computer skills were a must and expertise in programming was a definite asset. Armed with this knowledge he began his quest, however, his estimate of two hours was underestimated by about twenty minutes. He had logged on and found the necessary software quickly enough. After downloading and setting this up on all the machines he searched for a voice simulation program. After a successful search he typed in a message that was translated by a voice simulator to say:

> *'We are stranded on St. Santia in the Caribbean. A major catastrophe has hit the island and we believe there are only four of us left alive. Please call 809 555 6437 repeat 809 555 6437. We need immediate help.'*

Finally, he located a database of telephone numbers for the northeast seaboard. This took some time to download and copy to the other ten machines. As that was being executed he used another machine to download some software that could read a telephone list and automatically dial the number. After four rings the call would terminate and the actions would be repeated. If someone answered the call the message would kick-in and a buzzer would begin sounding on the PC. He estimated that at best, each machine could contact between two and three numbers a minute. Extrapolated, this meant each machine would reach in excess of 4,000 numbers. So he separated them by states. Two machines covering Maine, one begins at the first telephone number in the list the other machine halfway down the list. This was repeated for the Vermont listing. There were three machines for Massachusetts and New

York, each computer beginning with a telephone number at a different third of the list and finally, just the one list for Maryland. He felt this system would give the best bang for his buck. He activated the first machine and monitored the first few calls. Satisfied this was working correctly he repeated the action with the second computer. Once this was functioning correctly he invoked the rest of the machines and monitored them randomly for ten minutes. After a few minutes the alarms on one of the computers began sounding to indicate a connection had been made. He rushed over to the terminal, his heart thumping with anticipation as he jotted down the telephone number displayed on the screen. It was a New York number, quickly; he turned to the nearest telephone and began dialing the number. He held his breath as he finished dialing the last number and he waited anxiously for the ringing to begin. In his mind eye he could picture every click as relay switches between the islands and the mainland made the connection to that destination in New York. The first ring sounded, and then the second, then the sound of a telephone being picked up. A voice replied:

> *"You have reached Eva and Marvin Horowitz.*
> *We are not able to take your call right now.*
> *Please leave your name, number and a short*
> *message and we will return your call as soon*
> *as possible. Have a nice day."*

The disappointment was devastating, of course they were not able to take his call if they were both dead. But the answering machines would still be working and the software he had used couldn't tell the difference between a real person and a machine. As if to endorse his thoughts two more machines began sounding. With not quite the same enthusiasm as he enjoyed after the first successful call he walked over to each machine and noted the numbers. He dialed the numbers but as he half expected, they were answering machines that replied. Realising his oversight he decided it was fruitless to chase around responding to buzzers that would only yield one of the banes of modern living. Fortunately, the main objective of his efforts was successful so he removed the code to sound the buzzer, he was content to leave technology to robotically do his bidding and return to the other room and assist the others.

In the other room Bob was busy faxing a message similar to the one Tony had created by simulated voice. Marlene and Maria were dialing furiously on the phones. It may have been the intense concentration necessary to achieve what he had just produced on the eleven machines, or his frustration at his oversight to expect answering machines. It could have been the disposal of all the wasted bodies or simply their general circumstances that triggered his reaction when he saw Marlene dialing out on 555-6437. His response was to slam the door and scream at her, "You stupid fucking bitch - how the hell do you expect anyone to reach us if you're dialing out on the very phone we've told them to call?" The veins on his neck were protruding and his eyes blazed thunder as he grabbed the receiver from Marlene's trembling hand and slammed it into the cradle of the phone. It was an ugly situation, Marlene too was teetering on the brink and she was about to lash out at this male adversary and damn the consequences. This time Maria would not interfere, she was tired, both physically and mentally and anyway, Marlene was a big girl and could look after herself. Marlene was also tired, tired of this male chauvinist, she didn't deserve this sort of verbal abuse and furthermore, she was not going to take it. The adrenalin in her body was boiling, her delicate hands were forming a fist and her arm was in the action of swinging at Tony's jutting jaw, when the phone rang.

Chapter 8

CONTACT

St. Santia - Caribbean

They all stared in skeptical silence at the ringing apparatus as if they had never heard the sound of a telephone before. Bob was the first to react as he lunged between the two warring factions and slowly picked up the phone.

"Hello." Bob said apprehensively as if an apparition was going to suddenly jump out of the phone's earpiece.

"Hello," replied John Hamax, "just got your message, what the hell's happening?"

"We were hoping someone could tell us. Who is this?" Bob replied.

"My name is John Hamax. We, being me and my wife that is, had a little accident during the night. Almost died of a gas leak. Been sucking oxygen until we came around, only to find we were surrounded by dead people. We thought the whole country was dead - that is until we heard from you." John explained.

"Mr. Hamax, my name is Bob Grayling, I'm from Boston but on vacation here in St. Santia. Something has happened here that has killed everyone on the island. With me are three others, we survived because we were scuba diving at the time. We don't know what has happened but we need to get back to the mainland so we're trying to contact someone to help us." Bob was almost pleading as he summarized what had happened to them.

"Sorry son, I'm afraid it looks like we're the only ones left alive. It appears to me that anyone breathing through tubes survived this, everyone else is dead. How or why, I don't know. I'm sure somewhere out there are pockets of people who survived whatever it is that did this. If we bump into them we will tell them about you. I'm an old coastguard man, here in Maine. I know where you are and I know how to get there. But my wife and I, well, we're not as young as we used to be and we might not make it, but we'll try. I think you are in a better position if you stay there rather than try and reach the mainland. You've got plenty of fresh water, natural fruit and vegetables. Yep, stay there is my advice, we'll try and reach you and pass the message on to anyone we come across. By the way, you say there are four of you, is that all men or men and women?" John asked.

"Two men and two women." Bob replied, wondering why John had asked.

"Well guess what?" He smiled lecherously as he replied, "it looks like it is down to you to create the next generation, otherwise Man could be as dead as the dodo if you don't have kids." John offered.

"Yes, I guess you're right," Bob replied slowly, "look, we don't expect the phones to be up for much longer will you try and reach us tomorrow, say, at this number at 3:00 PM? By then we may have learnt more about what has happened?"

"Sure will, but just in case, if we don't talk or meet again - good luck and don't forget, the next generation is down to you." John laughed as he hung up.

On termination of the call Bob slowly and meticulously replaced the phone in its receiver in anticipation of future calls. He explained to the others who had called and how they had survived the devastation as well as their predicament. So now the others knew the gist of the conversation and the extent of the extent of the devastation but Bob had held back on the procreation of the species speech. As they digested this they all slumped down into chairs contemplating their future on the island with no other human or animal contact. After a couple of moments Bob slowly stood and broke the silence.

"There's something else that John had said that maybe hasn't dawned on any of you yet," Bob's tone was ominous and the others looked at him with trepidation as he continued, "we may well be the only breeding pairs of humans left on earth. We are responsible for the survival of the human race." All eyes were on Bob, and then they looked at each other. Almost immediately Tony stood and flung his arms in the air in exasperation, "just as you thought nothing else could go wrong - now we're told we have to breed. Great, just fucking great. Two fags and two dykes stuck on a deserted island and they are expected to breed."

Chapter 9

EXTENT OF THE DEVASTATION

Around the World

What John Hamax had told Bob was quite prophetic. All cross the globe there were people who had survived the devastation by the grace of one reason or another. Just like the USS Augusta, there were submarines of all nationalities carrying submariners, heading to their home ports, but the only one carrying women was the USS Augusta. A few women had been serving on submarines in the naval service of a few countries but at the time of the devastation there was none whose submarine had been submerged. In Kiev, San Diego, Norfolk, Marseille and Southampton commanders were desperately attempting to make contact with their bases. Communications between the vessels were limited for security reasons as paranoia began to run amok amongst the senior officers fearing a return to the cold war and all of its consequences. Something was obviously wrong, terribly wrong and anxiety permeated throughout the ranks.

One by one the vessels returned to shore, one by one discipline gave way to anarchy as the full reality of the devastation began to hit home. Some of the more disciplined crews maintained order but thousands of others broke rank and on reaching dock, fled in futile searches for their families and loved ones. In a very short period of time, across the vast lands of the former Soviet Union, North America, Asia and Europe these thousands of sailors reverted from organised, disciplined men to scavengers and warriors. The human race had returned to its roots of millenniums long gone.

Submarines were not the only source of survivors. Assigned to oil rigs in the North Sea groups of men and women had been working in bathyspheres on the ocean floor when the devastating microbes struck. Due to various situations a few of the women survived but none would ever bear children. In these bathyspheres and small submersibles, male and female crews lived through the devastation but for all of them, survival of the species represented a new meaning. Some of the bathyspheres were controlled by operators at sea level and with no one left alive their occupants died a slow death in their watery tombs. Of the bathyspheres that made it to the surface there were those that had no transportation back to the mainland. They rationed what few provisions they had and caught fish which kept them alive through the winter until the summer. But with the summer came dry spells and with little rain or the ability to distill water, rationing led to disease, which in turn led to death. Of those that did have serviceable tenders very few made it back to land because of fuel, navigational or operating problems. Of those who made it back to the mainland the few surviving women found they were a highly prized commodity. Congregating in the ports used by the oil companies to transport personnel and provisions to the rigs, the surviving men resorted to bitter fighting for ownership of a woman. Individual winners tried to take flight with their prize but they were hunted and tracked down by gangs of sex-starved men. Invariably, the man would be killed and the woman ruthlessly raped and relegated to being sex-slaves to one or more groups of men. Those women who didn't have the courage to take their own lives survived a short diminished life of degradation at the whims of men returning to feudal law.

Throughout the seven seas, there were divers, male and female, some professional, some recreational who too had been beneath the waves during that small window of time as the devastation passed over them. They survived, but it was only the beginning of their problems. Of the scores of scuba divers, very few women of childbearing age had been diving at the time of the invasion and none ever lived for their loins to bear fruit. A pair of female divers off the Great Barrier Reef in Australia surfaced to find the occupants of their boat dead and their attempts to start the engines proved fruitless. With no search parties and nobody to hear or see their distress signals they took twenty seven days to succumb to dehydration and thirst. There was a group of five men and three women diving off the Bermudian coast. Unlike the Australian couple, they managed to successfully start the boat's engines but being out of sight of land and owning a very poor sense of direction, they motored off into the Atlantic and their subsequent deaths.

Others arrived back on terra firma intact, only to be faced with the same devastation that had greeted the foursome of St. Santia. The shock for some of those people proved too much and the survival time for many of them was short. Of the others, many drifted aimlessly for the rest of their lives never coming in contact with another human being. Some were fortunate, they met others and would form small settlements but they rarely consisted of both men and women. If they did, the women were either unable to bear children or well past child bearing age.

All around the globe airplanes plummeted as their lifeless pilots were no longer able to help their mechanical structures defy gravity. A few plunged into the oceans with their cargo of ready-made fodder for the marine life. Others crashed into the ground, bursting on impact into a great ball of flame. These fires added to the carnage being created in homes and manufacturing plants as uncontrolled appliances, furnaces and vehicles began to run amok. It wasn't long before major centres like New York, London and Chicago were being consumed by incandescent firestorms.

Deep beneath the earth's surface were miners who had escaped the initial carnage only to be faced with a slow, horrid death in the darkness within the bowels of the earth. Because the microbes did not penetrate too far below the surface the miners were totally unaware of what was occurring topside until they realized the lifts and mining equipment failed to respond. The lifts and power supplies were controlled by the operators above ground and with no one alive on the surface everything came to a grinding halt. Ventilation gradually deteriorated, lights dimmed and extinguished but even more alarming was the water. The continuous trickles of water that seeped into the mines began to accumulate as one by one the pumps began to fail. It wasn't too long before the surviving miners were slushing around in ankle deep sludge that slowly reached to knee height. In some cases the miners were able to climb to temporary safety but alas, it was only delaying the inevitable as they succumbed to drowning or asphyxiation. In most cases the lights on the miners' helmets became the only source of light but their battery life was limited and emergency lanterns were not accessible in many of the mines. Some miners were able to climb the lift shafts and operate the equipment to save their co-workers but in other mines the pitch darkness and lack of quality air prevented any timely escape. But more significantly, for the benefit of the human race that is, in all the mines where survivors were emerging from the ground there was not a single woman to be found. Mining of course is a very much male dominated career path, especially in the deep mines and the men who did escape spent much of their remaining lives learning to survive.

There were others in hospital, in similar circumstances to John and Joan Hamax. Patients who were alive because they had been breathing from an artificial apparatus. Unlike the Hamaxs, however, they were either incapacitated or on life support systems, irrespective, with no one to tend to them they died in their beds.

There was however, one area that was exempt from the attack of the microbes, Antarctica. As the microbes travelled south beyond South America, South Africa and Australasia their breeding and life expectancies rapidly began to decrease with a lack of hosts to support them. So it was that the wild life of the harshest and most remote area on earth remained intact. Penguins flourished as did a few seals and whales basking in the relative summer waters of the Antarctic seas.

A few birds, albatross especially, continued to fly the skies. More importantly, at any given time, especially the summer months, there are approximately five thousand researchers stationed at the pole. At first these researchers carried on blissfully unaware of the devastation happening in the rest of the world. The first sign of a problem was the lack of response to any form of communication. The next sign was the non-arrival of the expected supply ships. These ships were eagerly awaited not only to bring fresh food and heating oil to the communities but to ship in relief teams and take others home. Without the essential commodities, very few of the researchers made it through the first winter and subsequent summer. Some became very resourceful and hunted seal and fish; enough to provide some additional clothing, oil and sustenance. But even these supplements were inadequate against the brutal Antarctic cold and none survived a second winter.

John Hamax wasn't to have known but he had just communicated with the only human, breeding pairs in the whole world who had any realistic chance of surviving the devastation. In the entire world, yes. But most ironically of all, 2,000 miles above the earth, safe in their space station equipped with all the life support systems you would need were a Russian male and an American female. Ironic because it was part of a top secret joint Russian and American mission to monitor human breeding in space. The American astronaut, Amy Lovett, was already pregnant but she and her Russian partner, Ivan Brantovich, knew they were in dire straits from the satellite pictures being fed to their space station of the bodies and the fires now ravaging their planet beneath them; and of course the now non-existent operational communications with earth. They had, only recently, been joined by a supply ship carrying two more Russians and in turn they had said their goodbyes to two others who left in the very same craft that they had arrived in. One of the new arrivals, Boris Denekin, was an obstetrician who was there to offer pre-natal care and ensure a successful birth. A pediatrician was scheduled to board just prior to the birth to monitor the baby but that was obviously not going to happen now. The other Russian was Petr Yenin a cosmonaut who was present to ensure the space station maintained its orbit and ensure all things technical are operating as they should. Both he and Boris were scheduled to leave just after the birth of the child. Realistically, assuming Amy survived the birth of their child, there existed enough supplies to live in their bubble for another six months, child and all. In addition to Boris, both parents were doctors and between them the comfort level of their combined abilities for mother and child to survive the birth and beyond were high despite the now defunct support from the ground. They would nurture the baby to see it make its first smile and then as their supplies are depleted they would all die a quick death from cyanide capsules, as any hope of rescue was nil.

Chapter 10

REALISATION

St. Santia - Caribbean

The emotional problems of being the saviours of the human race were slowly beginning to dawn on the four remaining inhabitants of St. Santia.

"No way. There's just no way. Like, no disrespects guys, but there's no way I'm having your baby, either one of you." Maria sounded adamant as she strode up and down with outstretched arms, palms up in the manner of the international meaning for 'stop'.

"Hey Maria, you've often told me you wanted children, now is your chance!" Marlene offered.

"Yea. By artificial insemination. Not being fucked by a dick that's only seen the ass-end of another guy."

"O.K. Maria, there's no need to get personnel." Bob was trying to calm the situation. "Look, it's been a helluva day and it will be dark in a couple of hours and we've no guarantee on how long the hydro will last. The immediate problem is to survive the next few days and determine how we do that. Hamax may be wrong, there could be thousands of people out there. Right now it's not worth thinking about. What say we get some food and sleeping stuff together? After all, we are going to have to get used to rising with the sun to make full use of daylight." Despite being in a state of agitation they all silently agreed and began collecting materials for the onset of darkness.

For the next couple of hours they went about their business in silence, engrossed in their own thoughts about the future. For protection, they were all to sleep in the same room, although protection from what was open to debate.

Despite their determination not to be pigeonholed into the normal submissive female roles Maria and Marlene began assembling the emergency rations and began preparing the food. There was a small kitchen area on the floor with a sink and a microwave oven. They carried over some of the rations and sorted through the tins of stew, chicken supreme, powdered soups, milk, coffee, tea and sugar. The cans of water and desalination tablets they placed to one side. They wouldn't need them right now, after speaking with the Hamaxs they now felt the water was not the problem. But who knows what was to befall them in the near future? Their selection for supper fell on vegetable soup followed by the chicken supreme with rice, washed down with colas from the machine found in the hallway which was unceremoniously prised open by Bob. The meal was to be cooked on portable stoves found with the emergency rations. Until now their conversation had been restricted to the cooking of the meal until an innocuous action on Maria's part forced Marlene to burst into tears. All four of them had been so wrapped up in their predicaments that the full realisation of exactly what had happened hadn't been able to sink in. It wasn't until Maria's pathetic attempts at opening a can of chicken with one of the can openers from the emergency rations that it hit her. It reminded Marlene of one summer when she was much younger during a camping holiday in Quebec with her family. As usual, they had brought everything except the kitchen sink and of course, a can-opener. The only thing her father could purchase from the store on the camp site was of the type Maria was struggling with now. A small, flat oblong shaped piece of metal with a sharp triangular piece hinged to it that did the actual opening of the can. Fiddly at the best of times but perfect for emergency rations and camping because it was light and required less space than a conventional opener. Michel LeCroix was a big man, with big, strong hands and arms to match. He had spent his entire working life working for the logging companies in Quebec, yet he was as gentle a man as you would ever find. But when it came to wrapping his large sausage like fingers around a tiny can-opener his lack of motor skills were revealed amid a tirade of Quebecois profanities, silenced only by Marlene's mother deftly and wordlessly opening the can. Marlene related the story to Maria while laughing through her tears. Instinctively, Maria embraced the sobbing Marlene. Maria's background had been devoid of family values, growing up in various orphanages and foster homes. Sexually abused by an overzealous foster parent turned her against sexual contact with men. Not having any known close relatives, no close friends, except Marlene, the devastation had saddened her but hadn't really penetrated her cold exterior. But seeing Marlene so upset brought the tears to her eyes and a brief reminisce of happier times. Slowly they separated, wiped their eyes and calmly resumed their dinner preparations.

Tony checked in to the communication room to ensure the computers were diligently processing their mundane instructions, he knew it wouldn't be long before the last volts of electricity stopped powering these dutiful, immobile robots forever. It was ironic, he thought that these objects of man's technological accomplishments which were supposed to revolutionise the world, would be silenced by what appeared to be some natural disaster. When all was said and done, in spite of mankind's command of science, advanced weaponry and interference with nature, Mother Nature was still the mistress in charge.

He checked each screen to ensure the list of numbers were being dialed correctly and waiting the appropriate time for a response before continuing with the next number in the list. As he oversaw the silent workers a telephone number appeared on one of the screens that held him hypnotically and froze his every movement. The exchange that was being dialed at that very second on that very computer was that of his own telephone number back in Boston. He knew if he waited long enough this machine would be dialing his own telephone number and all those hundreds of miles away the phone in his apartment would be forwarding his call to voice mail. The apartment in which he had invested thousands upon thousands of foolish dollars to provide a sanctuary away from the blinkered, bias, perverted thinkings of the general population. A big plasma screen TV, stereo equipment, surround sound, lavish furnishings and antiques littered the spacious pad that overlooked the harbour in Boston. He had been an only child and when his father died while Tony was still young his mother's health deteriorated and she had died only a year ago. The only living things he was attached to were his tropical fish and Bob. Bob was here with him but it would only be a matter of time before the fish died with no neighbour to look after them and no functioning heater when the hydro quit. He snapped out of the numbing depression that had embraced him. O.K. so he wouldn't see his apartment again, as for the fish, he could have his own tropical lagoon here. Life must go on, only now it would be a full time effort. Just as it was when his ancestors lived in caves and hunted food for their existence. Nevertheless, he needed to get some air to clear his head so he ambled down the stairs and through the front door of the police station to take a few deep breaths in the dusk air.

Bob began clearing some space between lines of full-size lockers. This would make sure both factions acquired some privacy, at least for to-night. The lockers were of the normal military variety. Tall, thin, tinny things painted army surplus green. With the exception of a few empty ones all had locks of various shapes and sizes. For no apparent reason he decided he was going to break open one of the doors. No guilt was attached to the act, everyone was dead but it was with some remorse that he picked up a crow bar from the toolbox and forced open the lock. At the top of the shelf were a few coins, a small bottle of what looked like rum and a Swiss Army knife. Hanging inside the locker were the owner's civilian clothes and on the floor was a pair of sandals which obviously belonged to a very big man. He pocketed the knife as he thought that would come in handy and was about to close the door when he saw the pictures taped to the inside of the door. There was a photograph of a young, voluptuous, black girl lying seductively on a bed wearing nothing but a smile. In the bottom right hand corner was the word, 'Thanks', a signature and three large crosses indicating kisses. Immediately below the pin-up was a snapshot of an elderly couple accompanied by three adults, two men and a woman. Beneath that, was a family portrait of a man, a woman and two children. The man in the portrait was one of the young adults in the picture with the old couple. This small time capsule obviously showed the owner of this locker with his parents and siblings in one picture and his wife and children in the other. As for the pin-up, that's something that will remain a mystery forever. These pictures of a happy functional family, whose spirits had been eradicated from the face of the earth reminded him of his family back in Albany, New York. His mother, a kindly soul, who forgave him for his sexual preference, unlike his father whom he still loved but hadn't spoken to in six years and now regretfully never will. He thought of his sister and the two nephews he had never seen. They moved out to California when his brother-in-law's company moved to Pasadena. They spoke often on the phone but anytime he mentioned travelling west to see them there was always some excuse from her homophobic husband that made it impossible. She hadn't said it in as many words but it was obvious her man had a problem with Bob being near the boys. He was surprised his melancholy wasn't greater. He was upset, but he would have expected the loss of his entire family to be devastating. Yet with the exception of a few other human souls scattered around the world, he was alive and the daunting task of remaining so, would not permit the indulgence of nostalgia or sentiment.

He slammed the door shut and continued with the task at hand. There was enough room to lay the sleeping bags side by side in their own segregated sections. Beside each sleeping bag he placed a flashlight and a truncheon, for reasons that were beyond him. At least, the box called them truncheons, to him or any other North American it was a nightstick. His task completed he went to assist the girls in preparing supper.

Bob rejoined the girls in the kitchen, offering compliments on the aroma of the food. After their spartan lunch and the hectic day they had experienced, the hot meal was the very thing they needed to lift their spirits. Just then Tony walked into the room brandishing bottles of wine, one in each hand, a white and a red. There was a bar nearby, who would have thought it, a bar close to a police station! He had entered the bar and from its fine wine cellar he selected a couple of bottles of their finest and even thought to return with four wine glasses. The girls served up the delightful repast while Tony took the orders for the wine. A cafeteria table was moved to the centre of the room and Bob draped it with a large St. Santia Police flag that would serve as a table cloth. The men set the table as the girls brought over their first meal as devastation survivors. A long cry from the all-inclusive hotel that they should have been dining at. Bob proposed a toast, "to-day has been the toughest day of our lives, but alive we are. We will have more tough days with even tougher decisions to be made, but at times like this we can pretend everything is normal. In fact, this is the new normal. Cheers!" He raised his glass and they all smiled, echoed his sentiments, touched glasses and took a sip of wine. They quietly ate their meals, speaking only when necessary and by the time they were finished, the sun was slipping beneath the horizon and it wouldn't be long before darkness enveloped the room. They had toiled constantly all day and now the meal was over the tiredness rapidly began to drain their ability to function. The electricity was still available but for how long? They decided to retire to their sleeping bags for a welcome early night. As soon as Tony and the girls had located their sleeping bags, flashlights and 'truncheons' Bob switched off all the lights and by flashlight he made his way to his allotted area. The quietness in the room was staggering. No sounds of insects, birds, animals or music could be heard and the darkness seemed to amplify the silence. Earlier in the day they had heard the sound of distant explosions but even they had subsided. It was all quite eerie and surreal. One by one, without a word, engrossed in their own thoughts, their flashlights were turned off and all four of them settled down and were soon fast asleep, until they were suddenly woken by the sound of a stranger dropping in.

Chapter 11

SURVIVAL STEPS

St. Santia – Caribbean

That night the only sounds that could be heard were the gentle breathing and light snoring of the four occupants in the room, until, that is, the very early hours of the morning. Then a quiet creaking sound began to emit from the floor above them. It got progressively louder as though a pressure was building and something was about to burst. Then burst it did. In a cacophony of sound the ceiling collapsed quickly followed by a torrent of water. The four occupants were awake with a start and they immediately reached for their flashlights and shone them in the direction of the commotion. There in the middle of this waterfall was a very large woman, arms raised and appearing to be coming towards them. Maria screamed as Marlene had hold of her night stick and was ready to defend herself and her lover. The others followed suit while Bob felt for the light switch. The lights came on to reveal a large police woman who had obviously been a victim of the devastation. She was hanging by her arms which were wedged between the beams of the ceiling, her legs had fallen behind a desk which made her lean forward giving the appearance that she was moving towards the four occupants. It had been a shock but everyone was safe and after further investigation it became apparent that a water leak had occurred above them so Bob and Tony climbed the stairway to determine exactly what had happened. For safety purposes they turned on every light as they went up the stairs and when they were on the floor above their sleeping area they gingerly walked across to the source of the leak. It wasn't difficult to figure out. There was a small women's washroom that they had missed when they were clearing out the bodies. Obviously, the lady had been in the middle of washing her hands when the devastation claimed her. The tap was slowly running with the plug firmly placed in the drain of the wash basin. Consequently, it had overflowed and eventually soaked though the flooring. The dry wall near the wall was the most exposed and the water had built up there until it was saturated and could soak up no more. It was only a matter of time before the buildup of water would prove too heavy to support both the wet ceiling and the large lady before inevitably giving way. Bob turned off the tap and removed the plug. Realizing there was no more they could do for the time being they retraced their steps downstairs turning off all the lights as they went. They explained what had happened to the girls and proceeded to free the young police woman from the ceiling, which was no mean feat being as big as she was. Eventually, they managed to extract her hands from the beam and man-handle her to the elevator. They pressed the button for the basement and sent her down to her final resting place with the other previous occupants of the building. The water had almost stopped running now, a few drops were still falling but the excitement was over and they all cautiously returned to their sleeping quarters to try and get some badly needed sleep, yet still wondering what was going to befall them next.

The next morning they awoke as generations of early man had done, with the dawn. And like those early generations, their first inclination was survival. As with most groups under times of stress and emergency the people looked to a leader and out of the bickering and animosity it was becoming increasingly obvious that Bob was theirs. During the body clearing Bob had noticed a large meeting room on the top floor of the building. On the door was a poorly, hand written sign naming it 'The War Room'. Bob found it difficult to imagine anything close to a war occurring on this picturesque island but figured this verbiage was another inheritance from British Colonialism. The good thing was that the room contained a white board, markers, reference books, flip charts and all the usual paraphernalia associated with a working meeting room. It extended the length of the building and provided a good view of the immediate surroundings. More importantly there was a large map of the island on one of the walls together with a pile of pocket sized maps. Bob suggested they go up there to discuss their next steps. It was only a couple of floors above them so Tony carried their larder, a purloined ice box obtained from their previous day's foraging, to the top of the building. There was a coffee maker in the room with packets of ground coffee and small containers of half and half creams in the refrigerator. So using some of their bottled water the girls worked out how to get the coffee going. Over a breakfast of bread, cold meats followed by fruit, washed down with juices, bottled water and a not bad cup of coffee Bob prepared to explain his game plan.

"What a great breakfast, healthy enough and could even be considered luxurious," Bob commented and as a segue he added, "but this meal will merely be a memory within a few days unless some drastic measures are taken immediately." They all realised this as Bob began to lay out what he felt had to be achieved.

"I have been giving our situation a lot of thought and I feel we should stock up on as much food and milk as possible. I have looked in the yellow pages for cold storage facilities. There are three on the island," using a point stick he indicated on the large map on the wall where they were. "The first one is just a few miles from here, the other two on the north side of the island. The closest one is the main meat packing plant beside the abattoir. If we can keep that one going, between the fresh fruit, fish and frozen meat we can at least survive until the generator packs up. After that, who knows? Still, the one thing we would be lacking is milk. So, here is my take on the situation. Tony and I will drive to the closest plant and make sure the generator is gassed up and has sufficient oil. Then, we will try and gather as much diesel fuel and oil as we can. Hopefully, there will be some cold storage trucks there. We will take one of the trucks and shuttle between the main plant and the other two and store as much as it can handle. We should make sure that the storage of goods are proportional just in case one of the plants break down. While we are setting up the plants I suggest you girls should find the biggest truck you can and load up on as much milk, cold meats and cheeses as you can find from the biggest of the supermarkets. Bring that to the main plant and we will divide it up for the other two plants. This should remain frozen and keep us going for quite a while. I've also found some old walkie-talkies so if anyone finds anything interesting or you're in trouble we're never going to be too far away from each other. I think we should also keep the protective gear on, gloves, masks, heavy boots and overalls. It's going to get stifling but I think that's a small price to pay with all the dead bodies we may encounter. Take plenty of bottled water with you, snacks and food, there will be plenty of them in the stores. Any questions?" Up until now everyone had been attentively listening but the pessimism in Marlene again showed its ugly head,

"And then what happens – after the milk runs out or the generators pack up? We gradually die of malnutrition with our teeth dropping out and dying a slow painful death."

"No, people have survived life-times with far more hardship than we will have to encounter. This is like a paradise compared to how the Innuits survived in the Arctic, or the Bedouins in the deserts." Tony chipped in hoping to break the tension that was beginning to well up.

"Yes, but they were born into it and had the experience of generations of learning handed down to them over thousands of years." Maria had jumped into the fray, not because she wanted to but she felt she had to defend her friend and show solidarity.

"Well, what about sailors in earlier centuries, they went years on ships to discover these very islands with less food than we have." Bob added.

"Yes and they developed scurvy, their teeth fell out and most of them didn't live past 40." Marlene retorted.

"But nor did they have the knowledge we have, scurvy was a lack of vitamin C, that we have in abundance." Bob countered.

"Bob, take a look outside, the next generation of flies and insects are beginning to hatch. In no time we are going to be bitten to death with all the dead bodies around. The flies will have a field day – we have become the endangered species." Marlene said. However, Bob, like all good leaders, listened and recognizing that here was yet another potential trouble spot that had to be eradicated, tried a diplomatic approach, "you're absolutely right, we don't know what's going to happen three months, six months or a year down the road. We don't know that whatever killed everyone else may not return. All I know is that we are on our own and we have to think of what we can do right now that will provide us with the greatest benefit. That is to preserve what food is available right now. The hydro will be out any time now – forever, as far as we are concerned. That's our immediate concern. Next, we find a place to live and clear up all the bodies within a mile radius."

"Just like that! There are thousands of bodies out there, it would take a lifetime to bury all of them." Marlene shouted as she walked to the picture window and pointed down at the outskirts of the square beneath them for emphasis. There were the bodies sitting on benches, on the pavements outside the stores and falling out of open car doors.

"My plan was to find a bull-dozer and a big back hoe and bury them in a pit, probably on the beach somewhere."

Bob replied but it was a good point that he hadn't really thought through fully.

"You mean like the Nazis did to some of my ancestors." Marlene said with not a little venom, "you probably don't realise this but I'm part Jewish, maybe not a very good one but nevertheless, there are certain things we Jews are taught –"

"Marlene," Bob interrupted with a sigh, "I meant like when I saw the city remove a dead leatherback turtle off of a beach in North Carolina. They dug a hole and buried it. My apologies if the notion upset you but I was thinking more of practicalities than anything else. I didn't know you were Jewish now I know that you are this is even more relevant. It's like Genesis, Adam and Eve all rolled into one. Only we don't have it all on a plate we're going to have to work for it. We have to find the fruits, avoid the forbidden apples and guard from serpents all over the place. Now I think this is the best approach to take and unless anyone have any better ideas we should get started."

"I don't think I can go into town by myself." Now everyone looked at Maria, she was staring down at a piece of paper towel she was twisting nervously through her fingers.

"You won't be. You will be with me." Marlene looked questionably at her, "That's what Bob just said, we try and find as much food as we can –"

"I know what he said. But I'm - well I'm scared. O.K. there, how about that. I'm scared. All those dead bodies and what if; well what if not everyone is dead." Her voice trailed to a whisper as she tore the towel into small strips absorbing the tears that dropped from her cheeks. It was a tense moment that should not be allowed to fester and Bob was quick to react.

"Maria, we're all scared. You wouldn't be normal if you weren't." Bob said authoritatively, "but our survival depends on immediate action and working our butts off for the next few days. God, probably wasn't too far out, work for six days and have the seventh off. But we must do whatever we have to do. As for other people, there are no other survivors. We are it. So let's do it." That said, Bob handed each of them a walkie-talkie and one of the pocket sized maps of the island and without another word walked out of the room. There was the briefest time that seemed like an eternity to him before he heard the sound of chairs being pushed back as Maria and Tony silently rose to their feet. They picked up their equipment and began to follow. As Tony, walked past Marlene he gave her shoulder an affectionate squeeze then she too rose, gathered her things and followed them out of the room. Bob felt it had been a poignant test of his leadership and he had come through it successfully. He didn't want to be a leader, he knew as leader decisions were made that were not always favourable to everyone but had to be made for the common good. In this case, he had considered the idea of matching girl/boy for safety but on second thoughts he felt that the more physical task of moving barrels of fuel, oils and meat carcasses while ensuring the generators are working was best suited for the men. Foraging for the best groceries was a no-brainer, Marlene and Maria would know what to get. Call it chauvinism, call it discrimination, call it a red-necked attitude, call it what you like; it was the best decision. Being a World War II history buff he recalled reading a book about Sir Winston

Churchill, a man who was thrust to power in a time of crisis and nobody questioned his leadership because everyone felt he was the right man for the job and of course they were correct. He also had to make decisions that were based on practicalities and not from the heart. It was mentioned in a book that during World War II he was made aware of an impending, massive bombing raid on the city of Coventry targeting the auto factories. This had been revealed through the recent breaking of the German code, Enigma. But to throw all their fighters and defences at the attack would suggest prior knowledge. Churchill knew that many more lives would be saved by not showing their hand. It was said that he stood alone in his office deep in the bowels of the Admiralty in London with tears running unabated down his face while Coventry endured one of the worst bombing raids on England during the entire war. Well there had been tears to-day but a decision had been made and the others had bought into it, that was leadership he thought.

Outside it was another beautiful day, not a cloud in the sky and with the sun just hitting the horizon it was still a comfortable temperature. Bob threw his stuff into the back of the Moke and looked around for a suitable vehicle for the girls. Across the street was a large white cube van strewn across the road. On the side it said 'ISLAND PAPER' with the company's telephone and fax numbers emblazoned in red on its side. No web site address, technology hadn't gained quite as much wide access amongst some of the islanders. He beckoned to Tony to follow him as he walked towards the cab. Inside the vehicle the dead driver was lying across the steering wheel. Being of manual transmission the van had stalled on the death of its driver. The ignition was still turned on but with a bit of luck there would be enough juice in the battery to start on its own power. They walked round the back and lifted the latch of the twin doors. Inside were cartons of paper towels, tissues, toilet paper and napkins. Each of the cartons was marked with 'Made Exclusively for Ramis Resorts by Island Paper', Ramis being the logo of the resort they were booked into on the island. How ironic, Bob mused, that here were commodities that would be useful over the coming months, courtesy of their hosts.

"Let's get the body out of the cab, back the truck up to the police station and unload. These are going to come in handy and they need to be in a sheltered spot. The girls can then use this truck for shipping the perishables." He closed the door and moved round to the driver's side. This was one time when driving on the left-hand side of the road was advantageous. The truck had veered to the right of the road before coming to a stop and they were able to remove the body from the cab out of sight of the girls who were now coming out of the police station. Rigor mortis had set in but the driver had been a slight man, probably 120 pounds soaking wet when he was alive, so they had little problem gently lifting him from the truck. Bald, just over five feet tall the dead man looked as if he would have been in his early sixties. He was dressed in blue jeans and a white tee shirt with the words 'Island Paper' on the front and back. Round his neck he wore a thick gold necklace that had a small crucifix attached to it. They reverently laid the body behind a parked car where the girls wouldn't see it. By coincidence both of the men were wondering about this man. Did he have a family? Where did he live? Throughout the rest of the day and in fact throughout the rest of their lives they would become far more 'matter of fact' when dealing with bodies, skeletons, carcasses and death. They would have to be; their lives depended on it. None of them had ever experienced death on such a large scale, then again, who had? With the body out of sight of the girls Bob jumped into the cab. He expected a smell, one of death maybe but instead he found out a little something about the driver. He smoked pot and judging by the sweet aroma emanating all over the cab, lots of it. For the first time since the devastation had hit, he smiled. Not a huge smile, but one nonetheless. A single key was in the ignition, he reached for the gear shift which was on his left side and made sure it was in neutral and with his right hand turned the key. With a lazy whirring noise the engine made a lethargic turn. His heart went in his mouth, not because this was the end of the world, they had already experienced that already but because it was the beginning of his plan and a set back at this first hurdle would have such a negative effect on their general mood. It was with great relief that the big engine fired almost immediately, of course this wasn't Boston in January it was the Caribbean and you don't need quite the same battery strength to get going here. Although looking at the state of the cab and the overall condition of the van, regular servicing may not have been a consideration and there probably wasn't much difference between the oil viscosity of this vehicle than that of one in the freezing cold North East U.S. While he was figuring this out and trying to work out reverse gear from the faded diagram on top of the gear shift's black handle Tony was explaining to the girls what they were going to do. Bob checked the gas gauge to make sure it had sufficient fuel for their needs, satisfied he then positioned himself so he could see Tony as he directed him as he reversed the truck onto the Police Station's driveway. The girls waited on the steps in anticipation. The truck was almost perfectly positioned to reverse straight up. Delicately, Bob maneuvered the truck up the driveway cautiously getting the feel of the worn clutch and gas pedals. Amazingly enough the handbrake worked perfectly as he was reluctant to shut the engine off in case it wouldn't start again. Nevertheless he wiggled the shift to neutral, cut the engine and climbed out. Tony had already opened the back doors and had jumped into the storage area. None of the cartons were heavy so they set up a chain. Tony moved the boxes to the back of the truck, Bob took them, one at a time, and passed them to Marlene who walked up a few steps where Maria climbed the remaining steps and carried them into the shelter of the Police Station. At approximately half way through the proceedings the men switched with each other, as did the girls, to help even the effort. The whole process took about thirty minutes and by the time Bob jumped down from the truck and closed the doors they were all sweating profusely in their overalls.

"Either of you ever driven a manual shift before?" Bob asked, looking first at Maria and then Marlene. Marlene gave a look of disgust and breezed past him shaking her head.

"You men think you are the only ones who can handle anything mechanical. I grew up next to a logging camp." Marlene reached for the door of the cab and looked back, "Oh and by the way, when you get to the bull-dozer part you may need some trade training – from a girl!" With that she climbed effortlessly into the cab and immediately restarted the engine.

"All I meant was-" Bob started to say.

"Humph" was the retort from Maria as she walked past them head held snootily high on her way to the passenger seat. Thankful that Marlene knew how to drive this thing as Maria couldn't recall ever getting into a manual shift vehicle, even as a passenger, until yesterday in the Moke. No sooner had Marlene stepped up into the cab and shut the door she put the truck in gear, revved the engine, released the clutch and gunned the truck down the driveway and onto the main road as though she was in the Indy 500 at the Brickyard. The men looked in awe as she took the corner and was soon out of sight. Without comment they walked over to their Moke, jumped in, Bob started the engine and sedately drove off in search of the cold storage facility. Even though they were headed in the opposite direction to the girls the sound of that cube van's engine revving and pitching as Marlene put it through its paces stayed with them an inordinate length of time.

As they drove to their destination Tony was doing his best to follow their route on the map while Bob skirted around the plethora of obstructions littering the narrow road. At first he did his best to avoid the bodies but after a while his reaction was akin to running over road kill on a freeway, as callous as it may sound. At a couple of crossroads they had no choice but to stop and maneuver vehicles themselves, unceremoniously dragging their occupants clear before parking, either by driving them or physically pushing them. At one point a fire, still smoldering in the remnants of a restaurant, had spilled onto the sidewalk and spread to a few of the stationary cars. Resulting in a welded, tangled mess of metal, burnt wire and human flesh, blocking the cross-roads they had arrived at. The Moke was a small vehicle but there wasn't a gap wide enough for it to find a way through, even on the sidewalk. To make matters worse the pungent mix of smells was almost overpowering, even though they were wearing their masks. All over the road pieces of the cars were scattered like shrapnel and shards of glass both from the cars and nearby shops lay atop of the carnage indicating that at least one gas tank had exploded. As he approached, Bob slowed then came to a complete stop.

"Well I guess that accounts for one of the explosions we heard yesterday." Tony offered as they sat in the Moke wondering what to do next. They discussed their choices, the bottom line was they could find an alternative route or somehow bull-doze the wreckage to one side.

"Where's Marlene when we need her?" Tony asked facetiously.

"Well, with a bit of luck we don't need her." Bob was looking past the crossroads to what looked like a gravel truck parked on a building site. "If that has a crash bar on the back we could reverse it into this junk and clear the road. The rest we can just sweep away. C'mon." He said as he leapt out of the car and walked on a narrow strip of sidewalk just wide enough for him to walk through. He was glad of his decision to wear boots as he heard pieces of glass crush with his every step. Ignoring the bodies and debris they strolled directly up to the truck and inspected the rear. Sure enough, there was the crash bar. A solid piece of welded metal that stretched the width of the truck to about nine inches from the ground. This was made law in the states back in the 60s as too many driving fatalities were occurring where cars crashed into the back of trucks, causing the cars to squash and wedge themselves underneath with little or no hope of survival for the occupants. There was no driver to remove this time and the truck started effortlessly. Bob quickly maneuvered the truck then reversed it into the pile of junk pushing it into what was left of the burnt restaurant amid a screeching of twisted metal. A cloud of ashes rose from the mound and a side of the restaurant that had remained standing after the fire came crashing down. Tony, armed with a pair of brooms, you can always find brooms on a building site, had followed the truck and as soon as Bob had driven clear began sweeping what debris was left to the side of the road. Bob returned, picked up the other broom and within a couple of minutes they had cleared enough of the road for them to be on their way again.

It had taken almost two hours to travel the three miles to the plant but now their destination was in sight and the road ahead looked clear. It was pure habit that had made Tony put his seat belt on but it was just as well that he had. Within 750 metres of their destination with a cry of 'Holy shit', Bob came to a sudden stop.

Chapter 12

GATHERING
SUPPLIES

St. Santia - Caribbean

With the encouragement from Maria of a "Yeeeha" and "go Marlene – you showed them girl," Marlene took the first bend a little quicker than she should have done – but no one else knew that, she was so intent on putting as much distance between themselves and those male, chauvinist, jerks. She purposely waited until full engine revolutions were being reached before changing gear as though she was driving in a Formula 1 Grand Prix. Briefly caught up in their euphoria they had forgotten both their predicament and their task. She had driven right through the town centre and a couple of appropriate supermarkets before remembering what they were supposed to be doing. This was partly because there were few obstructions in the road in this part of town to provide any serious reminders. There was an extra lane down the middle of the street, which was the path she took, clipping any cars that were parked in her way. Because it was a busier road there were very few bodies on the road except at crosswalks. Like Bob, once they had overcome the experience of that first squelchy sound of wheels compressing the innards of what was once a living thing it became just like squashing bugs. She also felt it was best not to slow down, the faster they went the more it minimized both the noise and the bump.

As they were approaching a relatively large supermarket about a hundred metres on their left Maria tapped Marlene on the shoulder. Without a sound she pointed to the store and Marlene reacted by slowing down and began looking for the best access. In front of the store was a small car park with two entrances, there was no cars on the main road obstructing the entrances but a line of cars both in and out of the car park blocked their path. Between the entrances was a grass verge lined with low concrete dividers separating the car park from a pedestrian walkway. She turned the wheel, increased speed and mounted the pavement scaling the dividers with a jolt. Neither of them were wearing seat belts but Maria wasn't quite prepared for the sudden change in direction both sideways and up and down resulting in her head banging rudely into the cabin roof.

"Jeez Marlene. You could have warned me," Maria said tentatively rubbing her head.

"Sorry. I didn't know myself until the last minute." Marlene replied, her eyes never veering from the path she was taking through the car park to the front of the supermarket. It was like a slalom and a bumper car ride combined as she weaved in and out of the least obstructed lanes knocking aside the vehicles in her way.

"You know what Maria?" Marlene said with a thoughtful expression.

"No Marlene what?" Maria replied still rubbing her head, only a little exaggerated now.

"When you go to a supermarket they usually have the milk in the back of the store forcing you to walk through the entire store just to buy a carton of milk. It's part of their marketing ploy to get you to buy more stuff." Marlene said.

"Yeah. So what's your point?" Maria asked.

"Well, why don't we just drive straight to the back of the store and any non-perishable goods we can pick up afterwards? And anyway, won't there be more stuff in the storage area at the back?" Marlene asked and stole a brief look at Maria. Maria thought for a second.

"You know what? You're right. That's why I love you. Always the practical one." Maria replied enthusiastically. By this time they had reached the lane at the front of the store. It was littered with prostrate bodies lying amongst dropped shopping bags and their scattered contents of groceries. Shopping carts, were strewn around the entrance, some upturned with their once purchased contents lying in pools of a drying, gooey mess of eggs, milk, beverages, jams and sauces mixed in with broken glass and soggy cardboard. Undaunted, Marlene drove on to the edge of the store as carts careered off the side of the truck adding to the havoc, as if anyone was going to care. As they drove down the side of the store they noticed the lighting in the store was off so it appeared the hydro had begun to fail. On turning to the back of the store Marlene slowed and then came to a complete stop to reconnoiter the loading bays used by the big trucks, there were four of them. At the far bay a truck marked 'MacPhearson's Dairy Products' had been backed up. Not only was all its doors still closed the sound of the small generator that ran the trailer's cooling plant could be heard above the noise of their own engine.

"We could be in luck here Maria my girl," Marlene said as she gently eased the truck parallel to the first loading bay so that the cab door was just past its entrance. Satisfied she had positioned the truck correctly she pulled up the handbrake, wiggled the gear shift into neutral and turned off the engine.

"C'mon. Time to change transport." And without a word of explanation, Marlene, with flashlight in hand, opened the door, got out and climbed onto the platform of the loading bay. A dazed Maria looked backwards and forwards from the dairy trailer to the open door a few times before following Marlene into the store.

The doors to all four loading bays were open so there was enough light to determine where they were walking. Marlene made a bee-line for the dairy truck and was in the process of pulling back one of the doors as Maria caught up to her. She only opened the one door to help maintain the cool temperature inside the trailer, however, she firmly secured the door to the side of the trailer – just in case it unexpectedly closed on her. She dreaded the thought of having to rely on Maria to open the door, she knew her all too well. The light was a little dimmer inside the trailer here so she used her flashlight to scan around. The trailer was half full of what appeared to be boxes of milk. Looking at the black stenciled description on the outside of the nearest box it stated that it contained '60 x 1 litre of homogenized - 1%'. Some boxes were marked '2%' but from a quick calculation Marlene calculated that there must be thirty boxes each containing 60 litres of various types.

"That's a good 1,800 litres here Maria. At a litre each per day that would be more than enough for a year – if we can keep it from going off.' She walked inside and carefully opened the nearest carton, just for verification. Sure enough, inside she could see the top row of 20 milk cartons. She closed the box back up by tucking its four tops underneath each other, walked back into the store and began to scout around. Maria brought up the rear like a loyal puppy dog. They were at the far corner of the building and right next to them was a small, battery-powered fork-lift truck, beside which was a battery charging system with electric cables attached to a spare battery. To the left of that was a cold storage with a wide entrance area that had thick, plastic blinds hanging from its mantle that during the working day prevented a lot of the cold air from escaping yet provided access for the fork-lift truck to enter. Marlene parted the plastic slats and walked into the cold-storage area. She needed her flashlight to augment what little light was coming through the entrance she had just entered and the one that was ahead of her leading into the supermarket. She noticed a couple of bodies ahead of her and another one to her right, she pointed them out to Maria who was following right behind her. Maria duly noted the bodies with little interest as she was more focused on the available goods as she randomly shone her flashlight around the boxes and skids of saran wrapped food products. There were cold meats, yogurts, creams and cheeses of all kinds. Despite the fact that the hydro here must have quit at some point during the night the room itself was still cool. Without hesitation Marlene took action.

"Maria, if I can get that fork-lift truck started we can load a lot of this stuff into the trailer. What I need you to do is take stock of what's here and help me load a good cross-section. O.K.?" Marlene asked, knowing Maria was the better shopper between the two of them. During their many conversations Marlene had learnt from Maria that as part of her many foster families she regularly had to help with the grocery shopping and cook for the various large families she had been part of at any given time. Now instead of buying food for a family short term she was storing food in the freezer for an indefinite period for four. Maria nodded and quickly got to work as Marlene returned to the loading area for the fork-lift, the first thing she needed to do was to dispose of the bodies. She managed to maneuver the tines of the fork lift under one of the bodies then reversed back to the loading bay. There she used the fork lift controls to widen the width of the two tines until the body dropped out of sight over the side of the loading bay. She repeated this exercise the three times necessary to ensure the area they were working in was clear of bodies. Each trip she recalled the conversation they had earlier regarding the disposing of bodies with a bull-dozer and how that had perturbed her. Now here she was doing much the same thing with no remorse.

Climbing over the boxes Maria began to take stock. Those cartons she could move she piled onto one of the wooden skids that Marlene could then hoist into the truck with the fork-lift. The ones she couldn't move and thought necessary she would point to as Marlene made her return trip from the truck. Unfortunately, Marlene was transporting the skids faster than Maria could move the individual boxes. In only a couple of hours the truck was full of enough provisions to feed an army for a year. No sooner had they cut the engine of the fork-lift they could hear the cackle of the walkie-talkie sounding in the quiet confines of the store room.

"Maria, Marlene can you hear me – urgent come in."

Chapter 13

DIRECTIONS
PLANNED

St. Santia - Caribbean

At the sound of the walkie-talkie Maria grabbed at the unit attached to her overalls and initially had difficulty freeing the clip. Finally she found the correct button on the radio and said, "Maria here go ahead."

"Where the hell have you been we've been trying to reach you for the last ten minutes? We thought something had happened to you." Bob, sounded a bit irate as he asked of their whereabouts.

"No we're fine. Doing what we've been told – doing a bit of shopping." The girls giggled conspiratively. Bob was already angry that he had been unable to contact them as during their loading the noises of heir packing and the sound of the fork-lift had drowned out the calls of the walkie-talkies. Now their tone seemed to anger him even more.

"Well get your butts over here – we need you." Bob told them authoritavely.

"Certainly mien fuhrer. Where's here and what's the urgency?" Maria replied wondering what on earth could be wrong.

"Of course, sorry." Bob mellowed a tad as he realized the girls could have no possible idea where they were and what they had found. "The cold storage we talked about? On that road just before you reach the cold storage there's a small farm. They rear chickens and there are about 50 chicks in incubating chambers that have just hatched and an awful lot more that are about to hatch. We need help. We've got some generators set up so the chicks are in no immediate danger except we don't have a clue." Bob explained to them and the girls were listening with growing enthusiasm. There's always something about babies, be they human or animal that brought the little girl out of a woman. More so when one considered all the death that had gone on around the world in the last 24 hours. Finally, after seeing nothing but death here is new life and they could be a part of nurturing that precious commodity. The result was that their eyes lit up with joy and they danced, giggled and hugged each other.

"Hello, hello are you still receiving me?" Bob asked wondering what the girls were now doing. They stopped their cavorting but still laughing Maria replied,

"Yeah, yeah the cavalry is on its way, over and out." Marlene, turned to close and secure the rear doors of the truck then they hurried forward to the cab and climbed in. Marlene quickly familiarized herself with the controls then started the engine. Despite the fact that the refrigeration unit had been operating all night the engine, backed by heavy duty batteries, started with no problem. After a final check that the refrigeration unit was still operating she slipped the truck into gear and they were on their way.

Maria became the navigator, using the pocket map from the police station, and with Marlene continuing her tryout for Formula 1 racing they arrived within twenty minutes, despite the obstacles. They had seen the Moke the guys had been driving from the main road and as they turned up the dirt track leading to the building containing the chicks Marlene gave a long pull on the horn to announce their arrival. Bob and Dave rolled their eyes at the superfluous sound of the horn. Even above the generators they had heard the sound of the truck's engine roaring along the main road for about the last five minutes. After all, it was the only truck engine working on the island, their arrival did not need to be heralded, however, the men were intrigued by the ladies new mode of transportation. Bob went outside to meet them and to lead the way to the chicks. It was now Marlene's turn to take charge and began barking out instructions to the others.

The buildings for the chicken farm were equipped with well serviced generators and what looked like a good supply of diesel fuel that would last a few weeks. On a hot island like St. Santia an electricity blackout for even an hour could wipe out all the chickens so the owners had been well prepared. All the new owners needed to do was to get the chicks hatched and rear them so that they were established enough to become free range. Again, Marlene's farming background kicked in. Living in the wilds of logging country self-sufficiency was a common practice and part of that practice was raising hens. True, Marlene had received no formal training in rearing battery hens but feeding and caring for chickens was not beyond her. She immediately took charge, organizing food, which was plentiful in clearly marked bags stacked in the building and ensuring the drip bottles were full of water. She ensured the temperatures of the incubators were correct, as clearly indicated on the outside of the large bath like bubbles. It was obvious to her from all the instructions and labels in the place that the people who worked there were not exactly university graduates and each time she came upon another piece of literature she silently pointed to it ensuring the boys were aware of them as they stood squirming helplessly as she quickly attended to the chirping chicks. To avoid further embarrassment, Bob and Tony decided to commence the removal of the dead chickens from the cages, beginning with those in the immediate vicinity of the chicks. It was imperative that the carcasses should be burnt to avoid the possibility of disease. What was also becoming obvious was the appearance of the flies. Those flies that were in the pupa stage of metamorphosis during the devastation were having a field day with all the dead bodies and carcasses in close proximity. Although all insects were killed in the devastation many of their off-spring were hatching in the heat and they had quickly re-established themselves as the most common order of species on the planet, especially the flies.

"You know what guys?" Marlene spoke to no one in particular, "if these flies and chicks are surviving I think what ever has killed everything has passed through. I'm taking off these overalls, it is going to be difficult to work like this – I'm quite happy to take the chance." With that,

Marlene removed her overalls and was soon down to her t-shirt and shorts. The other three looked tentatively at each other but in no time at all the rest of the group followed suit.

Following Marlene's instructions they now had the chicks stabilized. They estimated there were some 200 in the incubators contently foraging for food amongst their own broken shells that had hatched since the devastation. Dave and Bob returned from their cremation duties and once they realized their presence was superfluous they immediately left the girls tending to the chicks while they drove the truck that Marlene had arrived in over to the neighbouring cold storage plant. There they started the task of stocking the cold storage plant with the goods the girls had brought in the truck. It took a lot longer for the men to master the controls of the fork lifts in the cold storage plant than it had Marlene but by just after lunch everything was stashed away and secure. They grabbed some cold meats, cheese, chips and sodas, a positive banquet, and drove back to the chicken hut for a late lunch. Situated against the room housing the incubators was a canteen with adjoining restrooms. The canteen contained a half a dozen threadbare easy chairs that had certainly seen better days. Strewn between the chairs were a few old coffee tables and empty crates that appeared to have served as both tables and foot rests judging by the dirty state of them. In the corner was a large sink that didn't appear to have had a decent clean since being installed. Nevertheless, the water was still running on demand from the taps and with the help of some liquid soap they were able to clean up for lunch. Although there was little they could do about the stench beginning to emanate from the dead personnel and chickens in the adjoining buildings, they would deal with that as soon as they could.

Over lunch they reviewed their current status. They estimated that there was enough milk, bread, meat products, frozen and canned vegetables to last them at least a year, assuming the cold storage plant equipment remained serviceable. They certainly had enough fuel, assuming it doesn't decompose, to keep the generators going longer than a year but they didn't think the food would be up to much beyond that. Assuming the chickens could be kept disease free they expected more than enough fresh chickens and eggs for as long as they needed. There was fish aplenty to be caught in the sea so all that was left was the regular supply of fresh fruit and vegetables, which they would have to learn to sow, tender and harvest as there was certainly an abundance on the island. The only food source they couldn't replace was milk. There was an infinite supply of coconuts but whether the milk contained enough nutrients to become a good substitute for cow's milk they would have to research.

"There was a study carried out recently suggesting that not only did milk cause more harm than good but it didn't provide any basis for the long held belief that the calcium in milk did anything to help bones – so there." Bob stated nonchalantly as he contemplated the wrapping of a chocolate bar which coincidentally advertised the amount of glasses of milk that went into its manufacture.

"Bet the dairy farmers had a field day with that one." Marlene said.

"Shouldn't be a problem anyway," offered Maria, "as Tony said yesterday many remote cultures have survived without cows or goats to provide milk, I'm sure we will be able to."

"Funny," said Bob, "I thought cultures survived in milk." At first it looked as if the play on words would die a death until the others all groaned as one.

"Yeah, but cultures have to be frozen and we don't have Friesian cows!" Marlene retorted. After the most traumatic 24 hours of their lives it was the sort of relief they needed and the banter continued for a few more minutes with everyone laughing and trying desperately to think of a suitable pun. It wasn't until a crack loosely related to breeding brought the four of them and their sexual dilemma back to the forefront and the laughs died and they looked uncomfortably at the concrete floor that was covered in bits of straw and dirt.

"O.K., I hate to beef," said Bob, amid more groans, "but, we have to prioritise our tasks for the next few days." He stood up and walked over to a wall containing a white board that coincidentally held a list of names, presumably of the workers, and their duties for the next seventy two hours. Using the eraser he cleaned the board and then turned to the others.

"My suggestion is this. Because of the chicks, for the next few weeks we will move our base from the police station to here." He began to write as he spoke. "After lunch I have to go to the police station to take the call from John Hamax. While I am there I will grab our sleeping gear, some emergency rations, supplies and bring them here. Then we will commandeer a back hoe and we will clean out the remaining dead carcasses from the immediate vicinity, burn them and bury them. I don't think we can finish all of that to-day but hopefully we can by tomorrow. That should prevent the smell from getting too bad and diminish the chance of the flies from multiplying. Next, we have to look for more permanent homes. We need to be close to the beach, so we can fish, but high enough to avoid high seas. It also needs to be sheltered, have plenty of adjoining land and be as close as possible to the main fruit farms as we cannot guarantee transportation. Eventually any fuel we are not using will either evaporate or have a chemical breakdown. We will be able to transport some of the chicken hutches from next door to the new site, then we have to learn to live from the land. Thoughts?" There were nods of agreement all round. The girls were happy to be occupied looking after the chicks and avoiding the reality beyond their walls.

"Right, Tony, maybe you can continue finding more fuel for the generator. I'm off to the police station to wait for the call from the Hamaxes. I must remember our sleeping gear and a few extra things. Any requests for dinner? I know a nice little bar where they have an excellent cellar and a still functioning freezer"

"Ooh, beer and pizza," Maria said.

"A nice bottle of Chardonnay for me." Tony countered. Marlene just rolled her eyes, shook her head, waved them off and returned to the chicks. Bob smiled, left the room and went outside to the Moke. It was a beautiful day, the sort of weather they had eagerly anticipated when they left the U.S. He started the car and drove down the dirt track to the main road with the warm breeze blowing over his body. For the first time since the devastation occurred he was alone and his thoughts turned, not for the last time, to his mother. She had been spending the winter in California with his sister. For a brief moment he had an impulse to drive to a marina, find a big cigarette boat and island hop back to the mainland. From there to California with the hope of finding his family somehow surviving this terrible tragedy. What of his father back in New York? He hadn't wanted to travel south. He liked the seasons too much, so he would remain at home and just travel for a short visit later in the winter. Bob would have liked another opportunity to reconcile their differences. Suddenly, the tears were there, blinding his eyes and without realizing it, his speed had crept up dangerously high. A thump brought his mind back to reality, he braked and simultaneously wiped the tears from his eyes. He saw in his rear-view mirror the cause of the bump, it was the carcass of a dog lying in the road. That dead dog had probably saved him from a nasty accident. For seventy five metres ahead was a sharp turn and failure to negotiate the bend would result in an argument with a road barrier guarding a rock escarpment. Based on the volume of dents and assortment of car paint colours decorating the metal it had appeared to have won most of them. He skidded round the bend at a speed far greater than he felt safe doing so but managed to keep control, both of the car and his emotions. He was going to have to be strong, he was being regarded as the leader, not only by his own small group but also by the only other people known to them left alive, the Hamaxes. It would be the last time he grieved for his family, in the future, when he was alone, he would sometimes question whether it was cynicism but he felt it was more the sheer extent of the death, far beyond personal tragedy. He knew that if any one of his family had become seriously ill or had died he would have been on the next plane home, but losing every living person you had ever known, family, friends, public figures, sports stars, film stars, everyone except the three people you were stranded with; that was just far too much sorrow for a single person to vent.

He turned in to the police station car park and checked his watch, it was 2:50. That was another thing, time. They will be living by the sun rise and sun down, no meetings to attend, no trains or planes to catch, no movie start times or TV programs to watch. With no one to maintain the electricity or the phones he anticipated this to be the last time he would be communicating with anyone other than face to face and even that would be if Hamax could get through. Thinking back, one of his favourite acquaintances was one of the most reliable people he knew for turning up at a meeting, at least on the right date. Time was not a consideration for him, a couple of hours either side was reasonable and all of his friends accepted that. He often felt how much better life would be if one was not stressed by time deadlines – well he knew he was about to find out, in spades. As a token gesture to his new life style he unclasped his watch and warily placed it in the glove compartment of the Moke.

During the gathering of the equipment he would be close enough to the phone to get to it within a few rings and if it doesn't ring by the time he was finished it would be well past 3:00 anyway and he would just leave. He went about his tasks and at about six minutes past three the phone rang, crashing the eerie silence with its rhythmic shrill and startling Bob in the process. He recovered his composure and picked up the receiver on the second ring.

"Hi." Bob said breathlessly.

"Hello son, sorry I'm a bit late, got caught up doing things." The voice of John Hamax sounded livelier than it did yesterday.

"Hi Mr. Hamax, no problem. I was busy myself and hadn't noticed you were late. How's it going, any further news?" Bob sounded upbeat, so pleased to hear another human's voice.

"Not good son. Our worst fears are realized, it appears the damage is a world-wide phenomenon." This was John's assessment based on CNN being unavailable. "We were about to leave the hospital but my wife –"

"You really think it is a word-wide devastation John? Interrupted Bob.

"That's what it appears like son." John replied.

"My god, so many people," said Bob almost to himself, then he realized he was being selfish and thought John must have family too.

"I'm so sorry to ask John but have you lost family too? Bob was trying to be as diplomatic as he could under the circumstances.

"Yes I do as a matter of fact," John replied hesitantly, "have three daughters and five grandchildren," his voice trailed off as tears were being stifled and he took a deep breath as he composed himself. "Would like to have seen my daughters again, alive," he said. Bob thought that as difficult as it was for the four of them on this island they were not going to have to confront their dead family as the Hamaxes would. My God, how stressful is that.

"Well, I know they're gone," John went on, "I expect Darlene was still in bed so at least she would have been asleep at the time, I don't think she would have suffered much. Our Darlene was not an early riser, you understand. Poor girl was separated, second marriage. Anyway, none of her girls would have been at home, they would have been with their respective fathers. We won't drive over to find them, I don't think we could take that. So we will drive home, our poor dog, the neighbours and all. God, listen to me, I'm sure you have had problems of your own."

"That's O.K. Mr. Hamax," Bob replied in a soothing voice, "we got through the night O.K. and we've had a couple of breaks. We've found a chicken farm with incubators, live chicks and eggs and we are setting up shifts to try and hatch as many eggs as we can."

"Don't know much about chickens son, I'm a man of the sea but I know that if those eggs get cold even for a brief time, those eggs won't ever hatch." John added pessimistically.

"Fortunately, the hydro is still running on that part of the island and the incubators were still functioning." Bob tried to counter with optimism, "so we have set up a couple of generators. We've also found a cold storage facility with its own backup generators so over the next few days we are trying to find as much diesel fuel as we can to keep it going as long as we can. So for now we estimate we have meat and milk for the best part of a year then, if we can rear the chickens we have chicken and all the fish we can handle. We have to learn about coconut milk and how we can harvest that. Other than that, there are enough fresh vegetables we can grow here."

"Son, it sounds like you have it all planned out. I wish you luck. I'm not sure how we're going to fare, we have other problems," his voice was beginning to choke with emotion again, I used to hunt in my day and fish but I'm too old to do that every day, even if there is something to hunt."

"Mr. Hamax is -," Bob started to interrupt.

"Son, call me John, under the circumstances we can hardly be formal," John said.

"Right, John. Look if you are a man of the sea you must know boats right and navigation? Is there any way you can make it to St. Santia. We are going to need someone with the life experience you and your wife can offer." There was almost a hint of desperation in Bob's voice.

"Son, I don't think so. I'm in my 70s, that's a heck of a trip from Maine," John countered.

"John, you could drive down to Florida and find a nice vessel in Fort Lauderdale and island hop to us," Bob suggested.

"Nice thought but to be honest, I'm not sure I would be able to drag my wife away from her home," John relied.

"John, there's so much we don't know," Bob was pleading now, "cooking, growing, fishing, pregnancy, life. We're just four young people suddenly thrown together with no direction – we need help, guidance. We can't leave here, there's too much to give up. So could you please try and persuade your good wife to come and help us?" Bob was desperate now, he saw this as an opportunity to have a mentor, someone to bounce ideas and suggestions off.

"Son, that's a pretty speech and you are right, I just don't know that we can do it." John burst into tears, it was all too much for him. Bob felt so helpless. On the other end of the phone was a man in the twilight of his years and Bob was asking him to drive 1,200 miles with his wife through decaying bodies and carcasses, fires and who knows what other tragedies and then risk their lives on the open sea just to help them.

"John, I understand. Look, I wish you and your wife well. I'm sure you will be fine. We're young, there are books, CDs, videos and tapes we'll survive. Unfortunately, I don't think the phones are going to be working after to-day and we haven't come across any radios that could transmit to the mainland – even if we did I'm not sure we could operate them. So, this I'm afraid, will be our last communication. All I can say is, all the best," Bob said sincerely.

"Good luck son." John's voice was soft, cracking with emotion, "I just hope your next re-generation of the human race is better than the one we've had for the last few thousand years. I wish you well in your 'Garden of Eden'." With that, John Hamax hung up a telephone for the last time in his life. Not for the first time, Bob felt alone, very alone. That conversation had brought home to him the obstacles they faced, just to stay alive, never mind procreating the species, that was a major tribulation in itself. Suddenly, Bob realized that he was still half-sitting, half-standing against an old green metal desk holding the phone against his ear. He quickly snapped into action, replacing the phone on its receiver and gathered up the rest of their supplies and left the building. He loaded the things he had gathered into the Moke and walked over to the bar across the street to retrieve the requested orders. His heart was heavy as he entered the deserted bar and he saw the obligatory line of upturned bottles of spirits hanging behind the bar with their measuring attachments at their base. He went behind the bar, selected a glass and pressed it up to the bottle of Jack Daniels and waited for the dispenser to empty its measure into his glass. He watched as the glass module filled in preparation for the next shot and thought how easy it would be to just stay here and get absolutely legless drunk. But he knew he now had responsibilities and his life as well as those of his friends depended on him and getting drunk was not going to help. But still, he did down the shot and waited until the fiery liquid had been completely swallowed feeling its journey all the way to his stomach.

He slammed down the tumbler but before continuing on his scavenging duties he noticed a glass cabinet containing various items of clothing all emblazoned with the bar's name, '*The Olde Caribbean Cop Shoppe*'. The owners of this bar had obviously enjoyed free protection from customers working in the building across the street, hence its name. But what caught Bob's attention was a white, bucket style, sun hat frayed on the bottom edge, trendy but nonetheless practical. He had never been one for wearing a hat but driving around the island and working in the sun in just t-shirt and shorts he felt his wardrobe needed to be augmented by a hat. He casually walked over to the cabinet and opened the door, took out the hat that had caught his fancy and tried it on. It fitted him perfectly, he gave a nonchalant look in a mirror behind the bar and decided his makeover was complete. Behind the bar he found a cooler and filled it with what little ice remained in the freezer. He selected a couple of pizzas and a few Buffalo wings for good measure then placed them in the cooler before selecting some wine and a few beers. He closed the lid of the cooler and carried it outside to the Moke where he placed it in the back and covered it with a thick tarpaulin to help provide some protection from the sun for the short trip back to the chicken farm. He also decided to have another quick drink in preparation for the decisions he was making which would be shared with the others after dinner this evening. So he quickly returned to the bar, held the glass up to the dispenser. Unlike this drink, he thought, 'those decisions will not go down well'.

Chapter 14

CHANGE OF PLAN

The Arctic North Pole

The divers from the USS Augusta were in their element when toiling in the water; be it recovery, planting mines, underwater combat or exploratory exercises similar to the one they were currently undertaking. Even in cumbersome dry-suits, specifically designed for cold-water diving, supporting aqua-lungs and breathing apparatus they were as mobile and as comfortable as most people would be on dry land. However, the bulk of a polar bear bloated by its dying gases and fighting the laws of gravity almost defied their efforts. By tying ropes to the dead animal's limbs and running the ends of the ropes through the mooring grommets of the submarine they managed to haul the bear to the bulkhead. Once the carcass was floating tethered above the air lock it was a reasonably easy task squeezing the bear through the hatch. The real fun began when the water was purged from the chamber and they had to move the 1500 pounds of dead weight to the laboratory, at the other end of the submarine. There were other lighter, mammals available for post mortem but Ms. Delaney insisted on the bear as its respiratory organs were closer to that of humans than anything else floating in the water or so she claimed.

The bear had been tested for levels of radiation prior to handling the carcass and the results, as expected, proved negative. But without knowing the cause of death full medical security precautions were in force. The divers were secure, there was no skin exposed and they were still breathing from their tanks. So it was up to them to transport the bear to the laboratory. Every five metres was a door, which they secured behind them. As they passed from one secure area to another the air was purged and disinfectant spray was applied to every square millimeter of the corridor. The area was out of bounds to the rest of the crew until the all clear could be given. Once the bear arrived in the laboratory the bear was dragged on to an aluminum table where it could be raised for the grisly task of the autopsy. By this time the divers were sweating profusely in their dry suits but now they too had to endure de-codification before they could relieve themselves of their equipment. This was carried out by other suitably attired crew members. Meanwhile, Mary and Janet, clad from head to foot in surgical greens, immediately begun dissecting the late polar bear in an effort to determine its demise. The contents of its intestines revealed nothing unusual, the diet of seal and fish was normal with nothing contaminated. A visual check of its mouth showed no apparent cause of death, but then the sea would have sluiced any obvious evidence. It wasn't until they cut into the lungs that the cause of death was suspected - suffocation. The lungs and tracheal tubes were full of what could best be described as a white 'mush'. A sample of the substance was transferred to a glass square and placed under the electronic microscope. Both Mary and Janet took turns viewing the dead microbes in a futile attempt of determining what they were.

"Janet I've never seen anything like this. Where on earth could these things have come from? These type of organisms shouldn't be able to exist in temperatures like this!" Mary said incredulously.

"Where on earth indeed. That seismic reading. Could it have been a meteorite? If it was, then these microbes could have been carried from outer space inside the rock and on impact they could have been exposed to air and started breeding here." Janet replied.

"You can't be serious!" Mary stopped her probing and looked at Janet. "Mary, don't you remember when we were at school a researcher at the University of California broke open a piece of amber. It contained a bee that had died thirty million years earlier. Bacteria from that bee began to proliferate. What if some kind of bacteria had been transported through space for all these years and on being exposed to the atmosphere it too began to proliferate?" Janet suggested.

"It's possible. Improbable. But not impossible." Mary replied.

"It is more than improbable, I'm certain that's exactly what has happened." Before Janet had finished speaking she was already ripping off her protective gloves and reaching for the phone. She dialed the radio operator's number. The response was almost immediate.

"Able seaman Simpson," Sparks Simpson the submarine's radio operator replied.

"Simpson, this is Janet Delaney. I need to know, have you intercepted any radio signals from anyone reporting meteorite activity in the Arctic?" She demanded.

"As you know Miss Delaney, all radio communications are on a 'need to know basis' and I have direct orders from the Admiral -"

"Simpson - fuck your orders," she interrupted with exasperation, "we know there was seismic activity earlier that could have been caused by a meteorite. Now, yes or no, have you intercepted anything to do with meteorite activity?"

"I'm sorry Miss Delaney I can't answer that." Simpson dutifully replied.

Further exasperated, she took a deep breath and calmly said, "let me put it another way Simpson. If you have intercepted messages on the subject of recent meteorite activity then we may be experiencing a life or death situation, which I must report to the authorities immediately by going to the Admiral. Now, should I go and see the Admiral?"

"Affirmative ma'am." Simpson reluctantly replied.

"Thank you Simpson." Janet politely answered and put the phone down. She quickly undid the strings of her medical tunic and threw them into a laundry receptacle. It had been established that all the microbes were dead and no infection was possible. Janet and Mary carefully collected samples and together with the lungs of the bear they were placed in the medical freezer. Janet gave instructions to a nearby seaman to have the remains of the polar bear disposed of and the laboratory cleansed just before she called Simpson to transmit an 'all clear' message. To say that the seaman was not a happy camper was beyond being an understatement and under his breath degrading words of the woman's heritage were being muttered.

As soon as the all-clear message had finished Janet called the Admiral, she knew he would have been expecting her call and she was invited to his office immediately. Once they were out of their medical garb Mary and Janet left the laboratory to go straight to see the Admiral. The Admiral was accompanied by his chief medical physician, Lieutenant Moore, who, Janet learnt from the Admiral, was attending for consultation purposes. Janet ignored the tall slim man who in her opinion was a quack because he was in the military and could not possibly have had the necessary medical training to be a civilian doctor. She related her findings and a synopsis of the cause, which Mary agreed, was a feasible explanation. Quietly, Stanford listened to the summary while leaning back in his leather office chair and casually tapping his fingers together. Finally he asked.

"So you're saying a meteor crashed on earth, broke up and unleashed some sort of microbe that killed the polar bear?"

"It was a meteorite," she corrected impatiently, "it's a meteor when in the atmosphere, a meteorite when it lands on earth. But yes, that is the scenario we are suggesting."

He glanced briefly at Moore who merely shrugged his shoulders and nodded his head in acquiescence to the scenario being offered and then added,

"Would it be a '*meteorwrong*' if it landed in the sea?" This brought a rare smile to the Admiral's face that only made Janet even more indignant.

"Doctor, this is not a laughing matter and we need to investigate this further," Janet shouted, banging on the desk in frustration before continuing, "we need to contact other vessels to obtain their experiences to understand what the hell has happened because something most definitely has." After a few seconds silence Stanford raised Lieutenant Hargreaves in the radio room on his intercom and barked an order to contact Norfolk immediately. He wasn't sure if this breaking radio silence was the right thing to do but nor was he in the mood for arguing with these women and if anyone at headquarters would like to raise the issue he was prepared to give an explanation, in no uncertain terms, on how he felt about women's lib and the bastards who had authorised this scientific trip. Furthermore, based on his recent decision to finally retire from active duty, he really didn't care.

For a full five minutes Stanford and the women sat impatiently saying nothing until the intercom broke the silence startling everyone in the room.

"Sir, we are unable to receive any reply from Norfolk."

"Then try Greenland or Goose Bay."

"We have sir. In fact we have tried all wave bands, friend, foe or otherwise. We are unable to raise anyone sir."

"That's impossible. We obviously have a malfunction with our equipment," the Admiral's frustration was beginning to boil over, "my god Hargreaves you don't have to be a rocket scientist to work that one out."

"Obviously sir that was the first thing we checked." Hargreaves was calm as he replied, aware of his Admiral's lack of patience with anyone incompetent, "our diagnostic tests show no malfunction. Our tests have proved we are sending and receiving messages perfectly. We have also used backup communications with the same results. However, we are unable to receive a response from any live operator."

"Keep trying Hargreaves." Hargreaves was an experienced officer not known for shortcomings or making rash decisions and if he was unable to reach another party there was something seriously awry. As soon as he had delivered his order to Hargreaves he flicked the intercom button to the bridge and also that of the main tannoy.

"Bridge sir?"

Admiral Sanford took pride in his ability to remain fixed on an objective and to obey orders. That's why everyone on the submarine was surprised when using old-time vernacular, they heard the command, "full steam to Norfolk. All hands to stations – this is not an exercise. I repeat, all hands to stations, this is not an exercise."

Chapter 15

COMMUNICATIONS

Norfolk – Virginia U.S.A.

The USS Augusta sailed slowly on the surface towards its home base of Norfolk Virginia. It was early morning and weather wise it was a perfect day, blue sky, not a cloud to be seen with just a slight sea breeze. Admiral Stanford was in the conning tower dressed for the winter cold in regulation duffle coat complete with stripes on the epaulettes. Janet and Mary had earlier come topside in full protective gear to test the quality of the air. They had given it a clean bill of health and now Admiral Stanford was scanning the surface of the sea for activity. Apart from an assortment of listless vessels and the wake of the sea there was no movement to be seen. No birds following ships for scraps, no activities on shore, no gantries, cranes or vehicles moving. Silence, except for the waves lapping against the hull of the submarine. Some contact had been achieved with other sister submarines and they were making full speed to their respective home ports, in the case of one of them that was also Norfolk. But the

Augusta was the first to arrive. There were submarines from other countries, two British nuclear vessels headed back to Plymouth, one French off to Marseille and a few other conventional submarines that may or may not make it home with no supply ships to rendezvous with. So they would have to dock at a convenient port and take their chances. The Admiral, who happened to be the senior allied officer at sea, requested personnel numbers, male and female without having to divulge his own counts. As he suspected, the two women he had on board were the only women known to be at sea, or to his knowledge, anywhere else. Currently, only a handful of the crew had any idea of what had happened and that included the women. But everyone on board had some piece of the puzzle and in such close confinements rumours spread like wildfire and all the propensity for a potential mutiny was there. The Admiral gave this some serious thought. If the devastation was widespread, then the crew of the USS Augusta would be prone to looting and rioting unless discipline could be maintained. On docking in Norfolk, discipline amongst most of the men would break down, however, they were housing women and if word spread throughout the surviving Norfolk sea-fearing community that females were available they would be placed in a tenuous position. Admiral Stanford decided to refrain from broadcasting the news of the devastation to the crew until they were approaching Norfolk then, for their own safety, Mary and Janet would have to become prisoners on the submarine. A few of his officers and a handful of trusted crew would be designated to provide round the clock protection for as long as necessary.

The Admiral decided on a course of action and made no hesitation in acting upon it. He flicked the tannoy switch on the conning tower panel and made a broadcast "This is the captain speaking, all officers report to the war room immediately. I repeat, all officers report to the War Room immediately. Miss Briggs, Miss Delaney, please return to your quarters immediately. Thank you." He then gave an order to stop all engines before he proceeded to the War Room. As he made his way through the submarine to the war room he could feel the eyes of all the submariners on him. They knew this was it, whatever 'it' was. They knew that something was about to give but the Admiral strode to the war room with his customary vigour and swagger as though nothing untoward was wrong and after he passed the crew merely looked at each other and waited.

The last officer to enter the room was Hargreaves. This was standard procedure. The Admiral was a stickler for promptness and rather than enter the room and then leave to rustle out tardy officers Hargreaves never entered until all who were supposed to attend were present. He had also ensured that the two women were locked in their quarters, much to their chagrin, with guards posted outside. Everyone else was present and seated, Hargreaves took his seat and the Admiral began.

"Gentlemen, as some of you may know a catastrophe of momentous proportions has swept the planet. We all have families but gentlemen," the Admiral paused and looked round the room at each of his officers, "we must expect the worst. Our expectation is that few, if any people are left alive on the mainland." The Admiral waited as the full realization wafted over his officers and then sunk in. A few just stared glassy eyed some wept openly and a couple started mouthing godly references. Hargreaves sat by the Admiral resolute, having no living family, except for an older brother in Port Charlotte, Florida he had no one and he was married to the navy. He sat as if this was just another day at the office, awaiting the next order.

"Gentlemen," the Admiral resumed, "I know how tough this is for all of you. Our theory, and it is only a theory, is that a small meteorite crashed into the North Pole and unleashed some form of bacteria that has consumed every air breathing thing on earth, at least, certainly North America and Europe. Whatever it was now appears to have died out and we believe it is safe to return to the surface." The Admiral paused again, "our families have also gone." John Stanford knew from experience that the first reaction to bad news, especially the deaths of loved ones is disbelief and constant reinforcement is necessary until closure is achieved. At this point, the Admiral rose, Hargreaves and some of the other officers began to follow suit but the Admiral gestured to them all to remain seated. He stood to attention, back erect, shoulders back.

"Now, gentlemen we have to tell the crew. We have to be disciplined and remember we are officers in the U.S. Navy. We have a responsibility to our men, we made that pledge when we joined the navy. We also have an additional issue. The only two women known to be left alive are on this submarine. I'm sure there maybe others somewhere in the world but I don't know where. We have to protect them from the men on this ship and more importantly from those of other ships. So strict security is to be imposed. Until further notice no person other than existing crew is to set foot on this vessel. And no one is to mention the detachment of females we have on board. Is that clearly understood?" The Admiral looked around at his officers, not so much to see if they had comprehended but more to gauge their demeanor. One of his next orders would be to Hargreaves, to issue firearms to all the officers – except those that the Admiral felt were emotionally unprepared to handle them. First Lieutenant Doltry definitely fell into that category. He was still babbling and the Admiral knew he would have to be closely monitored.

"Gentlemen – attention!" The Admiral waited while the officers rose, some much slower than others. Some still with tears rolling down their cheeks. "Remember men," the Admiral reiterated quietly but forcefully, "we are U.S. Navy officers and every officer encounters a major challenge during their career which requires discipline and fortitude – this is ours. I know I can count on you. Lieutenant Hargreaves, standby to issue firearms." The Admiral looked grave as he completed his solemn speech. Hargreaves, all business, moved to the firearms safe in the corner of the war room that contained the pistols to be used by the officers during a code red state. A code red was the ultimate state of readiness, it was a state of war. The Admiral began to address the officers again, "you will each receive five additional rounds with each pistol and each pistol should be loaded – ready for firing. Gentlemen, at this point in time, not all of you will receive firearms. Those of you who will have them must be fully prepared to use them – on your own countrymen if need be. I am not going to stand in the way of any man who wishes to leave this submarine and find his own way in the world. However, I firmly believe that this vessel and the protection we can offer each other provides the best opportunity of preserving life than traveling aimlessly alone on a mainland fraught with frightening hurdles. Furthermore, I am not responsible for some of the other crews we may encounter, especially if word gets out that we are harbouring females on board. Right. When I call your name come forward to receive your firearm." Then turning to Hargreaves the Admiral continued, "issue arms to yourself first and then to me."

By nodding his head the Admiral indicated which of the officers would be receiving firearms, there was no dissention amongst those remaining unarmed. The Admiral addressed his officers once more, "I am about to call the ship's company on deck and repeat what I have told you. Hargreaves, please ensure the guards outside the women's' quarters can be trusted and then arm them. Lewis, shut down all internal communications." Hargreaves left the room carrying additional firearms for the assigned matelots, closely followed by Lewis. "Gentlemen, there may be some disorder, let us hope we can restrain the men, but if we can't - then use your guns. Are we ready gentlemen?" It was a rhetoric question and without reply he moved to the ship's tannoy system. "This is the captain speaking. All hands to report on deck immediately, I repeat, all hands to report on deck immediately – it's cold up there, dress accordingly." With that the officers filed out of the war room with the Admiral bringing up the rear. All the men were assembled and the officers in position when Admiral Sanford appeared in the conning tower ready to address the ship's company. Using a bull horn he related to the men much what was said in the War Room to the officers. After his speech, as to be expected, a few men broke down and collapsed to their knees. One man ran amok but was restrained by fellow sailors, most men were just too stunned to even comprehend or even believe what had just been explained to them. Some thought it was just another exercise but the eerie silence and lack of activity ashore made them realize that this was reality. After a few minutes pause while the commotion died down the Admiral nodded to Davidson, the Master at Arms and he, in turn, brought the company back to attention. The Admiral addressed the ship's company once more, "under the circumstances your obligation to this navy has ceased. When we arrive at base those of you who wish to leave are free to do so, however, disembarkation will be carried out in an orderly fashion and please give your name to the officer of the day as you leave the vessel. You will of course be free to return, we have often joked that the navy is your family. Now it is the truth and I will tell you the same thing I told the officers, this is probably the best place to be right now and if you do decide to stay – you will follow orders, not as a naval man but as a company man, and the goal of our company is to stay alive." At this point the Admiral paused briefly before continuing solemnly, "there is one more thing, you all know we have two women on board. This is information which is not available to other crews who you may encounter. Consequently, this knowledge is Top Secret and the sharing of this information will be considered treason and treason of course, is punishable by death, for either a civilian or military personnel. You may say those laws are no longer applicable, but gentlemen, morals are. And as captain of this vessel and for those of you who wish to remain, they will be part of our new order. But until we dock – remember, you are still under my command. Sir," he beckoned to the Master at Arms, "you may dismiss the men." The men dispersed in an orderly manner under close surveillance of the armed officers. The way the men had responded was testament to the discipline and respect for the command of the ship and bode well for the future. The usual barrack room lawyers offered their comments as they proceeded back to their stations or bunks, some groups were already planning what they would do on shore, others were too catatonic to even care.

Having given the order to continue on to Norfolk Admiral Sanford was returning to his quarters when the sound of Janet Delaney screaming expletives to his Number 2 forced him to change direction and confront the woman. As soon as he appeared in the gangway Janet turned her attention to him, as usual, needing to deal with the engineer, not the oily rag. "Admiral, I refuse to be locked up like a common criminal. I heard your speech and I wish to leave this vessel at the first available opportunity. I am quite capable of taking care of myself and I don't need some soldier wearing a uniform to protect me."

"Sailors Ms. Delaney, not soldiers," the Admiral replied calmly without a hint of condescension, "we will be docking in 30 minutes. At that time you will be free to leave the ship. Until then you are my responsibility and as captain of this vessel you will remain under armed guard for your own protection, whether you think you need it or not. Now, return to your quarters." Janet started to protest but the Admiral interrupted her with a stony glare in his eyes, "at once Ms. Delaney." The tone of his voice left no room for argument and she merely turned on her heel, went to her room and locked the door.

Mary had heard the commotion as she lay on her bed. But the words had not really penetrated as she fought with her own emotions as the impact of the Admiral's speech sank in. She was too busy thinking about her parents in San Diego, her younger sister, Irene, studying law at California State and her young brother Sean traveling in Europe. All dead. Impossible. It must be some kind of war game, but it didn't make sense when they were directly off shore, what was there to gain by saying that. She picked up her phone to call Janet but the line was dead. Thirty minutes before they could leave – it didn't give her much time to pack.

That thirty minutes seemed to take forever and both Mary and Janet were champing at the bit to leave. They felt the familiar bump as the submarine docked and the usual noises as chains and lines were secured. A couple of minutes later there was a knock, first on Mary's door and then Janet's. Both doors opened simultaneously, it was Hargreaves, "Mary, Janet, the Admiral wishes to speak with you in his cabin, immediately." Janet was through the door before Hargreaves had even finished and was already out of sight by the time Mary emerged from her quarters and was escorted to the Admiral's cabin. The Admiral was seated at his small work desk contemplating his hands that were splayed out in front of him, while Janet, not for the first time, was berating him for her treatment. Mary and Hargreaves entered and he closed the door behind him. At an almost imperceptible pause in Janet's tirade the Admiral intervened and held up his hands.

"Janet, Janet, my dear girl, for once in your life just shut up and listen. I do not believe you have fully understood the gravity of the situation. Not only has civilization, as we know it, been obliterated, you are, to our knowledge, the only females left alive. Do you know what that means? Over the next few days a few hundred men will be docking at this port and with no policing most of them will be running amok, undisciplined, unfettered and with no scruples. When they find out there are two females in the area you will be hunted down and," his voice trailed off as if it didn't bear thinking about. "Furthermore, as far as we know, you are the Human Race's only chance to provide children. As biologists, women of science don't you see your importance right now? I strongly advise you to remain on board where you can be protected, round the clock. We could leave here and travel to an undisclosed location where your safety would be almost guaranteed."

"Admiral, I can't speak for Mary, but if you think I am going to stay on board and become a sex slave for you and your men then, you are sadly mistaken. I wish to leave now and make my own findings on exactly what has occurred while we were at sea." Janet said adamantly.

"In which case may I suggest that you leave the ship now and we will give you a head start of one hour before the rest of the crew disembark. At which time I can no longer be responsible for your safety and welfare. No other submarine is expected here within the next twelve hours so that gives you plenty of time to get clear." The Admiral replied.

"How long do you intend to remain here Admiral?" Mary asked meekly. Although she saw the merit of the

Admiral's words, she also knew that she would accompany Janet.

"Hard to say Mary." For once the Admiral was like a civilian, he had never called her Mary before and his voice was different, less severe even compassionate. "It depends a lot on how many men remain, their attitude and of course what they want to do. This is no longer the Navy's submarine or my submarine, it belongs to the entire crew. It's a home for anyone who wishes to remain. We'll just have to see."

"Well thank you very much for you kind offer Admiral and of course your hospitality during the trip but I would like to leave now." Janet was back in control, seizing the opportunity, "so if you will excuse me, I will get my things and be off."

"Where will you go Janet?" The Admiral inquired, "how will you survive?"

"Oh don't worry about me Admiral. Goodbye." With that Janet opened the door and was gone leaving the others speechless."

"I, well I, better go with her." Mary stuttered and went to shake the Admiral's hand. She then turned to shake Hargreaves hand and as she looked in his eyes did she see a hint of remorse? The handshake seemed to linger a little longer than etiquette required and as she was leaving Hargreaves spoke to her and handed her a small communications device.

"Here, take this. Latest technology, it has a built in GPS and we can locate your whereabouts 24/7. It also has a two way radio that will be good within a few hundred miles of the sub. The battery is state of the art and should last up to a month with minimal usage. It also has a panic button."

Hargreaves showed her the mechanics of the device as he explained, "if you get into any difficulties press here," he indicated the small red button on the side of the device that was the size of a key-chain fob.

Mary took the device and put it in her pocket. With a last look in his eyes she replied "thank you. I hope we meet again. Soon." She turned and went running after Janet catching up with her just as she was picking up her luggage and moving towards the gangplank and land. Mary had a premonition that something bad was to befall them that in hindsight would have made them glad to have remained prisoners on board the submarine.

Chapter 16

DECISION TIME

St. Santia - Caribbean

It was just about dusk by the time Bob returned to their new base with the provisions. He was feeling no pain as a result of his couple of shots of liquor. Marlene was the first to comment on his hat.

"Ooooh cool hat dude!" she laughed. Marie just smiled.

"Wow Bob, all the time I've known you I don't think I have ever seen you in a hat except during winter," Tony said as he began to help Bob remove the items from the Moke. Bob just laughed and when all the items were inside and stashed away he reiterated the phone call to John Hamax. He concluded by telling a little white lie regarding John's intentions.

"John said they would attempt to make the journey down to Florida and island hop to us but they want to get closure on their children first so it could be a while." Bob felt that giving that tidbit rather than telling the rest of them the truth and that they were on their own would provide them with a little hope. This provided a good talking point as they prepared dinner.

That evening they had eaten their meal of beer, wine and pizza as they investigated the labyrinth of offices and rooms adjoining the chicken houses. The generators were connected to the main junction box so it was business as usual as far as the electricity was concerned, although they ensured no unnecessary lights were left on to conserve fuel. During their meanderings they discovered more washrooms that not only had sinks and toilets but functional showers too. But like the sink in the lunch room, it was doubtful if Mr. Clean had ever paid it a visit. On either side of the washroom were good sized utility rooms that could easily be converted into functioning bedrooms. They figured all that they had to do was clean out two of the adjoining rooms for bedrooms. The lunch room could be used as the kitchen cum dining room and by purloining the necessary furniture and utensils that they would need the result would be a comfortable temporary home for a couple of months. So they prioritized their tasks for the next day, during the morning Bob and Tony would continue to remove and incinerate all the dead carcasses, both human and otherwise. The girls would clean out the rooms and the washroom and take an inventory of what they had and what was required in the way of appliances and furniture. After lunch the boys would take the list of requirements and obtain the necessary articles. If they couldn't find what they were looking for onsite all they had to do was drive into town and grab whatever they needed. To date, they had not yet returned to their hotel so it was also agreed that the next day the boys would swing by the resort to pick up their personal effects from their rooms. Not that there was anything there that could not be replaced but they just felt it would be nice to have some of their own clothes and toiletries, at least initially. With that all agreed they retrieved their sleeping bags and just dossed down wherever they could.

The four new islanders were awake with the dawn, Marlene had made sure of that. The agreement had been to operate a 24 hour watch and it had been Marlene's turn for the graveyard shift. The girls prepared a cooked breakfast consisting of bacon and ironically, eggs, together with tomatoes, mushrooms, toast and marmalade. Their first meal cooked from scratch since the devastation and a veritable feast. During the meal they reiterated the day's activities that had been discussed the previous evening. Marlene was to catch up a little on her sleep and Maria would keep an occasional eye on the incubators and generators while she surveyed the place and started a list of things to make their new, temporary home as comfortable as they could. Everyone went about their tasks as planned and after lunch Bob and Tony took stock of the items that had to be obtained from the town, which was pretty much everything. So off they went while Marlene and Maria continued emptying out the adjoining rooms in preparation for the new furniture and giving the place a good clean.

Late afternoon Bob and Tony returned in a furniture truck and they off loaded the requested bedroom furniture, sheets and pillows and made up the beds. Once that was completed they returned to the furniture store to retrieve their Moke and drive onto the hotel to retrieve their belongings. On their way back they passed a garage that appeared to specialize in Mokes and there were a couple for sale on the front lot. They stopped and tried them out as they felt one more would make a good addition to their inventory. So by the time they returned, in separate vehicles, it was almost dark and time for dinner. Dinner that evening was a candle lit meal of barbequed steak, assorted fresh vegetables and a good Chardonnay while they discussed the day's events and how effortlessly everything had gone to plan. They now had two well-furnished bedrooms that any major hotel would have been proud of, clean showers and food on the table fit for a king. The generators and incubators were functioning well and the chicks seemed to be progressing. As a result, it was unanimously agreed that a night shift was considered unnecessary.

"Of course, the reason everything went as well as it did was because there was no people to impede us." Tony offered as he swilled a generous glass of wine, "no line ups, no tellers with attitude, and no Sunday drivers to slow us down. Nothing. So it is easier to plan – we are in complete control of our own destiny." The girls nodded in agreement and Maria was about to add something but Bob spoke first.

"You're absolutely right Tony, we are in complete control. Which brings us to the one issue we have to face that is considerably more difficult to plan." They all looked at Bob in surprise. He was sitting grim faced looking at each of them in turn. He had been waiting for the right moment to breach the problem and with the help of not a few glasses of wine he felt this was as good a time as any. "The world has changed and so must we. Tonight we must change partners." For a few seconds they looked at him incredulously and then all found their voices at the same time.

"Why?" Said Tony unbelievingly, "so, the world has changed we haven't we still love each other."

"We came here on a diving trip. Because we love diving and we love each other." Marlene shouted as she rose from the table and walked behind Maria and placed her hands lovingly on her shoulders. "You don't just change tribes, this isn't a TV reality show," Marlene continued. Maria responded by holding Marlene's hands. The tears were welling in her eyes and she bit her lip agreeing with her lover but knowing also that Bob was right. Tony was merely looking at the flickering candle shaking his head as if in complete denial. Bob was teetering on the brink. He held up his hands to silence them which only aggravated Marlene even more.

"That love of diving saved our lives Marlene. " Bob replied soothingly. "Why or how we were selected or how fate has played its hand who knows? But John Hamax is right, it is up to us to procreate the species. Whether we like it or not and the sooner we face up to that the better."

"Oh my God Bob, you have already been round these chickens too long. Listen to yourself. Now you have us breeding like those damn chickens." Tony offered petulantly. Bob was on the point of relenting when Maria spoke.

"Bob's right." Marlene paused and all eyes turned to her. "It's no good putting it off. We must do this. We must decide tonight who the partners are and make the break. The longer we leave it the tougher it will be." Marlene took her hands off Maria's shoulders and stood back absolutely dumbstruck.

"But why?" Pleaded Tony. So we have to breed, we chose some nights and do the necessary and we return to each other. Why wouldn't that work?"

"Tony, I don't think that is a practical solution." Bob replied. He saw Maria nodding her head in agreement. Marlene said nothing.

"But does it have to be to-night Bob?" Tony asked pleadingly reaching out for Bob's hand.

"It has to be to-night." A stoic Bob replied now he too was looking directly at the flickering candle as if it was the center of the universe. The others not realizing just how close he was to breaking down and reaching out to Tony to embrace him, kiss him and stay together. "I think we all know the match ups. But shall we pull straws for which room we will have?" He tried to smile but there was no feeling there.

"Marlene, which room would you like?" Maria asked.

"The one you're sleeping in," she replied not giving in to the pressure.

"No Marlene." Maria answered sympathetically.

"Just one more night" Marlene pleaded.

"No Marlene, now, which room would you like?" Maria's voice was wavering with emotion but she was resolved and Marlene knew that.

"We'll take the far room, it's closer to the incubators." Marlene answered with practicality.

"Fine." Maria replied almost inaudibly. Marlene slowly left to go to her new bedroom to prepare herself for a night with a man that a few days ago she didn't know existed. What's more, up until that point in her life, sexually no men had ever existed in her life. Unfortunately, the same couldn't be said of Maria. A child raised in various orphanages and eventually by foster parents, only to be sexually abused by an overzealous foster father. To the point that she had never intended making love to another man as long as she lived.

Bob stood up and blew out the candle. This was the signal for the others to retire for the night. Marlene had taken one last look at the chicks and she returned to the door of her new bedroom the same time as Tony, her new partner.

Chapter 17

TRAVELLING SOUTH

Norfolk – Virginia U.S.A.

Mary caught up with Janet just as she touched terra firma."
Janet, for Christ sake, slow down a little." Mary shouted
almost breathless. But Janet walked resolutely on, wanting
to put as much distance between her and the sub as possible.
This particular area of the docks was deserted, in as much
that there were only a few visible bodies and even they
were at a distance and could be easily mistaken for mounds
of garbage. Both Mary and Janet either chose to ignore
them or didn't see them. Either way, Janet maintained
an almost Olympic like pace and Mary struggled to keep
up with her. They continued for another twenty minutes
until they reached the security gate leading on to the sub
installation. Janet came to an abrupt halt as there in front
of them were the bodies of numerous Military Police. Janet
briefly glanced at the mouth of the nearest body. The white
substance she had seen in the dead polar bear on the sub
was prevalent on the man's face. She looked beyond the gate

at the many cars, on their sides, crumpled against walls, or just burnt out hulks of their once austere states. Beyond the road leading to the docks the freeway was just one mass of mangled machinery containing huge trucks, vans and cars of all types. They hadn't known what to expect, indeed, they hadn't given it a lot of thought, but they were now witnessing the results of their own theory and for the first time in her life Janet was regretting being right. After what seemed an age but was really only a few seconds Janet again took charge. She looked up and down the service road and noticed that although it had been busy at the time of all these driver's deaths there were gaps in the motionless traffic where people had instinctively pulled over to the shoulder at the first sign of their breathing difficulties. She also noticed the MP's jeep at the side of the gate and figured that a 4 x 4 was exactly what they needed. She strode over to it and peered in. The door was unlocked and the keys were in the ignition, some security she thought to herself. She quickly positioned herself behind the wheel and checked the gas gauge, it was full. How far that would get her she wasn't sure but a few hundred miles at least. She turned to Mary with her mind already made up and with a controlled voice, albeit croaky she shared her thoughts, "O.K. Mary, this is what I am planning to do. I am going to drive this puppy all the way to my home in Florida. Now, I know that there will be nobody there and nothing can ever be the same again but that's what I am going to do. At least there I know the area and the weather will be warmer. Are you coming or not?" Mary still stared at the wreckage on the freeway and thought of Jason and the protective cocoon he and the submarine offered.

"I don't know Janet, don't you think we would be better off on the sub. I mean look." Mary stretched out her arms in a gesture for Janet to view the carnage.

"Mary, it's done. There's nothing we can do about it. At least in Florida there is the sea, there are whole open plains of land where we can move around without hitting this." Janet too now pointed towards the freeway but Mary was still not convinced.

"We may never see another human, these men we are leaving may be all that is left. What about a new generation. As a biologist, don't you see? We need the men and we need them." Mary pleaded.

"No Mary, I don't need them. As for a new generation, that's neither here nor there. Whatever caused this could come back just as easily so what's the point? Besides, what future would the children have?" Janet asked.

"So that's it? You wouldn't have children because of the future? We have knowledge and even with no power or material things we will have far more technology than people had thousands of years ago when they were raising kids." Mary pleaded with Janet but her pleas fell on deaf ears.

"I'm not prepared to argue Mary. Are you coming or not?" Mary looked at Janet and then back in the direction of the sub. She thought if she said 'No' Janet may see sense and stay, but then again, she had known her too long and she was certain she would venture to Florida alone if necessary. Maybe if the sub was visible she may have decided to return to the sanctuary that was offered but out of sight out of mind and she certainly thought she was out of her mind. She picked up her bags and stowed them into the jeep.

Chapter 18

EMERGENCY

Norfolk – Virginia U.S.A.

The Admiral had watched the women's progress until they were out of sight and now truly on their own. If only the Admiral had known that at the moment he was hanging his binoculars on a hook in the conning tower the girls felt more alone than at any point in their lives. But he couldn't dwell on the problem, those members of the crew wishing to leave were now beginning to assemble topside. A few of the officers were there and about twenty of the men had arrived. The Admiral turned on the microphone and addressed the crew. All the men stopped what they were doing, those below decks preparing to leave and those who were staying and going about their regular duties.

"Men, those of you who are leaving, I wish you well, God bless. We will remain here until at least March 1st, by then all the other subs would have returned and we can discuss future plans with the other crews. I will try and obtain agreement on a schedule whereby you can always use this dock as a waiting station and a submarine will eventually be in port. We will leave provisions so if anyone wishes to return this will always be a base, a safe haven until the next docking. Remember that, if you don't find what you are searching for." The Admiral looked down at his watch, an hour had passed since the women had left so he continued, "Gentleman, you are free to leave. Good luck."

To a man, those who had already assembled to leave stood to attention and saluted, such was the respect they had for the Admiral. He returned their salute and for the final time in his illustrious career whispered 'dismissed'. Hargreaves was at the gangplank obtaining the names of those leaving and shaking the hands of each of them as they disembarked. No pushing or shoving just an orderly line like any regular furlough, again a testament to the discipline instilled in them during their tenure on this submarine. The Admiral was watching when Lieutenant John Smalls, the Communications officer, came on the radio.

"Admiral, USS Connecticut have reported an emergency, the crew has mutinied and docked at Wilmington." Until now the experience and sense of duty had kept any emotions from permeating that tough exterior of Admiral Sanford but the mention of Wilmington made his knees buckle and he unsuccessfully tried to stifle a sob. His 18 month grandson lived in Wilmington with his daughter in law, the widow of his son, a Navy Seal killed during a covert operation during the Gulf War. Not far away in Charlestown NC lived his daughter Lucille with his two granddaughters. Gone, all gone. Why bother? What was the point of carrying on? Suddenly, Hargreaves was by his side, all the men that were leaving had disembarked and Hargreaves took over.

"Mutinied? Who's the captain of that sub?" Hargreaves quickly asked.

"Was, sir. Captain Massey, along with most of the officers, was killed by mutineers. Boatswain Giles reported in, he said that a couple of the younger officers survived but he has taken temporary command as he doesn't feel the officers are capable of dealing with the situation." Smalls replied. At the sound of the name, Giles the Admiral snapped out of his reverie and managed to compose himself.

"Ha. That's Giles alright. Served with him many times, salt of the earth. Patch me through to him?" There was a couple of seconds pause as Smalls made the necessary switches and brought Giles on air. During that fleeting moment in time the two men on the conning tower stared into each other's eyes. The Admiral's steel blue eyes were flowing tears, the knuckles on his hands white with the effort of hanging onto support handles, defying his knees to collapse completely. Hargreaves knew what the Admiral was going through, he said nothing, which said everything. He merely, gently supported the Admiral's elbow as he brought himself back to his full height when Smalls came back on the radio.

"Boatswain Giles sir." Smalls said.

"Giles, its Admiral Sanford here give me a status."

"Sir, not good," Giles sounded hoarse as though he had a bad cold but was actually the result of almost being strangled during the melee until he fought off his attacker, "a group of the men took command of the sub and sailed her here to Wilmington. They killed all but two of the officers, and for all the good they are they may as well have topped the rest of them too." The Admiral smiled at this, not because the situation was humorous but the fact that Giles had taken charge. You couldn't wish for a better man to have on your side during hostilities but Giles hadn't always seen eye to eye with his so called superiors and was not backward in coming forward to say so. Invariably, he was right, but most officers wouldn't stand for the insubordination and he had been transferred more times than most sailors had had hot dinners. Giles continued with his raspy voice, "we were overpowered, and when we docked most of the men jumped ship. There are twenty of us left aboard. No serious injuries, a couple of bruises and black eyes but all fit for duty sir."

"I don't know Captain Massey but how could he lose control like this?" The Admiral asked.

"Well as soon as we figured out what had happened to everyone on land, well, let's just say he didn't handle the situation very well sir." Giles was for once being diplomatic.

"Good enough. For reasons we cannot divulge right now we are going to stay in port until at least March 1st. Can you make it up here to Norfolk?" The Admiral asked.

"Sure, I'll get the officers on it right away sir." Giles replied with a laugh.

"Good man Giles. By the way, we're all civilians now. There is no 'sir' anymore. We're considering ourselves a business corporation. But anybody who remains on board should do so by adhering to the rules. And it's good to hear from you again you old reprobate." The Admiral told the boson, a deep throated laugh could be heard over the airwaves.

"Thank you sir and I couldn't wish for a better man to report in to, navy or no navy. Congratulations, I guess that makes you the CEO! Of what I don't know." Giles said.

"Giles, this is ex Lieutenant Hargreaves, the men who left, did you get a sense of their intentions?" Hargreaves had more than a hint of concern in his voice.

"Not really. The king-pin is an officer, Lieutenant Linmore, a New Yorker. He was a trouble maker before we left port. Spent many a night in the brig. My bet is that he and most of his cronies will head north - back to the Big Apple. The rest will just scatter."

"Thank you Giles, good sailing and see you in a couple of days. Keep in open communication." The radio went quiet as Smalls removed the patch.

"You worried about the women aren't you Jason?" the Admiral asked. "Well, I shouldn't, it's a big country, and chances of them bumping into a bunch of mutineers are remote."

"Normally, I would agree sir. But I have a strong feeling the girls are headed south to Florida. The quickest route from here is the I95. From Wilmington to New York the best route is I40 then I95. I think the chances of them *not* meeting those evil bastards are even lower.

Chapter 19

HOUSE HUNTING

St. Santia - Caribbean

Bob and Maria's first night together was difficult, to say the least. Sexual activity could not have been further from their minds. They stayed awake until the early hours of the morning, talking, consoling, encouraging each other, trying to convince themselves that they would get through this, just like all the other events that had overtaken them during the last few days. In the other room, silence reigned. To Tony and Marlene, they felt like the participants of a forced marriage, thrust into matrimony against their will not by parents but by the hand of fate. No animosity existed between them, just a calm reluctance that this was potentially it for the rest of their lives. But for the remainder of the night they would be alone with their own thoughts, the future started at sunrise.

Marlene was the first to rise, checking the chicks and the fuel levels in the generators. Bob stepped into the hatchery yawning and stretching but wearing his new hat.

"Morning Marlene, how did you sleep?" Bob asked tentatively.

"Oh, pretty good, under the circumstances. How 'bout you?" Marlene replied with a surprising amount of enthusiasm.

"Ah, alright I guess. We talked for a while, that's all." The lack of any real intimacy was inferred.

"Same here. Didn't say much. Didn't do the deed either." There was conviction in her voice as if to say it would be some time before anything was to happen.

"Nah. First date and all that. But it will come" Bob replied as he started to get the coffee going.

"I'm sure it will." Marlene said giving him a mock wicked look. He smiled and gently punched her on the arm.

"Do you think we'll have enough diesel until all the chicks are hatched?" Marlene inquired.

"Hard to say, but if we are lucky we already have enough chicks to keep us going. But to be certain I would like to see this batch of eggs hatched and reared. Why do you ask? I would have thought there is plenty of fuel around." Bob looked at Marlene, trying to understand what she was driving at.

"Well, yes but with the hydro out the fuel pumps won't be working. How we get the gas out of the tanks I don't know. We'd have to siphon out of vehicles. Not impossible but time consuming and with all the other things we have to start working on it's something I'd rather not have to do." Marlene replied.

"Like what?" Bob asked as he turned to look at Marlene.

"Well, the food is not going to last forever, we're going to have to start a large garden. The water in this place is fed by a well pumped by the generator. When the generator stops, so does the water. We will have to find a place to live next to running fresh water. Once we find a place we will have to clear the dead stuff and furnish it, not just furniture but practical things. Tools, garden implements and we need to do it now, I think this should be a priority. Neither the generators nor the food we have are going to last forever. I know we discussed staying here for a while but I think the sooner we spend time looking for appropriate spots on the island to set up house the better." Marlene said. Now that she had mentioned it Bob couldn't understand why he hadn't thought of this before, it was so obvious.

"I didn't think we could leave the chicks that long. If something was to go wrong we'd lose everything. We can't take that risk." Bob said, trying to defend why this hadn't been raised before now. "However, we could take turns. Perhaps Maria and I can take a drive out to-day then you and Tony can go out tomorrow. If either of us find something appropriate the other couple can check it out and we can agree on it. How's that sound?" Bob asked.

"Fine, except I'd rather stay here. I feel I'm more qualified to handle things here and I trust Maria to make the right call." Marlene said despondently.

"Marlene, is everything alright? I mean, I know everything is not alright but this is tough for all of us you know?" Bob said with not a little concern in his voice.

"I know," she replied quietly, "it's just that…" then she trailed off. "I'll be fine. As long as Tony does his bit we will be having bonny, bouncing, babies before you know it." Marlene said with resignation.

"Marlene?"

"No really. I'll be fine. As you say, this is tough for everyone. I'll be fine."

"It sounds like you're trying to convince yourself."

"Sort of, but I don't really have much of a choice do I?"

"Guess not."

Over breakfast, a modest one of cereals, fruit and bagels, they discussed the day's plans. It was agreed, Bob and Maria would go house hunting, Tony would find a couple of tankers, one diesel and one regular and start a cache of gas. Marlene would see to the chicks, now that the heating, food and water sources were organized it would be merely a simple tasks of monitoring everything. If anything was to go awry there was no question Marlene was the right person to deal with any issue. Anyway, they all had their walkie-talkies and could contact each other if an emergency arose. Jokingly Marlene even offered to prepare dinner as she would have so much time on her hands while everyone else was out of the 'house'. However, they would all be on their own for lunch.

Bob and Maria began studying the map for a selection of potential sites. The main criteria was a water source but it also had to be reasonably sheltered from hurricanes. So they decided on a couple of spots on the west side of the island away from the rougher Atlantic seas. As a precaution, they packed sleeping gear, flashlights, two-way radios that had been purloined from the police station as well as spare batteries. They said their good-byes and were on their way as if they were newly-weds setting out on their honeymoon. Marlene and Tony watched and waved until all they could see was dust then without a word Tony walked over to the truck and was on his way to find a tanker. Marlene returned to the hatchery and began tending to the chicks.

To Bob and Maria it was as if they were an engaged couple off in search of that ideal first house. Only instead of a starter home in suburban Boston or rural Ontario it could be the most luxurious house they could find on a tropical island in the Caribbean. The roads on this part of the island were less congested but because they were narrower what vehicles were there were major obstacles. So it took the best part of the day of surveying various properties before they settled on potentially suitable houses. What they found was a pair of veritable mansions overlooking the ocean but sunk back into the hillside. They were separated by a fresh water brook whose source seemed to actually be in the hill itself. They knew the island was full of limestone caves, in fact that was one of the touristy traps that many people visited. It was even possible that the current was strong enough that in the future it would be suitable for providing some form of hydro power. But that would be later, more research would be required.

Both houses appeared to have been built at much the same time to similar specifications and obviously for some rich musicians as there were elaborate recording studios in both houses. There were diesel generators built into both houses and enough candles to last their lifetimes, obviously, used to power outages on this part of the island. The driveways up to both houses were spacious and extremely well paved, able to support high traffic. As there didn't appear to be anybody in residence in either house the number of dead things were at a minimum, a few maids, handymen and a couple of dogs and cats. They decided to spend the night in one of the houses so they radioed back to Marlene then spent the remaining daylight hours preparing for the night in their new house. There was a pick-up truck in one of the garages so Bob donned his overalls, that he had brought in the Moke and used the truck to clear away the dead things. He drove them to a beach out of site of the houses and dumped them ignominiously in a pile on the sand before setting fire to them. Even in such a short time since the devastation this act was carried out as if he was spraying insects, without any remorse or thought for the lives that these people and animals had had just a short while ago. While Bob was clearing the bodies, Maria had opened all the windows and strategically placed candles throughout the house, ensuring there was no immediate fire hazard if the candles were to fall. She had even found a freezer containing thick steaks, fries and vegetables, still frozen, courtesy of the automatic backup generators, and was in the process of cooking dinner on a propane barbeque when Bob returned. Bob removed his overalls and placed them back in the Moke then he went into the house and took a towel from a linen cupboard stuffed with luxuriously thick beach towels. He strolled down to the beach for a swim and to clean himself off in the sea. Emerging from the water he dried himself down and returned to the house just in time for a wonderful meal to be served on exquisite china plates, sterling silver cutlery placed on extremely expensive patio furniture. Maria had selected a fine Riesling from a well-stocked wine cellar that she had located at the back of the house, partially carved out of the hill. To add an extra touch of romance they were blessed with one of the most beautiful sunsets either of them had ever witnessed. There was even a propane gas heater that took the chill out of the air as a slight breeze began to waft in from the sea.

It felt almost surreal, only a few days ago they were in the depth of winter in busy cities amongst millions of stroppy, non-caring people, now, by a twist of fate, they were enjoying a fine gourmet meal without a person in sight, surrounded by opulence that they had only dreamed of, in one of the best climates nature could offer. The ambience created a romantic aura that relaxed them both and for the first time since the devastation they allowed themselves to kick back and to them they were the centre of the world. Unlike Tony and Marlene both Bob and Maria had experienced sexual encounters with members of the opposite sex but for different reasons they had settled for same sex partners. But fate had now changed that. They finished the wine and walked into the house, hand in hand, each carrying a lighted candle in their free hand. The dishes were left as if some imaginary servant was going to clear them away, but Tony and Maria, didn't care. They were already in the master bedroom, pulling back the satin sheets and snuffing out the candles.

Marlene had spent the day tending to the chicks and generally tidying the place up. Occasionally, she heard the sound of trucks as Tony parked another tanker in one of the old buildings surrounding the chicken farm. But apart from noting that on one occasion he left on a motorized bicycle she really didn't take much notice of his comings and goings, nor did she really care. She didn't stop for lunch, just had snacks on the go and it was just as well Bob and Maria radioed in to say they were staying over as she had been too preoccupied to even think about dinner. After talking to them and feeling their excitement she had a heart to heart with herself. It wasn't Tony's fault they were in this predicament, it wasn't anyone's fault, it just happened and they would have to work together to make the best of it just to survive, even ignoring the question of propagating the species. She decided that she too was going to prepare a nice meal, talk to Tony and clear the air in an attempt to make a fresh start. She certainly wasn't ready for the intimacy yet but like an arranged marriage, she felt it would happen eventually. The first hurdle had been jumped, she had accepted the situation, now she needed to work at it.

Meanwhile, Tony drove into town, well at least as far as he could. They had seen smoke last night but hadn't really taken much notice of it. Turns out it was the police station and surrounding buildings, a great source of emergency supplies destroyed. How the fire had started they would never know. Undaunted, Tony took the coast road and drove relatively unobstructed until he came to a dirt road that appeared to lead to nowhere. On a whim, he turned and drove for almost a mile, without seeing any other vehicles, bodies or even dead animals. Eventually, he arrived at gates topped with razor wire which appeared to be the only break in a chain link fence, also topped with razor wire that stretched either side of the gate down to the beach. The signs on the gates indicated that this was some kind of British military outpost, although for security reasons, Tony surmised, there was nothing to say quite why it was there. The locks on the gate were solid and for good measure a chain was lashed round the two gates fixed in place by a heavy duty padlock. He certainly didn't have the tools to make any impression on the locks and there was no way he was going to attempt climbing the fence and risk being lacerated by the razor wire. But the temptation of those buildings beyond the fence and the prize they may contain was too much. He reversed the Moke and retraced his tracks to the main road. Not far along the road was a truck that had been parked while making a delivery of furniture. The back doors were still open and swinging in the light sea breeze. Tony closed the doors and climbed into the cab. The engine started first time and he slipped it into gear and drove back to the army base. He turned onto the dirt road and slowed until he came to a complete stop. He fastened the seat belt and made sure it was securely tightened then resumed the drive back to the gates, only this time instead of slowing down he increased speed and at point of impact with the gates he closed his eyes and hung onto the steering wheel with all of his strength. With the sound of the headlights smashing against steel and the gates being wrenched from their hinges the truck burst through into the compound. Tony simultaneously applied full brakes and opened his eyes only to see one of the gates inches from the windscreen, fixed in place by the wire mesh wrapped firmly around the truck's bumper. The truck skidded to a stop, a mere five yards from the building nearest to the gate. After a few seconds pause, as the adrenalin rush subsided, he unfastened the seat belt, turned off the engine and stepped out of the cab to reconnoiter. The first building appeared to be an administration office and contained nothing of any use. The neighbouring building was the barracks and although it seemed capable of accommodating approximately twenty people most of the rooms were vacant, indicated by the army issue spring mattresses with no bedding. The few rooms that appeared to be lived in were immaculately tidy, beds made military style with nothing out of place, but again, nothing worth pirating. At the end of the building was a small medical centre, ironically, containing the only body Tony had come across so far. It did, however, provide some basic medical supplies, plasters, bandages, aspirins etc. but nothing he couldn't obtain elsewhere on the island. And that was it, hardly worth the effort, and then it occurred to him, where are the others, the other personnel. So far he had only come across one body, there must be others but where are they? Outside the medical centre was a Land Rover with the white medical cross emblazoned on its sides. He climbed in, started the engine and drove behind the barracks. A couple of hundred yards away, the hill sloped sharply down to the ocean, partially hiding a string of long, low, buildings almost resembling a strip mall. Tony drove towards the buildings. In the centre was a wide, almost hangar like building that appeared to be the motor pool. But inside was a fleet of trucks, far too many for the small detachment of personnel being housed in the barracks. A few bodies were strewn around vehicles that were obviously in the process of being serviced. On closer inspection of the trucks it appeared that they were transport vehicles, containing bench seats on the sides, obviously designed to carry many people, albeit uncomfortably. But for what purpose? They only thing Tony could think of was hurricane evacuation for the local civilians. Even though the hurricane season was a few months off, all the trucks were fueled up and ready to roll. It didn't make too much sense but it wasn't something Tony would dwell on as he continued to survey the buildings.

So far he had found a few medical supplies and a fleet of approximately fifty vehicles that had no real value except for the diesel fuel in their tanks. Not much of a productive morning so far, but that was just about to change. The next building housed eight fuel tankers, all full and ready to roll, all he had to do was drive them back to the farm. On further inspection of the tankers it got better, four of them were diesel and the rest were regular. There were even some motorized bicycles or mopeds as they were referred to, all fueled up, naturally. His game plan was simple, he would lash one of the mopeds to the back of a tanker, drive the tanker back to the farm and return on the moped for more supplies. But before leaving he thought he would finish foraging through the remaining buildings for other potential treasures. The next building contained wet weather clothing of all shapes and sizes, endorsing his assumption that this small military detachment was there for a natural emergency. There were Wellingtons, calf-length and also gun-boot style, sou'westers, coats, jackets, gloves and some garments he didn't even recognize. He chose a few for himself to take back to the farm, he figured there would have to be more trips to this spot so the others could take what they needed whenever they wanted. He tossed the clothes into the cab of the tanker and ambled over to the final building. He opened the door and let his eyes adjust to the dim light emitting from the few barred sky-lights in the roof. Lined up along part of one wall were stacks of portable generators of all shapes and sizes ranging from small four socket ones to hunking great towable rigs that would provide enough power for a small sub-division. In shelves along the wall were arc lights, flashlights, batteries and even industrial size cooling fans. Towards the rear of the building were stacked cartons of emergency rations, substantially more than was at the police station, more medical supplies and toiletries. He selected a few items at random and carried them to the cab of the tanker. He rolled open the doors of the garage and returned to the tanker, climbed into the cab and turned on the ignition. It started effortlessly, no surprise really as it had been meticulously maintained to be put to use at a moment's notice. Tony slipped it into gear and slowly drove the tanker out into the open. He brought the vehicle to a stop and climbed out to shut the garage doors. On retrospect, he wasn't sure why he did that but he felt it was the right thing to do. He drove the tanker gingerly along the roads, carefully negotiating each obstruction as though he was sitting on a cart carrying bottles of nitro-glycerin instead of a tanker full of low volatile diesel fuel. When he turned into the chicken farm with its ruts and uneven surface he was traveling so slowly an observer may have mistaken it for being parked. Finally, he arrived outside his temporary home and shut down the engine. He got out of the cab, untied the moped and repeated the exercise for one more tanker, regular fuel this time, before finally returning for the Moke. He decided that the moped might be a useful form of transportation so he placed that in the back of the Moke before leaving the military establishment.

On his return with the Moke he was about to go into the hatchery when he suddenly realized that it was late afternoon and he hadn't eaten a thing since breakfast. With that sudden realization came the inevitable hunger pain so he went into the kitchen where Marlene was preparing a meal. He silently went to the refrigerator in search of some cheese and biscuits to snack on. Marlene was the first to speak and explained that Bob and Maria had found two perfect houses and would not be returning that evening. Tony said nothing, of course he had listened in on the radio dialogue during his foraging. For a couple of minutes there was an uncomfortable silence, except for the sound of masticating cheese and biscuits. Again, Marlene spoke.

"Tony, look, I've been doing a lot of thinking to-day. I know I've been difficult and we both know that the situation is hardly ideal, but I've come to the conclusion we have no choice but to make a go of this. Whaddaya say? Right now it's you and me, Bob and Maria are going to be fine. Let's bury the hatchet and try and make the most of the rest of our lives." For a few seconds Tony stopped his chewing and didn't seem like he was going to respond at all. Finally, he swallowed and quietly replied.

"Well, that's interesting. *You* came to the conclusion, not we. Just like that, *you* have decided *we* have to make a go of it." He shook his head and spread his arms in a gesture of futility. "I'm out there busting my ass trying to find gas to keep these damn chickens alive while Bob and Maria are relaxing by the beach under the category 'house hunting' and you, you have been thinking." Tony replied sarcastically. This made Marlene furious.

"You have no idea what I have done to-day, aside from getting your dinner ready you ungrateful pig. Walking end to end in those hot, stinking, claustrophobic, chicken sheds making sure that we have food for the rest of our lives is not exactly a walk on the beach." She shouted at him, pointing the knife she had been using to cut up vegetables. So much for the 'clear the air' talk, she thought. She was too mad to burst into tears but she was damned if she was going to cook the dinner but then she noticed a slight smile on Tony's face as he looked up at her.

"You know," he said, "I think we're going to be alright - we're beginning to act like a married couple." With that they both burst out laughing and while they exchanged their day's efforts like happy school children, Tony helped her prepare dinner.

Chapter 20

RV DRIVING

Norfolk – Virginia U.S.A.

Driving to the highway had taken Mary and Janet almost three hours by either ramming other vehicles clear or transporting their luggage around obstructions and purloining other suitable vehicles. Many of the vehicles had run out of gas as the microbe attack had come so quickly that the occupants had no opportunity to switch off the ignition, so the engines had continued running until their fuel was exhausted. Most of these were automatic transmissions, the manual shift cars just stalled but of course these were in the minority. However, most of the heavy duty trucks were manual and they too had merely stalled, so for the most part these were the type of vehicles they were seeking. Once on the main highway they had lucked out by coming across a recreational vehicle that judging by the Baltimore Orioles cap the elderly driver was wearing had originated locally and was obviously on its way to warmer climes, probably the Sarasota area to watch spring training. The fuel tanks were full and the beds didn't look as though they had been slept in. The tidy living spaces also indicated that no serious driving time had occurred. It was stocked up with food, both canned and packaged, some fruit and vegetables that were still passable. It also had a refrigerator and freezer that were well stocked and their contents still relatively cold. Given the outside winter temperatures, the coolers had retained enough chill to have kept its contents from turning bad. On one of the tables was an open map and slumped beside it was a white haired old lady. It appeared as though that was the last thing she had looked at. This could account for why the vehicle was parked on the shoulder with the motor turned off; they were possibly, ensuring they were on the right road.

Once its two occupants were removed and unceremoniously deposited on the tarmac shoulder Janet and Mary climbed back into the vehicle and Mary started the engine. With the fuel indicator showing full and the low hum of the appliances functioning they felt they were going to be O.K., if they could retain this vehicle all the way to Florida. At the impact of the devastation most of the drivers naturally turned to the shoulder on the slow lane, where possible, so the shoulder on the fast lane was relatively clear. This also avoided other vehicles that had been entering the highway at oncoming ramps and service areas. A few times there was no choice but to gently 'bull-doze' vehicles aside, however, they chose their opponents carefully, inflicting marginal damage to their new home. At one of the service centers, avoiding the prone, listless bodies, they stocked up with a few items from convenience stores, especially personal hygiene items and toiletries. There were a couple of up-scale fast food restaurants with industrial freezers and with no heat being generated in the buildings their contents were still frozen. They managed to stuff a few coolers with ice and meat such as steak, chicken, ham and other meats as when they arrived in Florida they knew all they would be living on would be fish, fruit and vegetables. They agreed only to drive during daylight as the obstructions were too numerous and too difficult to maneuver in the dark. During the day they arranged to drive in shifts, and hoped it would only take a few days to arrive in Florida. Unfortunately, they could only do that if conditions were perfect with even limited obstructions on their route. However, a brief storm hit them and blanketed the road and all the stationary vehicles with snow; not only making the driving treacherous but in the dwindling light, perspective was difficult as the snow cover made everything appear as one. Even at a reduced speed obstructions were not apparent until they were right on top of them. They decided to stop to consider their situation. Over a meal of cold cuts, bread, chips and a delightful cup of hot tea it didn't take them long to figure out that the day's events had caught up with them, they were dog tired and driving through the night was completely out of the question anyway. It certainly wasn't worth the risk of driving zombie like through the night when there really was no hurry to arrive. So after their meal they selected a bed and trying to keep as much normality as possible, dressed into their pyjamas, and were soon fast asleep.

The next morning Mary awoke with the sun rising on what looked like a beautiful day. It was cold in the vehicle and judging by the frost on the windscreen it would be even colder outside. Although there was an adequate shower they had decided the previous evening that they were not sure of the water availability in the tanks and if and when they could replenish it. They had stocked up on bottled water so they were in good stead for drinking water. They had both used the toilet but from now on that would only be used in emergencies to conserve water in the tanks. Using the old camping formula, 'if it's yellow, let it mellow and if it's brown flush it down'. Mary made do with a quick body wash as she heard Janet stir and begin to get herself dressed. Over a cup of tea, orange juice and cereal they discussed who was going to drive first and for what period. It was decided that Janet would drive for as long as she felt capable and Mary would carry on with the vehicle's inventory that she had started the previous day. They both had brought their laptops so she was using database software to categorize items and make notes of what she felt was missing that they would need during both the immediate future and the long term.

With Janet driving and Mary rummaging through the back of the RV this, once more, left them both isolated with their own thoughts. Janet, an only child always used to getting her own way, the daughter of wealthy parents and brought up in a sprawling mansion just outside Naples, Florida. Her father owned a construction company and had successfully bid on huge profitable contracts with the theme parks around Orlando. Because of his involvement with Sea World Janet obtained a summer job there during her early teens and she had never looked back. Although she had never seen eye to eye with her parents, obviously, she loved them very much and fortunately the concentration necessary to avoid obstacles on the highway was keeping her mind occupied on the present and not dwelling on her parents' demise. But secretly, she was hoping there was just a chance, albeit slim, that somehow her parents had survived. They had been on a cruise in the Caribbean, via the Panama Canal and although it would have been early when the devastation hit, maybe, just maybe, her parents, both avid divers, had been underwater at the time.

In the early light any obstructions were easier to detect and negotiating around them was relatively easy. There was one slight scare when after a stretch of open highway Janet had to brake to avoid a car pinned into the guardrail. Although they were only traveling at a moderate speed, the back of the RV lost traction on the snow and began to sideslip. She quickly corrected the skid and used it as a wakeup call to remind her that there had been no road crews out during the night clearing and salting the roads - and there never would be again. But having regained her composure it also brought the thoughts of her family back to mind. She realized she must stay focused if they were going to weather even this part of the long journey that was ahead of them and from that point on she rarely thought of her family again.

In the back of the RV Mary felt the sideslip and inquired whether everything was O.K. Janet assured her it was so Mary continued with the inventory and the thoughts of her family. At the time of the devastation her mother and father were living in San Diego with her two younger sisters, one working as a hairdresser, hoping to open her own store one day, the other at college studying law. Mary too, lived in hope that somehow her family had survived, maybe the devastation hadn't been as widespread on the west coast, but the scientist in her knew that it had. So for the next little while, as the snow melted under the bright sun and diminished even more as they traveled south, she continued counting thinking about her family and the happy times they had once enjoyed.

Around mid-morning Mary inquired as to how Janet was feeling. Mary had spent the last ten minutes scanning through some travel literature that the original owners had collected for their trip. It was typical tourist information but included in the pile of pamphlets was a map of all the outlet malls in each state on the highway. They would soon be at an exit that boasted one of the biggest outlet malls on the interstate and she suggested Janet come off the highway at that point so they could take a break and provide them with an opportunity to obtain a few items she thought would come in handy. Twenty minutes later they were in the car park of the large outlet mall trying to decide where best to park. It was indeed a large mall comprising of many outlet stores housed in an L-shaped building that appeared to represent only part one of the construction phase. The land to the right of the building was in the process of being prepared for phase 2 that would complete the other half of the construction to produce a horse shoe shape of shops around a massive parking lot. There were not many cars in the expansive car park so they drove around its perimeter looking at the shops to decide on where to stop first. At the top of the shopping list were a few more coolers, ice packs and frozen meats which they thought they may find in the food court or at one of the outdoor equipment stores. The electrical system could support a few more appliances so they were looking for a store that would have some of those plug-in coolers that worked both off mains and car cigarette lighter outlets. There was a national department store that they thought would also be a prime candidate, which happened to be the flag ship of the mall. So they made a bee-line for the front of the store, which was situated in what would eventually be the middle of the mall, turned off the engine and climbed out into the cool air.

Inside the store they ambled along looking at various items ignoring the few dead people littering the aisles. Now that they could have anything in the store it seemed to take away the luster of shopping. But nevertheless they did pick up a few cosmetic items and more toiletries as well as some of the more practical items. They found their way to the camping section and found what they were looking for. They also found through the 'Employees Only' door a motorized flatbed trolley that they used to stack eight coolers, all-in-one tools adverstised as '*perfect for surviving in the wild*' and various items of practical all-weather clothing. Fortunately, the building was single-storey so they did not have much difficulty returning to the front of the store with their new found possessions until they came to the revolving doors. Of course the customers' entrance had not been built to accommodate the industrial trolley, even the doors to the side were not wide enough. So, they jammed open the side doors and wearing their new vests to brave the cool air they began to carry their trophies back to the RV. Mary was the first to the back of the RV so she placed the boxed cooler on the road and reached up with both hands to simultaneously open the back doors. Startled, she jumped back as a man's voice lewdly said, "well, well, well. What do we have here?"

Chapter 21

SHOWDOWN IN THE MALL

Somewhere off the Atlantic U.S. Coast

Aboard the USS Connecticut the news of the devastation hadn't been as obvious as it had been to the crew of the Augusta. The sub had been approximately 100 miles from base carrying out exercises on the Atlantic seaboard when all communications with base and sea going vessels were suddenly lost. Concern enveloped the members of the submarine as all attempts to restore communications proved fruitless. Without any incoming orders Captain Massey made a decision to raise periscope depth in an attempt to obtain visual communication from one of the destroyers participating in the exercise they were part of. The view the commanding officer saw through the periscope was that of one of the U.S. Navy's finest, aimlessly drifting through the gentle swells of the Atlantic, seemingly, out of control. He immediately ordered surfacing procedures. Further attempts to communicate with the destroyer using lights and semaphore were to no avail and finally the captain ordered a porter, in the form of a fast moving dinghy, to be launched and accompanied by a small party of men captained by Lieutenant Sheldrake. They motored towards the destroyer and as they approached the vessel their loud beckoning received no replies and with no way to board they were forced to throw up grapnel hooks so that two of the men could scale the ropes to the ship's deck. As soon as the men reached the top of the ropes and saw the bodies of the seamen laying on the deck they shouted back to the captain that he needed to come aboard. Not prepared to climb the rope himself he ordered the men down to the lower deck to open the loading door used to accept crew and supplies while at sea. The Captain and remaining crew maneuvered the dinghy to the middle of the ship and waited for the doors to open. After what seemed an age the doors were finally opened by two very grey faced seamen holding handkerchiefs over their mouths. As soon as the doors were opened one of the seamen dropped to his knees and vomited over the side, much to the disgust of the Captain and crew. The other seaman slumped against the side of the bulwark with his head between his knees. At first the Captain had thought the men had contracted some disease but they began to explain what they had found throughout the ship. At first the Captain couldn't believe what he was hearing so he climbed aboard using a short rope ladder tossed to him by one of the boarders. He was closely followed by the rest of the dinghy's crew who were also intrigued by their sea mate's findings. Even the helmsmen wanted in on the excitement so he secured the boat to go and see for himself.

Stepping over the bodies the Captain made his way to the bridge and opened communication with his sub. Like the seamen, having seen all the death he was experiencing great difficulty in speaking, but he managed to explain what they were witnessing and while the rest of his party tried unsuccessfully to contact land bases and other vessels he concluded that whatever had happened was not restricted to this destroyer. Unfortunately, the dialogue was unwittingly being broadcast to the whole of the sub and by the time the dinghy returned, panic had set in and many of the younger ensigns had already lost control and they had physically overpowered the officers on the bridge, killing most of them, including Captain Massey. Any senior non-commissioned officers who tried to oppose them were badly beaten and on his return Lieutenant Sheldrake was immediately knocked unconscious but to save punishment, the other men agreed to join the mutineers and were spared. A few other officers survived but were badly beaten, all except Lieutenant James Linmore, a young up and coming officer who saw the situation as an opportunity to gain control and grab power. He actually joined in the mutiny and once all of his peers were overcome he shouted out that they were returning to base and began barking out orders. At first, there was some dissention but being a hulk of a man, 6 foot 4 inches and 220 pounds of fat free muscle, he used his physical attributes on the nearest two sailors and once they had been floored with a punch to each of their heads the rest of the mutineers began following orders. Resembling a pirate of old he selected a band of the men to press gang the rest of the company into helping them man the sub back to the mainland. Those who refused were locked up in the brig and if they were officers, badly beaten or in the case of some of them, remorselessly beaten to death.

Wilmington – North Carolina U.S.A.

Because of their close proximity to shore it hadn't been difficult to plot a course to the mainland and at full speed they were soon back at base. As soon as the sub docked many of the mutinous seamen jumped ship and headed for their homes in desperate attempts to seek out their loved ones. Of the remainder, ten of the men, including Linmore, banded together and commandeered vehicles to head inland. Linmore, who held a pilot's licence, didn't think there was any merit in returning to his home in New York so he decided to make his way to a municipal airport just outside Wilmington with the intention of flying across country to L.A. or San Diego in the hopes that some pockets of life had survived. Failing that, at least they would be in a better position, geographically, to head even further south to Mexico or even Central America in a search for survivors. Once the mutineers abandoned ship the prisoners in the brig managed to break out, some decided to go their own way but the rest of them stood behind the wizened old boson, Giles, as he organized medical assistance for the wounded and manned the radios in an attempt to obtain contact with anyone he could.

Linmore and his motley crew commandeered a couple of Sports Utility Vehicles that were parked at the dock gates and they arrived at the ground school of a municipal airport just outside Wilmington just thirty minutes later. But by the time they had driven onto the apron another five of the mutineers had decided to drop out and went their own ways across the great country that is the United States. Their feeling was that they had already cheated death once, they were not going to risk climbing aboard a small plane in the hands of someone they knew only as a sea-fearing man, especially with no backup services like air traffic control. After all, they were seamen, if they had wanted to fly they would have joined the Air Force. In the former, they were somewhat unjustified as Linmore had been flying since he was a teenager and it was really only his size that prevented him from becoming a naval fighter pilot. In the latter, they had a case, as with no up to date weather reports Linmore could only plot a course based on dead reckoning and using charts he had found in one of the ground schools on the airport. Without weather reports and the upper wind speeds he would need all of his navigation skills to travel across country.

While Linmore was putting together a collection of charts, navigation equipment and airport data the others were gorging themselves on what they could from the small canteen annexed to the training school. Once Linmore had all he needed they returned to their vehicles and drove to the first of four hangers that were close to the ground school. Linmore saw a suitable plane immediately, a Cessna 190 that would comfortably carry the five of them to L.A. Unfortunately the Cessna was at the back of the hangar and getting the plane onto the apron meant moving three training planes out of the way. He ordered the men to clear a path as he began a thorough walk around of the Cessna using a checklist he had found inside the cockpit. He checked the fuel and oil levels, control surfaces and tires mentally ticking off the items from the checklist until he came to the items concerning documents to carry on board. These he disregarded, concentrating only on those checks that were pertinent to safety. He calculated the load balance and figured that without any baggage, a full complement of passengers and a full fuel tank take-off would be iffy. But with no trees or buildings obstructing the runways he was confident that a gradual climb on a cold day would be within limits. Once the way was clear for the Cessna he told the men where to sit to ensure an even load and after they were all seated and buckled in he started the engine. He dispensed with explaining the emergency procedure to his passengers and once the engine was purring nicely he went through all the engine checks, back up alternators, carburetors etc. Satisfied everything was in working order he eased the plane through the gaping hangar doors and onto the apron. Despite the fact that he didn't anticipate hearing any radio traffic he donned the headset and tuned in to the emergency frequency. Judging by the windsock he decided that runway 340 was most favourable. As he was taxiing to the holding area, he became a pilot again, lost in his own little world and as a pilot, having the whole world's airways to oneself was a joy beyond belief. He arrived at the holding area and much to the surprise of his passengers did a complete 360 degrees as old habits forced him to carry out a final check for other traffic in the skies, it would have been nice to have warned his passengers of his intentions but then he was not a nice person. Not surprisingly there was no other traffic either in the air or on the ground so he expertly taxied to the centre of the runway and started rolling for takeoff.

Despite the trepidation of some of his passengers the takeoff was one of the smoothest they had ever experienced and the first couple of hours of flying were uneventful. For most of the passengers this was their first experience in a small plane and being able to view the ground and all the landmarks, albeit punctuated with signs of the devastation, time went very quickly. But nature decided to show another of her ugly sides. Linmore had to navigate around a weather system that was ahead of them and as he did so he temporarily lost his bearings. With strong upper winds he found himself far further north than he had anticipated. At that point they were faced with a wide weather system and his attempt to climb above the clouds proved unsuccessful and snow began to settle on the Perspex windscreen. He dropped altitude and decided he was going to have to put the plane down. He searched around for a suitable landing area but the snow that had quickly began to settle made the quest difficult. The thruway, with no traffic moving on it was a logical choice, but he couldn't find an empty stretch long enough to provide a safe landing strip. Then he saw a mall with a vast, almost empty car park. Because of its recent development there were no trees to obstruct an approach so he felt that if he positioned the landing diagonally across the lot it would provide sufficient distance to safely land the plane. He certainly didn't need any panic on the plane so he explained to the rest of the men what he was doing and assured them that this was normal and everything would be fine. His approach was spot on and his feather like touchdown brought relief to the men as they arrived safely back on terra firma. From the air, the relief of the car park was made to look flat by the thin layer of snow that covered it. Unfortunately, for the men in the plane, it disguised the speed bumps placed every twenty yards along the access roads between the rows of car spaces. Consequently, just after touch down, traveling at 70 miles an hour, the Cessna clipped a speed bump which not only threw the plane back into the air but also spun it 45 degrees. Linmore carried out a remarkable feat of airmanship to retain control and after a couple of more unexpected bumps they eventually came to a stop with everyone on board, badly shaken, but safe. Although they did regret making pigs of themselves at the airport's canteen and three of them were unable to hang on to their digested food. Through habit, Linmore proceeded through a full shutdown while the passengers quickly exited the plane and ran towards the mall. Just as well, the stench in the plane was now unbearable. Not that it mattered, nobody would be flying the plane again, it was totaled having hit three speed bumps, at odd angles during their diagonal approach, the fixed landing gear had partially collapsed sustaining irreparable damage to the prop as it ground repeatedly into the asphalt.

At the entrance of the mall was one of those chain roadhouses providing '*fine eats, happy hour and great company*'. Until then, having been tea total since they originally set sail almost a month ago and just having lived through one of the most harrowing experiences of their lives all they were interested in was some very hard liquor. By the time Linmore had joined them they had each consumed a half of bottle of their choice as if it were a soft drink. Their shattered nerves were beginning to return to normal.

The mall was almost devoid of bodies, the devastation had hit in the early hours of the day and opening time was not until mid-morning so only a few dead workers and security guards were lying scattered around the mall. They did a quick reconnoiter of their surroundings, bottles in hand, and came across a bedding store that was conveniently situated next to the bar. They each tried a selection of beds and each one decided on where they were going to sleep that night before returning to the bar for some serious drinking. One of them was the sub's cook so on their return to the road house they helped him prepare a slap-up meal from food that what was readily available in the refrigerators and freezer, then proceeded to get absolutely shit-faced drunk and crashed out on one of those famous orthopedic mattresses. They would decide on what they were going to do in the morning. Linmore said nothing, he knew that this was not the time to pull rank and assert his authority. He simply nursed a malt whiskey, tucked into the food, a T-bone steak, cooked to perfection accompanied by a baked potato with all the condiments, asparagus tips and baby carrots. It was surprisingly good and he gave his sincere compliments to the chef who obviously took great pride in his craft despite the circumstances he was in and the rabble he was part of. When at last the rest of them had drunk themselves silly and retired to their bed of choice Linmore laid down on one of the bench seats in the restaurant and slept.

He didn't sleep too deeply but when he heard the sound of an engine he was in that state between dreaming and awaking and at first he had trouble differentiating between the two. When he knew he was awake he lay still, listening for the sound again but failed to hear it. It wasn't until he heard the sound of a door closing, closely followed by another that he knew the sound was real and he quickly rose and looked out of the window from behind a curtain to see two attractive women walking away from a parked RV. He watched them enter the mall and then he tip toed to the bar entrance, peeked through the door as the women checked the store directory. He knew that if they turned right and went through to the bedding store it would be impossible not to see the comatose men, they may be fooled into thinking they were casualties of the devastation but the noises the men would be making as they recovered from their drunken stupors would soon put paid to that. It would result in the women leaving as quickly as they arrived. Fortunately, as though responding to his wishes, they proceeded down the aisle away from the bedding store and once they were out of sight he went to wake the men, which he had to carry out quickly and quietly. He managed to do this one at a time, albeit with great difficulty. His plan was for all of them to wait in the RV and whichever door the women approached he would wait for the women to open it, surprise them and hold their attention while the men exited the other doors to grab them from behind. It was almost thirty minutes before the women returned, the men had even had time to brew a carafe of coffee in the RV's kitchen and down a few bottles of water in an effort to clear their heads. The women were hauling a flat-bed trolley topped with coolers and camping utensils and as expected, were approaching the back of the RV. Linmore beckoned to the rest of them to take positions at the side doors and as soon as the back door swung open the men opened the side doors and jumped out.

Mary stood dumbfounded as two of the men each grabbed one of her arms. Janet experienced the same fate except in her case a third man was pawing her breasts with a lustful smirk on his face. Janet was shouting at them to let her go and putting up a brave fight but Mary stood defiant in front of a smiling Linmore, despite the rank breath of the drunken seamen in close proximity to her face. "Well don't be impolite lads, help the lady up." Laughingly they lifted Mary into the RV, not without a little grope of her buttocks as they did so. Once up there Linmore pinned her arms to her side in a vice like grip and leeringly said to the others, "me and this nice young lady are going to have a little chat so why don't you go and play with her friend?" Then he shut and locked all the doors. Once alone inside, his smile disappeared and his demeanor changed as he tore off her clothes as though they were made of paper, threw her onto the bed and proceeded to rape her. Not satisfied with straight sex he forced her to commit acts of depravity that she had never experienced. Mary tried valiantly to fight off her attacker but he was far too powerful and a after a punch on the side of the face that had left her almost unconscious she could offer no further resistance.

Linmore's sexual appetite appeared insatiable and Mary's torture continued for the rest of the morning without a single word being uttered by either of them until finally Linmore got dressed, tied her to a Captain's chair and left the RV for the roadhouse. Inside, he downed a couple of swift shots of the same malt whiskey he had been drinking the previous evening. He could hear the jaunts of the men in the bedding store echoing through the mall. He topped up his glass and went to see how they were faring with their new sex toy. As he approached them Roots, a nickname given to the large African-American saw Linmore and detached himself from the other drunks. One of whom was in the process of raping Janet once more, encouraged by the others with every thrust. By now, Janet was just lying there, no longer required to be held down, as she was for the first hour, much to the delight of her captives. Now, they were just screwing a piece of meat, her mind retracted into the recesses of her brain, so deep, that clinically, any medical personnel would think it would never come back. Her body badly bruised and her insides torn by the repeated abuse of these men.

As Linmore drew closer, Roots broke away from the others and stood in a menacing stance, between him and the rest of the men. Roots real name was Sebastian McCourt and was a torpedo man aboard the sub, Right now he had his hands behind his back as though he was concealing something. Linmore was aware of this and tried a diplomatic tact by stopping, raising his glass towards them and saying with a wide grin, "bottoms up eh? If you will excuse the pun." But Roots was not amused and encouraged by a concealed Magnum he was holding and the support of Uncle Jack Daniels he reproached Linmore, "you know, asshole, who gave you the right to take that girl for your own when the four of us have to share this one?" Roots asked menacingly.

"Because it was agreed I was in charge, but hey," he said holding out his arms in submission, " if sharing is what you want, no problem, I can go and get the bitch and you can all have her – I really don't give a shit." Linmore replied nonchalantly but nevertheless becoming very wary of the man facing him.

"Nobody agreed you were in charge asshole, you did that all by yourself," Roots stated as by now the stand-off had gotten the attention of the others, the man who had been gleefully banging away at Janet stopped and eased himself off to the other side of the bed and like the others, watched, knowing that something big was going down.

"Hey, Roots, if that's how you feel, no problem, I'll just take off and leave you to the girls," Linmore replied, still giving that sickly smile. In his own mind he felt he could take this behemoth of a man standing before him, Roots was even bigger than Linmore, muscular and agile but dulled by a day's steady drinking. Linmore on the other hand had consumed very little alcohol so he switched the glass of whiskey from his right hand to his left and approached Roots with an outstretched hand, "I'll just shake your hand and be on my way." Linmore's thinking was to use surprise on Roots, he knew that once he was incapacitated the others would do nothing. He would then take the girl from the RV, drive to another airport and put some miles between him and these low-lives. But as Linmore took his first step, Roots shot out his arm, sinews showing taught as he revealed a .44 Magnum and pointed it directly at Linmore.

"Stay where you are." Roots ordered Linmore. He had wanted no part of the burly officer, like Linmore he felt he could take the other down but to be on the safe side he revealed the gun he had found in the desk belonging to one of the security guards. The other men were standing now, watching in horror at the events unfolding in front of them. With venom in his voice Roots hissed, "don't call me Roots. I hate that fucking name. Nobody is going to call me that again especially a fucking officer. My name is Sebastian." With that, he squeezed the trigger. A bullet went through the chest of Lieutenant Linmore, killing him instantly, but it didn't come from the Magnum being held by the man they called Roots.

Chapter 22

RESCUE

Norfolk – Virginia U.S.A.

Hargreaves was ashore, supervising the procurement of necessary provisions for the remaining men left on board, when his radio was activated. "Hargreaves here – what is it?" He was surprised to receive a call and his tone reflected it.

"Sir, Sparks here." Sparks was the radio man back on board the sub. A middle-aged man, whose retirement years were long overdue, who had been raised in one of those boys homes that were common years ago. But as he had no family, the Navy was it and the sub was his home. So when the choice to leave was offered, he chose to stay, for reasons similar to the other dozens of men remaining, no family and no home. What the people who jumped ship were going to find, was beyond him, but that was just him. "Sir, you know the radio receiver we have here for those new communication devices we were issued a while back?"

"Yes Sparks, what about them?" Hargreaves replied with not a little concern.

"Well sir, strangest thing, we are receiving a 'panic' signal and it indicates its location as down in Georgia. Everything seems to be serviceable, just thought you might like to know." Other than Mary nobody was aware he had given her the device so Spark's nonchalant attitude was no surprise.

"Thanks Sparks, would you notify the captain and call an all personnel meeting to be held in fifteen minutes time." Hargreaves replied calmly. It had slipped his mind to tell Sparks that he had given Mary one of the devices, he should have done that. But true to form, Sparks had done the right thing. He knew it had to be an emergency and Hargreave's worst fears were becoming a realisation.

"Certainly Sir," replied Sparks. Hargreaves was about to admonish him for the nth time for calling him Sir but like so many of the other remaining sailors it had been banged into them so much over the years that it was what they preferred and as Admiral Sanford had said during a private conversation 'if that's the way they want it who am I to tell them different'. He called the men to finish what they were doing and as they were getting into the trucks to return to the sub he heard the tannoy message being broadcast by Sparks for all personnel to meet on deck in 15 minutes time. At least he said 'meet' and not 'report' that was some progress. It only took a couple of minutes to return to the sub and a few more to load the provisions aboard. By this time, Admiral Sandford had arrived on the bridge and a few of the other men were milling about on deck wondering what could possibly have gone wrong now. Hargreaves briefly filled in the Admiral before addressing the men.

"Two days ago when Mary and Janet left the ship they were issued with a state of the art communication device that amongst other tricks included a 'panic button' that would not only inform us of an emergency but provide us with their exact position using its built in GPS. To-day, we received such a signal and I believe the girls are in some kind of trouble. There is a possibility that they have been kidnapped by some of the mutineers from the Connecticut, however, that is just conjecture at this stage. I personally feel somewhat responsible for their well-being so I am leaving, immediately, to offer assistance. Now, obviously, I can't order anyone to accompany me but any assistance would be greatly appreciated, however, I have a feeling it could be dangerous. We don't know their demise, whether if they have been kidnaped and if so by how many or even if we can even locate them, let alone being able to return to base." Almost as one, every man stepped forward to volunteer, a sense of purpose suddenly providing an opportunity from the loss of any reason for carrying on living. After all, these were still fighting men trained to spring into action as and where necessary. Hargreaves sincerely thanked them all but after serious consideration and consultation with the Admiral he selected just five, the youngest and fittest of the volunteers. He diplomatically stated that the remainder still had to provide backup and manage the base with the Admiral. That was until one of the men, Seaman DeVersa a man in his late thirties and slightly overweight, stepped forward again and indicated he wanted to speak to Hargreaves in private.

"Look, sorry DeVersa, the decision has been made, there's not much time, we need to get as far as we can in daylight and -," Hargreaves was walking away from the man and really was not in the mood to enter into a debate but DeVersa interrupted him.

"Precisely. And I can help you do that Sir. I am -," DeVersa was adamant and had to break into a trot to maintain pace with Hargreaves. But Hargreaves was equally as adamant.

"DeVersa, I must insist, we have just a few hours -." Hargreaves was still trying to keep a lid on his growing infuriation with the man's persistence but the man wouldn't cease.

"Sir," DeVersa shouted emphatically, turning the heads of the other submariners who were just out of whispering earshot, "I am a helicopter pilot, Naval trained." That certainly got Hargreaves attention. He stopped and whirled round to look at DeVersa.

"But, but you are the ships cook DeVersa, what are you talking about?"

"Busted Sir. In my younger days, did a lot of binge drinking. One day, during one of my better ones I somehow managed to find my way into a chopper and cracked up a couple of other stationary helicopters while attempting take-off. The Navy wasn't too pleased, but nobody got hurt so I was court-martialed, demoted and sent to the slammer for six months where I learnt to cook. But I can fly Sir, they can't take that away from me. You know there's a helipad on this base, I could find a chopper and have you at your destination in a couple of hours. Trust me Sir, I can do this." DeVersa was pleading but Hargreaves didn't take long to make his decision. "Alright. You're in. Take one of the jeeps to the helipad, fire up one of those birds and we'll be right behind you." DeVersa didn't need any further encouragement, he ran to the fleet of jeeps they had been using since they had arrived and leaped into the front seat. With a screech of tires reminiscent of any GI portrayed in a Hollywood World War II movie he was driving down the dockside to the helipad.

One of the selected men, Sergeant Grover, was the one remaining Navy Seal from the small detachment assigned to every U.S. submarine. For this operation Grover would be in command, unconditionally. Hargreaves would be just another subordinate and yes, it was a military operation. Orders would be followed implicitly and immediately, if no one could accept that – they were free to bail out. But there was no dissention and after gathering guns, ammunition, star bombs and a few other goodies that Grover could muster they boarded the jeeps. Hargreaves gave the team an update regarding their transportation arrangements. Not surprisingly the rest of the team looked at each other in complete bewilderment, the cook is the pilot? But Hargreaves insisted everything will be fine, although he wasn't a hundred percent convinced himself but he would live with his decision for expedience sake. After a few encouraging words from the Admiral they were off.

As they approached the helipad they saw a Sikorsky S-70L, with its rotors engaged in preparation for take-off beside it was DeVersa's jeep. The surprising thing was that the noise of the helicopter's engines couldn't be heard above the sound of their own transport as they pulled up and transferred to the helicopter. DeVersa, although grounded, had kept abreast of the latest technology and explained that upgrades had been made to the fuel tanks, engines and exhaust systems, based on stealth technology and this model was intended for covert operations. When all the men and equipment were safely stowed on board DeVersa lifted off with a smile of satisfaction on his face like that of a small boy who had just found himself alone in a store of wonderful toys. It was wasted on the worried looks of the rest of the men, who still saw him as the ship's cook. As he manipulated the controls the helicopter rose and angled into the direction indicated by the navigation aids. Their fears would have been diminished had they known that DeVersa knew this aircraft like the back of his hand. In his flying days he had trained pilots at North Island, San Diego and there was nothing about these puppies he didn't know.

True to DeVersa's word, they were within a few miles of their target in a couple of hours and Grover ordered him to fly low and bring them down a couple of miles from where the signal was emitting which according to the map appeared to be a large mall. Even though these engines were quiet, they were not silent, neither were they invisible. DeVersa landed in a small clearing surrounded by trees covered with kudzu and was ordered to stay behind with communications open, as the others made their way to the mall. As they edged closer to the mall Grover instructed one of the men to run low and fast to the corner of the main building and take a peek to see if there was anything to be seen. He returned to say there was a plane, probably a five seater, in one corner of the car park and a RV parked outside the main entrance. Grover went to look for himself and on his return he felt they would be too exposed moving along the outside of the building and decided to go round the back and see if they could find an open door. About half-way along the building was a metal fire door that, ironically, judging by the numerous cigarette butts lying around appeared to have been used by the store workers for the purpose of going outside for a smoke. Grover gingerly tried the door and softly opened it enough to poke through a probe that enabled him to see what was inside. The entrance led into a narrow hall way between stores. There were no lights working, but the glass ceiling in the aisles allowed in enough natural light for him to see that the aisle was empty. Quietly, they filed through the door into the hallway, Grover waited until they were all in and silently shut the door. He gestured to them to stay where they were as he crept to the aisle and repeated the process with the probe. There was no activity in the aisle so he gingerly peeked his head around the corner of the store. He could faintly hear voices to the left and knew that was the direction to go but he felt uncomfortable leading a group of rookies through unknown territory against some hostile, possibly armed, mutineers. Nevertheless, that's what he had to do. He crept back to the men waiting in the hallway and whispered to them, "there are some men to the left of us but I can't see where. Walk to the edge of this hallway and when I tap you on the shoulder, quietly walk to the other side of the mall, crouch down and wait. When we are all out I will lead on. From here on in it is all hand signals and silence is key. I will use 'stop', he raised a flat hand in the air, and 'go', a waving action forward. If I want people to cover, I will point to where I want you to go and how many of you. The next ones in the line are the ones to go. Understood?" Everyone nodded their agreement. He then made sure everyone put in their ear plugs and checked each one of them to ensure they had been inserted correctly. He walked back to the aisle, took a quick look and tapped the shoulder of Hargreaves, the first in line. The next to go was Seaman Jon Graneski, an ammunitions man, a third generation Pole, who had never seen action of any kind, before now. He was closely followed by Seaman Manny Hernandez, a first generation Mexican who normally worked in ships stores, along with the next man, his buddy, Seaman Stenich from Minnesota. Last but not least was Petty Officer Third Class Lewes a veteran of the Gulf War and a few other skirmishes that the U.S. government would have denied his any involvement. Grover waited for Lewes to cross and went to the front of the line and waved his hand to indicate them to move on. As they slowly moved along the stores, hugging as close as possible to the store fronts the shouting of what sounded like a small group of men was getting louder. They were approaching a bend in the aisle and Grover raised his hand and everyone stopped. He cautiously crept forward and slid the probe along the floor just in time to see a big man slowly walk across the aisle from what looked like a bar and entered a bedding store. Within a few seconds the shouting was reduced to silence and then he could hear the voices of only a couple of men. He indicated that he wanted two men on the other side of the aisle and then he beckoned the men on. He quickened his pace as one of the voices began to sound threatening and he reached edge of the bedding store. He positioned the scope just as the big man he had just seen enter the store hold an outstretched hand to a big African American. He could also see a group of men watching the proceedings and there lying on a bed was the motionless, naked Janet. He ran in a stooped position to the entrance of the mall and quickly rolled silently through the door and stopped behind one of the beds on display. Lying between the beds gave him a clear view of the two men and as he began to position his automatic rifle the African American pointed a gun at the other. It took Grover just a couple of seconds to make a decision and then he fired his gun killing the target of the armed African American. With a slight but accurate shift to his right he fired a round through the chest of the African American. The time taken between the two shots was imperceptible to human instincts and before the other men realized the gun shot had not come from the magnum being held by Roots, Grover was on his knees and with his marksman skills fired shots into the heads and chests of the men standing around Janet. Satisfied that all the men he had seen in the bedding store were incapacitated he immediately ran across to the bar and tossed a star bomb through the doorway. This was where the first man had come from and he didn't know if there were others. He had only counted four men and Graneski had said the plane he saw was a five seater so he wasn't taking any chances. But when he rushed the door, firing a couple of rounds into the ceiling for good measure, there was no one to be seen. The other men had remained where they had been told to stay and he turned to face them, removing his air plugs as he did so. This was an indication to the others that it was over.

Hargreaves stood and looked through the glass into the bedding store. His eyes fell on Janet lying naked, motionless on a bed. He dropped his equipment and rushed to her, ignoring the bodies of the mutineers. He didn't need to have medical training to understand Janet had been through hell and was in immediate need of medical assistance. "Grover," he shouted out, "get on the horn to DeVersa and tell him to get his ass over here, we need to get back to the Augusta - now." He told Hernandez and Stenich to find some red sheets, go outside and lay them in a cross in the parking lot to give DeVersa a landing space. Other than that, there was nothing he could do for Janet right now except to give her some reassuring words, hoping she could hear him, and cover her with warm blankets. One man stayed with Janet while the remainder searched the rest of the store for Mary, to no avail. They were just about to move to another store when the voice of Hernandez came through on the radio," sir, there's some banging coming from the RV parked outside."

"Dammit, I should have thought of that," muttered Hargreaves but before he could reply Grover was back in operational mode, "nobody move or make a sound," he said as with lightning speed and the stealth of a large cat he was at the entrance and taking in the RV. Obedient to the last, Hernandez and Stenich were staying quiet without moving, but standing in full view of the RV. Under normal circumstances Grover would have blown a gasket but the sight of the Mexican and the Minnesota farm boy standing there reminded him he was not operating with combat troops, they had done the right thing by not opening the RV. He was still concerned about a possible fifth man, the fact that they were still undetected and the banging still persisted could mean that he was in the RV with the other woman. He ran over to the other two men in a crouch, his eyes never leaving the RV, gun poised and ready for firing. He whispered instructions to them that they were to take a side door each, he would take the back and on the count of three, indicated by a count with his fingers, they would storm the RV screaming as they did so to create as much confusion as possible to anyone inside. They took their positions and on three they screamed like little girls. Unfortunately, only the back door was unlocked, where Linmore had left Mary only a few minutes earlier so Grover was the only one to find a terrified, naked Mary wrestling with the cords that tied her and kicking against the side of the RV for leverage. Mary stopped. She was about to let out a scream of her own when Grover slowly put down his gun, took off his helmet and said "Sergeant Grover, USS Augusta ma'am. We got your message."

In the time it took Grover to untie the cords holding Mary and covering her in a blanket, Hargreaves had reached the RV and held her in his arms. She looked up at him and whispered apologetically, "I pressed the button as soon as I could." The sound of the approaching helicopter drowned out Mary's relieved sobs as she clung to him with all her strength before passing out. They retrieved two emergency stretchers from the helicopter and carried the women back to the chopper and laid them between the seats. With the operation over Hargreaves was now back in command, he quickly barked out orders to get extra bedding from the store to make the girls as comfortable as possible. Hargreaves quickly rifled through the RV gathering as many of the obvious personal belongings as he could, based on what he could remember them carrying as they walked away from the slip just a couple of days ago. DeVersa was issuing instructions as to where everything should be stowed and once everything was on board he indicated where everyone should sit to balance the load. Then Hargreaves realized Grover was not on board. He jumped from the helicopter and ran back to the mall. He burst into the bar to see Grover sitting silently at the bar sipping whiskey from a small glass. He was a spent force, typical after a sortie where the adrenalin had been running so high for such a short period of time and the comedown is so great. Nevertheless, he jumped to attention at the sight of Hargreaves.

"Sorry sir, didn't realize you would be ready this quickly - just needed that," Grover said apologetically as he gathered his things together and began running to the exit.

"Perfectly understandable Grover." Hargreaves calmly replied running out of the mall behind him. On the helicopter everyone just let Grover be, he had carried out his part. As soon as the two of them were on board and the door was shut DeVersa lifted the chopper into the air and they were on their way back to the sub. DeVersa radioed to the sub with their ETA and a request for all medical personnel to be available to attend to wounded passengers, they didn't mention the women as they did not want to take the risk that others were listening in on the airwaves. Fortunately, back on board the sub, Lieutenant Moore, the chief physician had remained with the crew. As he had been involved immediately after the initial discovery with the polar bear he had had more time to contemplate the consequences. Like everyone else, his first impulse was to return to his immediate family, his wife and two teenage children, unable to comprehend that everyone had perished. But the scene beyond the security blanket of the docks and the sight of the bodies with the same white stuff that was found in the polar bear now emanating from every possible orifice of not only these poor people but birds, dogs, cats, every living thing was enough to convince the doctor in him that there would be nothing he could do for his family. So he returned to the sub where he felt his services would be best suited for the living. But it came well after a long meeting with Uncle Johnny Walker.

Moore had been briefed about the circumstances and had gleaned enough to know that surgical procedures would be consistent with that of rape victims. With one trained medical orderly at his disposal, Petty Officer First Class Cecil James, Moore seconded the services of two more men to prepare the operating room. They used a buddy system to arrange the instruments and equipment and to demonstrate the correct way to scrub and dress. Moore showed Chief Petty Officer Sewell, the ship's engineer and James was with Seaman Recruit Franks. James was just a teenager out of Iowa who had only been in the Navy six months and was still deciding what trade to pursue. Of the remaining ship's crew that Moore found on hand were the Admiral and Sparks. Sparks was needed to maintain communication and the Admiral will never know how close he had become to being an orderly in the operating room.

At the helipad DeVersa made the gentlest touchdown he had made in his entire career. Within seconds Grover, who was back in military mode, was out of the helicopter and sprinting for one of the military ambulances parked by the helipad. By the time the others had hit terra firma Grover had reversed the nearest ambulance up to the helicopter and Hargreaves began opening the rear doors. Grover moved through the back of the vehicle to join Hargreaves and they carefully took hold of the stretcher bearing Janet as it was passed to them. Janet was still in a deep coma and they secured her in the bunk on the left before turning to collect Mary who had come around during the flight back. She desperately wanted to see to Janet but was restrained by Hargreaves. As soon as she was secure, Grover returned to the driver's cab, the men outside closed the rear doors and with sirens wailing they were on their way to the sub. The rest of the men didn't wait for DeVersa to go through his shutdown procedures but jumped into the jeeps that they had driven there only a few hours earlier and followed the ambulance at full speed.

Grover stopped with the back of the ambulance at the gangplank to the sub and the Admiral was on hand to open the doors.

"David is waiting for you down in the infirmary," he said and then stood back as the two men unstrapped Janet's stretcher and carried it quickly but carefully from the ambulance, up the gangplank and down below. The Admiral had been listening to the radio dialogue, albeit cleverly disguised to protect the women, and was aware of both women's conditions, so knowing that Mary was awake he climbed into the ambulance to offer a few consoling words but he had hardly done so when the jeep transporting the other men pulled up and they unceremoniously pushed past the Admiral, unstrapped the stretcher and carried Mary to the infirmary.

Down in the infirmary David Moore did a quick examination of Janet which only confirmed his earlier theory. Her insides were badly torn and would need immediate surgery to repair the damage. By the time his decision was made Lewes and Stenich had arrived with Mary. He made a cursory examination of her and concluded no serious damage had been sustained, at least physically, and he gave her a sedative that would calm her for at least the next four hours while he was carrying out surgery.

During the surgery, Sparks manned the communications room, mainly to talk to the approaching Connecticut and monitor for any other craft. Identification tags had been retrieved from the dead mutineers and Sparks explained as much as he could to his counterpart, Radiohead, on the Connecticut, without divulging the existence of the female passengers. As he read each of the names off the tags of the killed, Radiohead replied 'bastard' as he made a note of the name to report to Giles. The Admiral paced the War room like an expectant father while the men who had carried out the exercise showered, cleaned themselves up and ate a slap up meal prepared by the recently returned ship's cook and pilot, Seaman DeVersa. He had calmly returned to the sub and resumed his position in the galley and began preparing the meal as though nothing had happened. After the meal they joined the Admiral in the War room and they all waited. After five and a half hours the doctor came in, poured himself a quick scotch and turned to the group.

"Well, the operation went well. She will be fine but it is extremely doubtful that she will ever be able to have children, her insides are badly scarred. Furthermore, I am extremely concerned about her mental state. The coma she was in, well, it could be sometime before she recovers, if she ever does. But, as we know, she's a strong woman and she may just surprise us yet, let's hope she pulls through because I have a feeling, despite being a cold hearted bitch, we could use a brain like hers during the next little while. Cheers," and he lifted his glass in salute before downing its contents in one gulp.

"Thank you doctor," the Admiral replied, "and what about Mary?"

"Medically, she's fine, just need lots of TLC." Moore directed his comment at Hargreaves who blushed slightly but offered no response.

"Well gentlemen, what you men did to-day should go down in the annals of American Naval history except it no longer exists. I'm very proud of you. I think this calls for a celebration. The Admiral served alcoholic beverages to those who wished to indulge, DeVersa just smiled and shook his head and accepted a glass of cola instead. The Admiral made a toast and his face turned stern as he was just about to say something of profound importance to the group when the whoop of another submarine's siren stopped him.

Chapter 23

ROUTINE

St. Santia - Caribbean

During the ensuing months significant progress was made as Bob, Maria, Tony and Marlene set up house merely a few hundred yards away from each other. They had built separate chicken coops in an attempt to stop any disease killing off their main source of fresh meat. In addition they had left a few free range chickens at locations around the island that they supervised regularly. A few times a week Bob and Tony would take a small sail boat and net a few good fish to supplement their diet. They usually came back with a couple of good red snappers, grouper and Spanish mackerel. Neither of them were particularly good sailors but they figured that the gasoline was not going to last forever and sooner or later they would have to learn to sail. The consensus of opinion was that it should be carried out sooner, while they had working engines for backup. The good thing was that they had a fine selection of sailboats to choose from and after reading various training documentation purloined from local sailing schools they practiced individually in a pair of sun fish class boats, gradually moving up to the 26 foot MacGregor, a hybrid sailboat and motor boat, with a powerful outboard motor that gave them the best of both worlds. They found that at the speed they were comfortable sailing they could use fishing lines to troll and on a successful catch they would stop the boat of the day and throw in some nets, based on the theory that where there's one fish there's going to be a lot more. Which, in their experience appeared to work for only thirty percent of the time. The MacGregor also had fish finder equipment that had, by trial and error, brought them considerable success. Again, however, they knew this technology would not last forever and finding fish in the sea was not a well-documented subject and would have to be gleaned from years of experience. Nevertheless, the amount of fish they were catching was more than ample for their needs and with a forced moratorium on fishing limits they expected fish populations to grow exponentially and would be limited only by Mother Nature's tried and tested formula, survival of the fittest.

In addition to their fish and poultry expertise they were learning to live off the land. Vegetable plots had been dug and fruit trees planted, all in locations conducive to their survival, based on the various books and pamphlets found in the garden centres. Their whole schedules had returned to basics, up at first light and in bed by sun down, exhausted and too busy too think too much about their pasts, although it was always lingering in the background. The only exception to this was the celebration of Marlene's birthday when a surprise party was thrown and a few drinks, more than what they were used to, were consumed. It was a beautiful day and the others had convinced Marlene that they needed more information on hurricane survival. She was quite prepared to go but expected Maria to accompany her, but Maria feigned a sickness, Bob and Tony had arranged to work on the boat, so, in a huff, Marlene had driven into town to find books and pamphlets on the subject of hurricane survival. Tony and Maria had already begun preparing food that morning and as soon as the Moke was out of site Bob joined them and the three of them went to work setting up table and chairs on the beach. With her driving, it only took Marlene a couple of hours to drive into town, look round the library, what was left of the police station and tourist information offices and return with a plethora of documentation. On her return, she was a little put out to find everyone on the beach playing volleyball using a net that had been strung across a couple of conveniently spaced palm trees. They beckoned her over and as she approached them her anger was increasing with every step. They had set up a wind breaker so she couldn't see the celebratory feast awaiting her. As she got closer the others stopped playing and approached the wind breaker from their side which Marlene had not yet noticed being focused on giving them a piece of her mind. She was just about to do just that when she saw the table with all the food together with party favours and the others burst into a rendition of 'Happy Birthday'. She had forgotten it was even her birthday and her anger quickly melted as she realized that the trip to town was just a ruse to get her out of the way but she gave each of them some abuse anyway, which of course was expected.

Each of them had procured a birthday card and a little present which Marlene gratefully opened. The food was great and the wine was even better and as the afternoon turned into dusk the mood turned a little somber as Marlene remembered some of her favourite birthdays spent with her family and they all started to share their own personal favourites. But before everyone got too melancholy, Bob remembered a poem and with the sun setting on the beach, the full moon beginning to rise and the waves gently lapping against the shore he chanted the verse:

> "Beyond the beach there lies the sea,
> And 'neath it all, tranquility,
> While men have ventured to the moon,
> The fish have swum their vast lagoon,
> No bills to pay, no words to say
> No scales of justice to be weighed,
> No wars to fight,
> No hate that spite,
> Is it no small wonder, that part
>   of the moon we see
> We named, Sea of Tranquility."

"That was beautiful Bob." Marlene slurred.

"Yes Bob, it truly was, who wrote that?" Asked Maria.

"I think it was that popular poet Anonymous, I think he wrote more poetry than anyone else in history." With that they all burst out laughing and they toasted the poet Anonymous and discussed the poem as though they were a book club analyzing each line of the stanza. They liked the play on words, fish and, scales but more importantly how it is now so appropriate to their situation, it was as if the poem was written for them.

"Just one thing Bob." Marlene began, "What makes you think this Anonymous person is a 'he'?" There was no venom in the question, not like there would have been a few months previously, instead it was a genuine inquiry. Bob thought for a moment and replied,

"I've always thought it was an abbreviation for Algernon E. Mouse," then added as an afterthought, "von Trap," and burst out laughing at his own conclusion which proved infectious and the jokes continued. They drank some more wine and with an effort made their way home to bed. The next day the chickens were not fed quite when they expected to be.

As a first priority they had cleared the immediate vicinity of bodies, human and animal, and as necessary they had extended the clearing to other parts of their, what they reverently named, properties. This extended to as far as they wanted it to be. A concern remained, the lack of other meats, which they knew would not be serious as an excellent diet could be had without red meat, although there was nothing quite like a well barbequed steak when you hadn't eaten one for months. Not to mention a pork roast, lamb chops and the mouthwatering list goes on. But by far and away the biggest threat to their survival was their lack of calcium provided by dairy products and more significantly milk. Certainly, they had enough frozen products to last them a couple of years with enough fuel to maintain the freezers, assuming the fuel wouldn't breakdown but what would happen then? Coconuts could provide a milk substitute but not to the extent of a good, cold, pint of milk. Although, a couple of years earlier, Bob and Tony had taken a diving trip to French Polynesia. They had learned that the islands in that part of the South Pacific were populated by small groups of natives arriving in outrigger canoes containing only what they could safely carry. That included tools, poultry and pigs but not large animals like cows or horses. They had flourished without the luxury of dairy products. But this did not remove the feeling of trepidation from the girls' minds. This concern was further exacerbated when after dinner that night in their respective houses they got together for coffee in the pagoda that was between their properties. Bob and Maria had an announcement to make. Bob calmly said, "we are pleased to announce that Maria is expecting a baby."

Chapter 24

NEW LIFE

St. Santia - Caribbean

Tony and Marlene were thrilled.

"That means, what, due in October, November time." Marlene almost screamed with joy, "that's fantastic."

"Yes congratulations." Tony offered and they were all on their feet hugging and laughing.

"We will have to have a celebration, with limited alcohol of course." Marlene said and so it was that a celebratory meal was staged. A new buzz of excitement surrounded the foursome and a different type of relationship began to develop between Marlene and Maria as she began to mother Maria to ensure she wasn't overdoing it. However, that only lasted a few weeks as sure enough it was Tony and Marlene's turn to announce her pregnancy. Their announcement was also followed by the prerequisite feast of celebration but without the free flowing drinks of alcohol. Just a glass of wine for the ladies, from the cellars of their fine properties, courtesy of the previous owners and a pint of beer for the men.

By consensus of agreement they resurrected a tradition from biblical times, working hard Monday to Saturday and resting on Sunday. They knew that survival depended on maintaining their crops, raising their chickens, fishing and keeping the freezers operating as long as they could. This meant they were working solidly from sunrise to sunset and unless they took a little time off occasionally, they would be burnt out very quickly. So they decided that except for the tending of the chickens and the usual meals, Sunday would be a day of rest. On this day they would relax, play, make things and consume a traditional roast selected from one of the many freezers they were maintaining, together with a small tipple of what they fancy. Now there was a new purpose to Sunday, an opportunity to search the island for baby clothes, cribs, toys and all the other paraphernalia associated with a new born baby. So once the necessary chores were completed and the breakfast things cleared away they took their two mini Mokes into town to shop. They took two in case one broke down as their servicing prowess was limited to changing the plugs and oil and their hope was that they could keep them going until their gas supplies ran out. Sure, there were other cars but none that were as good on gas and as versatile as their mini Mokes. So with the girls in one car and the boys in the other they wended their way down the hill and into town.

The boys had done a great job, with some assistance from Marlene, of clearing the bodies from the main roads into town but in the stores remnants of decaying bodies were still visible and unfortunately one species of land life that had survived, other than themselves and the chickens, were insects. Usually a buzzing or swarm of bugs was a dead giveaway that a body was in the area and unless they really had to, they circumvented the place and tried a different location to obtain what they needed. Up at the houses they had so far succeeded in keeping the insect population out with various insecticides and sprays but without any natural predators it would only be a matter of time before the insect population encroached on their properties. Soon the flies would have no dead bodies to feed upon and they may diminish but there were so many other insects that would thrive in a non-human world. Bees of course, could be an asset and honey could be a great source of sugar and easily harvested, however, there was enough honey available in the stores on the island and it was a commodity that would not deteriorate with time. Furthermore, none of the four had any experience in the field of apiary so while they had supplies in the stores, learning how not to get stung was not a current priority.

As the summer progressed, along with the sizeable increases of the girls' bellies, trips were restricted to short walks to the beach. The men made sure they had carried out any of the heavy duties and the girls tended to the chickens, plant preening and preparing meals. They were well aware of the hurricane season from June to November and they had prepared procedures for waiting out a storm. It had been agreed that the recording studio in Bob and Maria's house would make the best storm shelter. The house itself was the furthest of the two away from the sea shore and had a slightly higher elevation, reducing the risk of a potential tidal surge. The recording studio was an inside room, built for sound proofing with insulated padding in the floor, walls and ceiling. There were no large trees or other buildings in the immediate vicinity so nothing was expected to come crashing through the roof. To date, a couple of bad storms had hit the island but by no means were they of hurricane force. As a dry run, during one of the storms they had spent the night in the studio to ensure that if the real thing was to occur, their provisions would be sufficient to last at least a week. This included appropriate cooking facilities, bottled water, sanitary equipment, flashlights, first aid equipment and enough food to last them the duration. Fresh milk, fruit and vegetables would be brought with them during the siege. Permanently stored under the banks of switches and knobs that were originally the recording mixing equipment was their bedding, spare clothes and a collection of heavy duty tools such as axes, mallets, saws etc. just in case they were forced to bash their way out. Chicken tunnels had been dug into the side of the hill so that in the event of a storm the chickens would be protected, providing they had the sense to go to them.

Without the aid of weather forecasts they were left to their own devices to determine the onset of a hurricane. To a certain extent, the weather told its own story. The wind speed would increase and the surf would begin to crash on the shore. But if it all started at night, their reaction time could be greatly diminished. To reduce this risk, heavy duty wind chimes were hung on the verandas of their bedrooms. The normal, daily land and sea breezes would not usually be sufficient to invoke the sounds of the heavy chimes. But the force of a wind from a tropical storm would waken them from the deepest slumber. Such was the wind one night that they decided to put their own evacuation plan into action. Marlene was the first to hear the chimes and she jumped out of bed to check the huge barometer that hung by the wardrobe. It was down to 960 mill bars. She didn't need the quadrant on the dial that indicates '*Stormy*' to tell her there was a major weather system approaching. She immediately woke Tony, he listened and agreed that they should call their neighbours. Using an industrial set of walkie-talkies purloined from the army camp they informed Bob and Maria. Within fifteen minutes Marlene and Tony duly arrived at their friends' house, all excited as though it was a group of adolescents having a sleep over. Tony and Bob grabbed some flashlights and went outside to secure all the storm shutters around the windows and doors in both houses, again grateful to the architects of the houses who had built them to withstand a category five hurricane. They could see, even through the dark, the white caps of the waves as the wind churned up the sea down on the beach. Meanwhile the sound of the heavy wind chimes cascading against each other providing the tell-tale sign of at least a tropical storm. They returned to the house and joined the girls in the recording studio and once in there, they were oblivious of any weather phenomena occurring around them. They all slept peacefully and all awoke at their usual time. After checking their luminous wind-up clock to confirm it was indeed time to rise, Bob quietly went upstairs to the front door and gently opened it, expecting a strong gust of wind to blow the door away. Instead, the sun was rising amid a beautiful blue sky and apart from some excellent looking surfing waves, which was unusual on their side of the island, and some palm fronds littering the beach everything appeared normal. Putting on his shoes he went outside. By now, Tony had joined him and they quickly reconnoitered their immediate area and satisfied themselves that everything appeared to have withstood the storm. The chickens were pecking for food as though nothing had happened and their garden was still standing. By now the girls were outside and already brushing away some of the debris blown in with the wind. Over breakfast they discussed their evacuation procedures and were pleased with their preparations and site selection and felt no updates to their emergency procedures were necessary.

"Of course, you could never had accomplished this level of awareness unless I had retrieved all that documentation from the town." Marlene chipped in, between mouthfuls of toast and marmalade, which brought groans from the others. However, there was some small truth in that statement, their supplies had been based on some of the facts they had read from the notes and it was reassuring to know that in the event of a full scale hurricane the studio would provide a safe haven and their supplies would be sufficient to last a week.

Routine continued like this until one early evening in early October when during the innocent task of opening a jar of beets Maria unexpectedly went into labour. Bob immediately raised Tony on the walkie-talkie and he and Marlene were there in a flash. This was the moment they had prepared for, albeit a few weeks earlier than they had calculated. But all those classes they had participated in, amongst themselves of course, all the videos they had watched, all the reading they had done all appeared to go out the window. Bob was in a bit of a tizzy, after all he thought, they were basically a quartet of young innocent people who had never witnessed, participated in or had experienced anything to do with the birth of a child. The one person who could hold this situation together was the one going through the pain of contractions and without her calmness, panic was beginning to set in. Marlene was holding Maria's hands trying to comfort her but as far as taking charge was concerned, she was leaving that to the men. The situation was dire and getting increasingly desperate by the second. Just as they were entering full panic mode there was a knock at the open door and a man's calm voice was heard to say, "good evening. Could you folks use a little help?"

Chapter 25

NEW AWAKENINGS

Portland General Hospital – Maine U.S.A.

After that first phone call from St. Santia all John and Joan Hamax could think about were their own three children and five grandchildren. Needless to say, Joan was inconsolable; she needed to get closure on her off-spring. So against John's better judgment the decision was made to voluntarily check out and leave the sanctity of the hospital even though it had functioning heating together with ample food and drink being readily available, albeit temporarily. Two of their three children were scattered throughout New England so John planned what he thought would be the most expedient itinerary to get to them, starting with Darlene in Portland, then Brenda in Bangor. Their eldest John Hamax IV was a computer designer living in Silicone Valley, California and it hurt to think that the chances of seeing him, his wife Elena and their two children Dave and Darcy before major body decomposition set in were totally unrealistic. Darlene their divorced daughter had, in turn, had three beautiful daughters, Amy, Gracie and Denise.

The Hamaxes had arrived at the hospital with nothing except their pyjamas so they searched through the immediate closets in their ward to put together a decent wardrobe to face an East Coast winter's day. They also gathered some thick blankets and not for the last time, plenty of water and food. They wisely thought that under the circumstances it would be prudent to use the stairs. It would be ironic to survive a major catastrophe only to find themselves trapped in an elevator with no hope of escape. But there was no way they could carry all their newly found wares down three flights of stairs to street level. So they used the elevator for the goods, placing everything on the floor and pressing the ground button before deftly moving out as the doors gently closed, unwittingly using the same modus operandi as the new inhabitants of St. Santia. The exit signs were still lit by the emergency power that had kicked in when the main power died and they were just passing a heating vent by the stair doors when Joan, still with tears coursing slowly down her aged cheeks suddenly stopped. John immediately suspecting a relapse dropped the coats he was hanging on to and went to her. She instantly held up her hands and said, "listen! Can you hear that?" John always admired his wife's acute hearing but in this case he wondered if she was still suffering from the effects of the asphyxiation because he couldn't hear a damned thing. "No listen," she repeated with a sense of emergency as she cocked her head in an attempt to hear more clearly.

"Come closer to the vent," she ordered as she grabbed his sleeve to pull him closer. He tilted his head closer to the wall, straining himself to concentrate all his thoughts on listening to he knew not what. Then he heard it, albeit very faintly. It was a sound he was all too familiar with, the sound of a crying baby.

Chapter 26

MORE NEW LIFE

Portland General Hospital – Maine U.S.A.

Joan returned to the bank of elevators to review the floor directory identifying all the hospital's departments, there it was, '4 – Maternity'. The sound was coming from just above them. With a sense of real purpose Joan returned to the exit door, "we have to go up one" she instructed John. Forgetting they had only just woken up from a near death experience by asphyxiation they started walking up the stairs. Their breathing, or lack thereof quickly reminded them to take the stairs very slowly, albeit with a sense of urgency. It took them a couple of minutes to scale that one flight of stairs but when they opened the door to the 4th floor they were rewarded by the sound of not one baby crying but two. There, in a sealed room, were a number of incubators, all containing little bundles. A quick scan of all the incubators showed that four babies were still clinging to life, but without the constant care of attending nurses and pediatricians, other babies had already succumbed. Of the four that were still alive one of them was a boy who was badly deformed and desperately struggling for breath, his little lungs straining with every intake of air. Joan scanned the equipment's dials and determined how to increase the level of oxygen indicated by a valve on the incubator. This temporarily eased the baby's laboring but she felt it was only a matter of time for the poor child. In another incubator was a baby girl, she was so tiny, obviously born premature but she was still alive, albeit barely and again Joan felt there was nothing she could do for her. Although she was a trained nurse she had neither the skill, the training nor the knowledge to be in a position to help those little ones survive. The thought came to her that all over the country other babies, in the same situation as these poor things, were slowly dying with no one to attend to them. A sudden burst of purpose enveloped her, there were two other children, a boy and a girl, that appeared to have a good chance of survival, she was determined to save them. She made a decision that prior to the devastation she would have thought cold hearted but the best she could do for the sickly ones was to make them comfortable and she would concentrate on the two babies that she felt she could nurture to survival. Neither of the healthier looking babies gave the impression that they were premature and by the way they were bawling at the top of their lungs indicated they were in good health but just plain hungry. They may have just been placed in the incubators for precautionary reasons because on the face of it there didn't appear to be anything wrong with them.

Joan snapped into action, she quickly found some bottles of baby formula and mixed up the contents as per the instructions on the label and using the available equipment waited until she thought the mixture was at the appropriate temperature. Her biggest challenge was to feed the baby using the appropriate apertures offered by the incubator but once she worked that out Edward, as indicated by his name tag, was sucking at the bottle for all he was worth. Joan had decided to feed the boy first as according to his chart he had been born before the young girl and his feed may have been more overdue. During this time while Joan was silently taking action John had stood in the background, knowing that when his wife was on a mission it was beneficial for all concerned to stay the hell out of the way. But suddenly she ordered him to come over to the incubator and keep an eye on Edward while she repeated the process for feeding Amilia. On receiving the bottle Amilia also began to feed with the same relish as her neighbor. Joan gave a smile, it appeared that the two feeding babies were going to be O.K., unless there was something wrong with them that was not inherently obvious. After the babies were fed Joan walked over to the other two surviving babies the premature girl had passed and with a tear in her eye she continued on to the other remaining survivor. He was still breathing but each breath was very shallow. She reached through one of the incubator's access holes and touched the tiny infant. His head turned towards her, whether he could see her or not, she will never know, but his tiny hand clutched her finger as he gave out his last breath.

During the next two days their time was occupied feeding and changing the babies, their own family was put to the back of their minds until finally the emergency power failed. John had been foraging for food, which wasn't difficult. There were three fast food restaurants in the food court of the hospital and of course the hospital kitchen, each one of which was equipped with well stocked freezers and refrigerators. Add to that the many confectionary machines situated on every floor they had actually been eating quite well. But now with the emergency power depleted they had to move on and risk removing the babies from the warmth of their incubators and into what would be the cold of a New England winter. Fortunately, John had preempted this and they were prepared for it. During their first day he had been outside scouting for an appropriate means of transportation. Outside, in the car park he had his pick of assorted SUVs including a custom stretched Hummer. Tempting as that was he located the hospital garage and inside were a couple of ambulances, not just ordinary ambulances but 'in the event of a disaster' type ambulances the size of an RV. Inside was just about everything imaginable from a medical standpoint and wouldn't you know it? Two incubators. The ambulances also had a small refrigerator and freezer that contained various medical items whose purpose he didn't understand. During lunch John and Joan discussed their options and agreed that whatever the items were in the refrigerator and freezer could be tossed as they wouldn't know what to do with them anyway. John would then stock the cold storage with as much food as he could get in there and pack as many non-perishable items as he could.

First of all John checked out the ambulance to understand its controls and what it could do. It was a standard shift powered by a regular fuel engine. He started it up and listened to the engine purring with power. Adjusting the settings on the various heat controls the inside warmed up very quickly and with the engine still running he checked out the incubators and all the other features behind the driver's cabin. Not only was it the size of an RV, amidst all the medical paraphernalia and machinery like an RV it had a small cooker, pots, pans, cutlery, a small microwave oven and a functioning toilet and shower. There were six beds, two of them fixed and four more that were hinged to the side of the vehicle for additional patients. Unlike an RV there was no TV or video but he didn't think there would be much use for those anyway. After satisfying himself that this was the best alternative in terms of vehicles he test drove it around the parking lot and was very satisfied with its handling. He parked beside the entrance closest to the restaurants and kitchen and began to strip the vehicle of all the items he felt they would have no use for. The ambulance had even been stocked with 'walkie-talkies', which John had purloined on his first discovery. They had tested them out on the floor, while Joan stayed with the babies and also as he went down the stairs and out into the parking lot. He would say, "can you hear me now?" To which Joan would reply, "yes I can hear you." As she humored him as he played out a recent television commercial advertising a widespread telephone network. Once they were happy the radios were functioning to their satisfaction, they agreed that even if there was nothing to call about John would call on the hour, every hour. If John forgot, Joan would contact him and if either received no acknowledgement at any time it would be considered an emergency. Occasionally John would call to ask Joan a question regarding the stocking of the ambulance but for the most part during that couple of days Joan looked after the babies and John started to prepare for their next adventure. They had talked about what was next, and Joan wanted closure on her own children, so it was agreed that their first priority was to go to Darlene's house. Not knowing about the fuel consumption of the ambulance and afraid that they could be stuck without any power John needed to find a trailer that he could attach to the hitch bar on the back of the ambulance. This he could fill with emergency gas and food rations. To satisfy his curiosity, having never driven one before, he choose the Hummer to locate a suitable trailer, his rationale being was that it too had a hitch bar. His disappointment was that he didn't have far to go. The west wing of the hospital was being refurbished and a plumbing contractor had a perfect solution to his search. It was one of those covered trailers that substitutes as a workshop and inside were cupboards and trays of all sorts. He managed to rid the trailer of all its contents with the exception of a few useful looking tools and an industrial size, cordless, drill fitted with a pump for siphoning water. He felt this would be equally as useful for siphoning gas, once he had replaced the old hoses with new ones, of which there were ample in the trailer contents.

Attaching the trailer to the Hummer did not prove as difficult as he had anticipated. The front of the trailer could be raised or lowered by the turning of a handle for a telescopic stand and wheel. All he had to do was negotiate the ball of the Hummer's hitch bar directly underneath the front of the trailer and lower, which he managed to accomplish, first time. Then he pulled out the holding arm of the telescopic wheel, lifted it up and reset the holding arm securing the wheel in its driving position. The new rig was ready to roll, next stop, gas. Again, John was fortunate he didn't have to drive far, across the street was a large gas station, unfortunately, meandering through the static traffic with the trailer proved to be a bit more of a challenge. He tried to use the Hummer as a battering ram but all the reversing he needed to carry out proved both difficult and tiring with the trailer. Moving to Plan B, John walked across the street to the gas station and found twenty government approved gas cans of various shapes and sizes. The power for the pumps was no longer available, so undaunted, he lifted the cover of the station's fuel reservoir, slid down a piece of pipe taken from the plumber's trailer and began siphoning gas into the containers using his new found tool. Once they were all full, he walked them over to the trailer using a trolley from a nearby delivery truck. He secured the gas tanks to the rear of the trailer that could be closed off from the rest of the storage area. All this had taken a significant amount of time and not once had he remembered to call Joan. At five past the hour the 'walkie-talkie' squawked. He picked it up and acknowledged,

"Sorry, got wrapped up in things and forgot to call, I'm fine." John said meekly.

"Oh I knew you'd be fine, I'm just reminding you to call that young boy on the island." She replied authoritavely.

"Shooot, gotta get to a phone, will catch you later." Fortunately, the phone behind the counter in the gas station had long distance and referring to the number he had written down on an 'Emergency Patient – Triage' form he dialed the number.

After the emotional phone call with Bob, he sat in the gas station booth, idly unwrapping a chocolate bar and trying to understand why he suddenly felt so drained. He knew he wasn't a young buck but he was not prone to emotional swings and crying on the phone to a stranger was completely out of character. He could only attribute it to the events suddenly coming into focus exacerbated by the physical effort he had been exerting all day. He remained seated for a few more minutes while he finished the chocolate bar and chugged back a soda pop. Suddenly he realized that he had been so caught up in his own emotions he had failed to tell the young man about the two babies they were taking care of. Immediately he redialed the number and waited as the phone started to ring in the St. Santia police station cursing all the while at his own forgetfulness. There was no reply and rather than remonstrate himself any further he slammed down the phone and with a loud shout of 'well, this won't do', he was back on his feet and continuing his preparations.

The next day, after feeding the babies and wrapping them in warm blankets, John and Joan each carried a baby down the four flights of stairs to their new mobile home. Up until that point, Joan had not seen the ambulance and she was impressed with its features and the expert way John had packed all the necessary baby paraphernalia in the storage compartments. John had started the engine earlier so the inside was already nice and toasty. They carefully unwrapped their bundles and Joan placed the babies in their respective incubators, securing them with specially designed straps ensuring they would not be tossed around during the journey.

They had agreed to continue with their original plan and travel to their daughter's house. It took them the best part of three hours to arrive and when they did, John was forced to break open the door while Joan fed the babies again. With their charges sound asleep, Joan felt it was safe for both of them to leave the babies on their own while they went into the house. They slowly climbed the stairs to Darlene's bedroom and found her lifeless form in bed. Darlene was always a slow riser and as expected, she would have been in a deep sleep when the devastation hit, fortunately death would have been mercifully quick. The serene look on her face reflected this and reminded John of when she was just an innocent young girl and he would look in on her before leaving for work. Remembering this brought a tear to John's eye and it rolled down his cheek as Joan positioned his lovely daughter and covered her face with a sheet. They wouldn't be able to bury her, the ground was far too hard for John to dig a grave and they just couldn't bring themselves to create a pyre for her. They had seen so many bodies that it would only be right to leave her where they found her. As they assumed, their granddaughters were not in the house, they would be with their ex son-in-laws. As much as they would like to see them, they decided that they would not make any further visits. They had been lucky with Darlene but after seeing all those bodies on the way, most had obviously died an agonizing death and Joan had no wish to see the death masks of her grandchildren or her other children. She would remember them as they were, in her mind's eye. By now it was getting late and they decided to hunker down for the night in the ambulance and return to their own home in the morning. After a light meal they cat napped in between the feeding times of the babies and slept on the surprisingly comfortable beds. At first light they ate a breakfast of cereal and coffee, saw to the babies and with one last look at their daughter's home, started their journey home to at least get into their own clothes before planning their next steps.

At their own home they found their poor dog, Pippa, lying in his familiar spot on the mat at the front door. It was ironic that they owed a debt of gratitude to the dog who, instrumental in saving their lives, was subsequently stricken by the devastation. John took off his borrowed overcoat and covered the dead animal with it. They immediately went upstairs and changed into their own clothes, carefully avoiding the dog excrement that had been trodden up the stairs during their rescue. They then went to their immediate neighbours houses and offered the same courtesy to them by at least covering their bodies with sheets. It was strange, even though all of their family, friends and neighbours had been wasted by the devastation they were still functioning with minimal emotion. A similar affliction had affected the people on St. Santia and the personnel on the submarines. It was as though human emotions reacted differently between the deaths of a few relations to that of thousands. The brain, unable to focus on one or two individuals has to try and balance the grief across thousands with the net result being a zombie like state bereft of the usual passion.

After John repeated to Joan the substance of the phone call with Bob in St. Santia they both felt frustrated, being so far away and unable to help. But they had decided that returning home would be for the best, for now, for many reasons, not least of which was knowing where to find all that they would need for the babies. However, on their return, the smell of gas was still prevalent, even though it had been pronounced safe by the local fire department, according to the notice pinned to their front door in a cellophane wrapping. Their original plan was to sleep in their own beds that evening as they felt it was now safe to move the babies from the incubators to cribs that had been retained for their own grandchildren. But with that smell of gas Joan would not risk the health of the babies despite the clearance notice. As a result, they took turns showering, surprised that the water was still hot, and changed into their own clothes. For the rest of the day they pottered around, in between the regular feeds and finally went to bed, with great reluctance in the ambulance parked outside of their home and the family bed. At around seven o'clock John awoke to find Joan had left the ambulance. The babies were still sleeping so he quietly dressed and went outside in search of his wife. He walked to the house and opened the front door to the sound of cutlery and saucepans clattering in the kitchen. The aroma of bacon and eggs, his all-time favourite meal, was emanating from the kitchen beckoning him to the table. For a brief moment, the devastation had not entered his mind and it was reminiscent of his time on the coastguard when he would arrive home at all times of the day or night after a rough shift but on awakening, Joan would be ready with a breakfast fit for a king. As he walked into the kitchen there on the table was a plate of bacon, two eggs, tomatoes, hash browns, baked beans and toast. Their cooker was natural gas and so far, service had not been compromised but that would only be a matter of time. They ate in silence, him devouring his cholesterol laden meal with relish, her, a piece of toast and jelly, until Joan spoke.

"You know, I think we should go to St Santia." For a moment, silence reigned once more, well apart from the masticating of toast and other breakfast food items. John, was dumbfounded, caught in mid-mouthful he slowly shook his head and swallowed his food as he realized what the purpose of this breakfast was really all about.

"John, there is absolutely nothing for us here and the babies would have a future. You told me yourself, on the phone to that young man, they need us. I think we should go."

"But I thought you would want to stay here. It would be dangerous crossing that water. What if we were to break down? What if we missed the island and drifted off into the Atlantic? Anyway, have you forgotten something? You don't like small boats." John replied with a bit more gusto than he felt was necessary.

"John, really, we've lived in this house all our married life, that's over 50 years. We have had the opportunity to live in Florida, Arizona, anywhere we wanted to but no, you have always had an excuse for not moving. Face it, it's not me who doesn't want to leave the sanctuary of this house, it's you. As for small boats, we have the pick of boats and we can get a nice luxury yacht. Wouldn't the risk be worth it to help some children in need? After all, there is nothing left for us here, nothing." She let the words hang for a moment, of course she was referring to their lost children and grandchildren but John inwardly felt she was right, what was the point of staying here?

They decided to spend the rest of the day grabbing a few mementos and photographs and packing the ambulance with suitcases stuffed with clothes, more tools and of course an ample supply of food and water for themselves and the babies. They purloined an additional cooler that could be plugged into the cigarette lighter and they filled that with cold meats and fruit from a local grocery store. That night they spent their last night outside the house that had given them so many great memories, made love in, countless times, and conceived three children. That night they made love one more time, not as vigorously or as passionately as they had once done but equally as satisfying.

In the morning, the water in the house was still hot, courtesy of natural gas, so they showered and dressed. Joan cleared up the kitchen, an act that John thought was superfluous considering they would never be returning and nobody else would be visiting, however, that's what Joan did. After coffee and cereal for breakfast they packed a few last minute items in the ambulance. They held hands and both gave a final look at their home, each amidst their own thoughts. After a few seconds Joan tugged her husband's hand and said, "come on, we've a long way to go."

They had decided to head for Fort Lauderdale, that's where the best pick of the yachts would be. That would be Interstate 95 all the way from Portland with plenty of places to grab gas, food and places to sleep. There were few obstacles on the interstate that they couldn't either get around on the hard shoulders or push out of the way. Occasionally, they would have to reverse and go northwards to take a diversion. They would go southbound on the northbound lanes or drive on the grass verges but eventually they would be back on track. Bodies in the road were no longer considered obstacles. The first few, they stopped the rig, got out and carefully moved them aside to avoid driving over them, after a while this became too taxing and time consuming. After driving over the first few, driving over them became like speed bumps and an inconvenience. They decided they were going to sleep in a motel, just to stretch their legs and avoid cabin fever, but the silence, the dead bodies and darkness made it far too eerie. They had no trouble sleeping on the ambulance beds and the feeding routine had become the norm. After seven nights of sleeping rough and eight days of maneuvering round crashed trucks they made it to the sun drenched shores of Florida and more specifically, to the luxurious boats of the Fort Lauderdale marinas.

After driving around the outskirts of Fort Lauderdale, they found an uninhabited beach house with a large driveway, close to a large marina. They investigated the house and found it suitable for their newly expanded family, except that the hydro was now unavailable. They set up cots and enjoyed a dinner of canned meat and vegetables cooked over a camping stove. The next day, John's first priority was to find a suitable generator to supply the house with hydro as he felt they would be here a few months until he could find his sea legs. Using a Mercedes convertible found in the garage of the house, he drove around until he found what he was looking for. On a construction site was a mobile generator attached to a pick-up truck and in the back of the truck were two big barrels of diesel fuel together with a few smaller tanks. This would not only solve the short term problem but would provide a solution for transporting additional fuel when he had to replenish the tanks. He ditched the Mercedes and climbed into the pick-up truck. Relieved that the truck started first time he slowly made his way back to their new premises. Once the hydro was running and the babies settled, John did much the same as the foursome on the island, tried to fill their ample freezer with as much frozen food as possible, under the watchful guidance of Joan. Unlike the islanders, his selections were limited to large distribution stores and hospitals where generators had kicked in after the hydro had finally died. After a couple of days of scouring the area and checking yellow pages for suitable depots, they felt they had done enough. Most of the generators had finally drained their fuel and any that still functioned were on fumes. The next task was to ensure they had sufficient baby formula and diapers, which was infinitely easier with the variety of drug stores nearby. With all the gathering completed they felt they were reasonably settled, it was time for John to find a boat.

During the trip down to Florida, John had devised a game plan. True, he was an experienced seaman with an excellent understanding of the tides, waves, navigation and potential weather changes. This knowledge was based on a career in boats. Boats with engines. An engine has the propensity to break down, especially on long trips. He was able to fix simple problems but a major problem with no assistance would find you drifting at the mercy of the sea. That was suicide. He decided, therefore, that their best option was to travel to St. Santia in a sail boat with spare sails and a powerful engine, just in case. That brought up another problem. Apart from a few trips with friends he hadn't sailed since he was a kid. So his plan was twofold, to read up on the basic points of sailing, select a reasonably sized yacht to practice with, probably about 24 foot and while he was relearning the ropes, look for a suitable boat to sail to St. Santia. He explained his approach to Joan and she supported him 100%. So, in the morning, after breakfast, as old as he was, he knew he would have to keep fit to fulfill their plan. He began by carrying out a few stretches, took a walk on the beach, culminating in a gentle swim in the ocean before putting his plan into action.

It didn't take him long to satisfy all of his personal demands. In a marina a few miles away was an excellent sailing school specializing in keel boat sailing using 24 foot Shark sailing boats. The school had an education center containing volumes of good teaching aids together with videos, DVDs and educational films. Many of the boats moored in the marinas had video/DVD players and once their batteries were fully recharged using their own engines John became a student once more. He would spend a couple hours watching the visual aids and a few hours a day sailing the Shark. It wasn't long before he could maneuver the boat to any point, regardless of the wind direction. In between his learning and sailing he used a little fishing boat with a 10 horse power engine to check out the boats moored in the marina. After considering many of the beautiful boats he came upon a Hunter 36 that was loaded with a bank of four batteries and not only a solar generator but a wind generator too. It appeared that the boat was being prepared for a long ocean trip as there were spare turnbuckles, lines, main sail and jib all carefully stowed throughout the boat. The boat was also set up for a spinnaker but he discarded that as he knew it would take him all of his time to handle just the main and the jib sails. The galley was spacious with a microwave, fridge and in the stern there was even a small washer/dryer. The diesel engine looked brand new and was powerful enough for even high seas. He raised Joan on the walkie-talkie and she agreed to check out the boat. The marina was only about five miles away from their house and as there was no traffic it took him only minutes to return home to pick up the 'family'. He was now driving a bright red Ford Mustang convertible but he had to switch to the 'Escalade' to secure the babies in the back seat in their baby chairs. On arrival at the marina, Joan was impressed with the choice of vessel, she tentatively boarded the yacht and with some difficulty negotiated the steep stairs into the cabin. She carefully inspected the washroom, shower, main bedroom, galley and the CD system. With her arthritis she was not thrilled with the steps to get back on deck but felt that other than that it was an excellent choice.

John maneuvered the 'Chosen One', as they had christened it, to a slip that could be easily accessed by Joan. She would clean out the boat to her satisfaction and begin making a list for provisioning the boat for their trip. John gradually stocked up with baby formula, diapers, both disposable and non-disposable, non-perishable goods, clothes, first aid equipment and of course the photographs of their family that they had brought from home. In addition, John had upgraded to a bigger practice boat until he was ready to take out their 'Chosen One' for sea trials. By late July, John had mastered another Hunter 36 that he had found in the marina and after a few weeks of trials and day trips out into the ocean he felt they were ready for a short trip on their target boat. They planned a trip to the Keys for a couple of days to get used to being on board for a few nights to ensure they had everything they would need for a longer trip. The boat was equipped with auto helm and all the lines led to the cockpit so the boat was reasonably easy to handle single handed. It would be very difficult for Joan to help with the lines due to her arthritic hands but with the aid of the winches she was taught what to do in the event of an emergency. So one fine July morning they set sail for the Keys. Using the engine they left the marina, crossed through the Intracoastal Waterway on their way into the Atlantic. There was a favourable wind so for that first day they just used the mainsail and before evening they made their first stop just south of Miami at Coral Gables. They were both very pleased with themselves. Joan was accustomed to the galley and John was just so comfortable sailing. If anything, the babies were sleeping better at sea than they were on shore and during the day they had enough room to crawl and play topside albeit with their life jackets on. The next day, after a hasty breakfast, they were on their way again. Only this time, Joan, the person least likely to set foot on a yacht smaller than a cruise ship, had got John to rig up a hammock on deck and was happily reading a book during the babes nap time while John navigated the open seas. They had set up a baby monitor so that they could hear if either of the babies woke up. By the next evening, just before dusk, they were sailing into a marina at Key Largo. They selected a slip and Joan flipped the fenders over the side of the boat while John maneuvered the boat against the dock. John deftly stepped off the boat and attached the spring lines before attaching the bow and stern lines. With the boat secured and without the glaring sunlight the babies had been brought topside in their cots to enjoy the fresh evening air prior to their evening feed. Tired but very proud of their achievement, Joan was breaking open a bottle of wine to celebrate and she was just handing a glass to her husband when the babies both suddenly awoke and started crying. However, it wasn't sudden hunger that tore them from their slumbers, it was the sound of a Coast Guard klaxon being pulled on a boat approaching them at a great speed of knots.

Chapter 27

TRIP TO ST. SANTIA

Key Largo – Florida U.S.A.

The Coast Guard boat was of the type used to intercept boat loads of immigrants from Cuba or the occasional drug runners laden with narcotics unloading from ships traveling from South America that remain outside of U.S. waters. The boat was fast, very fast. It also required a lot of gas but that wasn't a factor that appeared to be bothering the current skipper of the craft, Danny Martinez. Danny slowed his craft and proceeded to moor a couple of docks down from them, John was already off his boat and on the dock to assist with the lines. Danny walked towards the surprised man wearing a big grin on his friendly looking face. John noticed that he was a reasonably big man, about six feet, extremely well built, tanned and good looking. As Danny neared him he held out his hand in greeting.

"Hi, Danny Martinez is the name, named after 'Danny Boy', it's the Irish in me but boy am I glad to see someone else still living, I've started talking to myself, which I never thought was a good thing. Haven't seen another soul since my sub landed back in January, what would it be now August, September? Who knows and what difference does it make eh?

"Hello, my name is John," replied John, "I think it's September but I've lost track of the days. But we hadn't expected to see anyone. How did you know we were here?"

"I was fishing out in the ocean when I noticed you heading into the marina." Danny replied. "Nothing else out there so you were easy to spot."

"You say you were in a submarine? Does that mean there are others around?" John asked hopefully.

"Not round here, not that I know of anyway. I was brought up in this area. So, when the sub got back to shore we were given the option of staying or leaving. I felt I would be better off down here. Plenty of fish, I can sail, great weather and if things got bad I know I could always get up to Norfolk where other crew members may still be around. Best of both worlds."

John slapped his hand to his forehead in exasperation, "I should have thought of that. We've actually driven all the way down here from Maine to help some people on the islands when we could have got help from professionals. Hell it was only a few hours drive for us – why didn't I think of that?" Just then Joan appeared, she had managed to get the babies back to sleep and came over to introduce herself. She went on to explain to Danny the phones calls they had with the people on St Santia and the quest they were on.

"You know," said John as his face lit up as it does when a great idea forms, "we may be better off driving back north to get help from the submarine crews rather than try and make the trip ourselves, after all, this is hurricane season and we will have no warning once we set sail."

"Professionals? I left the sub because of the trouble." Danny replied, "mutiny was rife and many of the crew were fighting amongst themselves. No, I don't think that would be a good idea. Anyway, I know these waters, the winds and the climate. Why don't I travel with you to St. Santia, we could island hop all the way, we can make it. We would have two well laden boats if anything went wrong with one we could easily make one of the islands on the other and find another boat." A sense of relief swept over Joan, although it had been her idea she had not been looking forward to the trip at all and Danny was making it all sound so easy. Not that she didn't have faith in her husband's ability, but on a voyage like this, anything could happen and they weren't exactly spring chickens anymore. Now, being accompanied by this hunk of a man, who also happened to know what he was doing, she felt much better about the journey.

"Well, now that's settled," Joan said, "why don't I rustle up some dinner and you guys can plan the trip over a cold beer or two."

"Great idea, I've got all you need in the boat. I 'commandeered' a cold storage truck on my trip south and filled it with some staples. My base is still Miami, where I have a big military generator keeping the food cold but I travel with a few goodies in the small freezer on the boat. I can leave the generator for about 5 days at a time before it needs refilling. So, on the menu to-day is T-bone steaks with fries, Guinness, of course or wine if you - ." Just at that point, one of the babies started crying very loudly, Danny looked mystified until they explained to him the story of their other passengers. He was captivated and couldn't wait to see the babies, all the more reason he felt to get to St. Santia toute de suite.

Over dinner they swapped stories and began to plan their expedition to St Santia. Danny had a fully equipped Catalina 28 docked in Miami for those occasions when he felt just like sailing. He felt it was the perfect size to sail solo yet still had all the necessary amenities. At first light, he would return to his base and prepare his sailboat for the trip. Danny showed John and Joan his marina's location on the chart and gave them the exact position for their GPS, it was expected they would make it there before sunset the following day. They would take a couple of days loading and planning contingencies and then the flotilla of two would be on its way. With the main business out of the way and a couple of beers softening the mood John asked the question that had been bothering him since they met,

"So Danny, you say your father was Irish, how come you use Martinez as your family name?"

"John," Joan scolded him, "that's his business."

"No, that's O.K. ma'am, I can tell you, what difference does it make now? My father was Irish and he met my mother in a bar in Cuba, you know the story, in any bar in any part of the world there's an Irishman. Well, in Havana, that was my dad. They married and he managed to get them both to the states, legally, I might add. How he finagled that I don't know. Not long after, I was born in Miami. You see, in Havana, my father was a big fish, he was into a lot of things, some legal some not quite so above board. In Miami, he was a fish out of water and suddenly, one day he was gone. I never saw him again and my mother, although extremely upset never said why he left but from that day on we reverted to my mother's maiden name. He still sent money, lots of money, I could never claim I had a poor single family upbringing."

"So where was that money coming from?" Asked John, now quite intrigued, "did he return to Cuba?"

"According to my mother none of her family ever heard or saw of him again and my mother never knew of his whereabouts. Every so often mom would receive a phone call from him, never at home though, and a meeting place would be arranged where someone would show up with an envelope of cash. My guess and it is only a guess is that he was involved in gun running for the fighting in Northern Ireland."

"Good Lord Danny!" Joan put her hands to her chest in amazement, "whatever would make you think of a thing like that"

"Well I went through a brief period where I fell into the wrong crowd at school. My grades were beginning to slip and I had not exactly been respectful to my mom. Well, one day, on my way home from school, Two men grabbed me and pulled me into the back of a truck. A third man was in the driver's seat, but he didn't even look back. I thought they were perverts and I began to kick and scream but the truck had tinted windows and was sound proof. One of the men spoke, in a very gentle voice with a thick Irish brogue very similar to what I could remember of my father's.

"Its O.K. son, we're not here to hurt you. We're here with a message from your da." I looked at him and relaxed, his eyes were ice blue and they seemed to penetrate right into my soul.

"He understands your school work is not up to snuff." I didn't know what that meant exactly but I got the drift. "Well son," he continued, "if you persist in hanging around with that no good gang and carry on treating your ma the way you have we may have to pay you a little visit. Trust me, you won't want that. Do we have an understanding? Well, I don't have to tell you, one look at those cold eyes told me he meant every word of it.

"What did you do Danny did you tell the police? Did you speak to your principal?" Joan asked with concern.

"Oh no, I know I was only a young teenager but I'll never forget those eyes and the calm matter of fact way he delivered the message. These guys were for real and not bothered by the authorities. I just nodded my head, got out of the truck and never received anything less than straight A's ever again. About a year later I was helping my mom take some groceries out of the car when a car came by, slowed and the tinted window on the passenger's side was rolled down only slightly. Just enough to see those eyes and I heard a voice say" well done son" before the car drove off. I never saw them again but for that reason, I think my father was involved in something that prevented him staying in the States, at least legally. But as I said, it really doesn't matter anymore." There was a brief lull in the conversation, but not for long as Amilia decided she was ready for a feed. Danny, smiled, gave a quick toast, drank the last of his Guinness, bade them all goodnight and returned to his boat.

The next morning John and Joan heard the deep guttural sounds of the Coast Guard boat cough into life. They heard the engines gently increase speed as it cruised out of the marina then burst into a roar as it reached open water and in no time the sound disappeared into the distance.

"He seems like a very nice man John."

"He certainly does dear. He seems very keen to help out."

"I think it is the opportunity to meet people of his own age. After seeing nobody for all this time it was probably amazing to meet other people but the prospect of interacting with others of his own generation must be quite exciting for him."

"You're probably right dear, but bumping into him has been most fortuitous because it wasn't a trip I was relishing."

"I know dear." Joan tapped his hand a couple of times, "I know," then she got herself out of bed to make the coffee.

With favourable winds the Hamaxes made their destination by early afternoon and there was Danny waving and preparing to grab a line to secure the boat. During the next few days they loaded the boats and planned the trip to St. Santia. It was estimated that the first day would be the longest sail day, after that they could island hop to their heart's content.

It was a beautiful day as the flotilla of two left the marina to set sail for St. Santia. The sky was blue the winds were out of the west and the sea was calm, it was perfect. They had stocked up the on board freezers with as much as they could from Danny's stash. They had even added a couple of small freezers to the Hunter as John had the power capacity. Not taking any chances, John had ensured the boat had a fully charged bank of four heavy duty batteries to supplement the wind and solar generators. In addition to the spare sails he had stowed, there were enough jerry cans in the stern, full of diesel to keep their powerful Yanmar engine going there and back if necessary. As further safety precautions, he was towing a small painter with a small gas engine, a single sail and a pair of oars, just in case. On board was an Avon, ready to inflate, also with a small gas engine and paddles. Each of the small boats was stocked with emergency rations and first aid kits. The precautions didn't stop there, not only were the fresh water tanks full, the forward salon was full of bottled water and there were enough saline tablets to purify the Gulf of Mexico. No, John was taking no chances, despite being accompanied by an excellent sailor in another fully equipped boat. Allowing for stopovers, they planned on taking just under a month to make the trip, subject to weather conditions. The first part of the trip would be the worst in that it would be the farthest between two points of land so Danny wanted to sail right through the night, which John was a little reluctant to do but in the end he agreed. Once they were in the Bahamas they could island hop all the way to St. Santia and rest accordingly. Up until day four, the winds were still out of the west making it a very easy sail and both sailors were able to take cat naps. For John it was easy in that Joan took the wheel, between tending to the children, while John slept and she would only wake him in the event of a major wind shift, so far that hadn't occurred, Danny meanwhile used the autohelm to keep on course. As the sun set on day four the wind died and their sails flapped aimlessly on their masts, they were forced to revert to their engines. It had been agreed to keep the emergency channel open on their radios, however, John had also insisted on pilfering some military walkie-talkies to use as a backup. Danny came over on the radio.

"They are the Turks and Caicos islands on our port side. As the wind has dropped I think this would probably be a good time for an overnight stop. We're on the lee of the island here, in the morning we could sail through this strait and we will be in open water and we can pick up the wind again - over."

"Thanks Danny, I think we could do with a stop, remember, we're old farts and not used to all this physical activity, not a young buck like you. We'll just follow you in - over."

"Good idea John. Look, I just have to use the head so I'll be out of earshot for a couple of minutes – over." John climbed back up to the cockpit, Joan maintained her position at the wheel as John secured the sails and placed the fenders on both sides of the boat, not knowing which side he would have to berth. John was just about to take back control of the wheel when the radio crackled into life once more, only this time the voice wasn't Danny's.

Chapter 28

CHANCE MEETING

Norfolk – Virginia U.S.A.

In the distance the crew of the Augusta could make out the USS Connecticut making a beeline towards them. Giles had, as instructed, kept in radio contact to periodically report their position but they had left it until the last minute to surface, then immediately hit the siren. That had caught everyone's attention and as they approached, the entire Augusta crew, with the exception of the doctor, who returned to attend to his two new patients, went over to greet their compatriots on the incoming sub. The officers immediately reported to the Admiral, apologizing profusely for the lack of control exerted during the mutiny but also praising boatswain Giles for taking control and organizing the remainder of the crew. The Admiral attributed no blame to them under the circumstances and reminded them, they were no longer in the navy, there is no navy and they were no longer accountable to him, however, if they wanted to stay, they were welcome, as long as they followed the rules.

When this was relayed to the remainder of the Connecticut's crew only two of the submariners decided to take their chances away from the sanctuary of the naval yard, the rest remained. Now with a complement from two subs there was enough crew to comfortably sail both. There would have to be some skill balancing and movement of personnel from one sub to another but in itself that would not pose a problem. They would also have to arrange for some trade training as in some areas they would be vulnerable if a crew member went sick. Alternatively they had an abundance of crew from the Weapons Department whose skills were now made redundant. But the Admiral knew that unless he kept the men busy, trouble was only an argument away. The two crews had to be brought together with a purpose and not for just the sake of keeping them busy. He pondered that thought overnight and the next morning he called a meeting of the senior members of the crew, both officers and other ranks. He put forward a business model where he was the CEO of a shipping company that traveled the world looking for potential business opportunities. They traveled in ships owned by their company with crew employed by their company. Anyone in the company can make suggestions as to where they should travel to look for opportunities. Decisions would be made by a democratic voting process, everyone on the ship had one vote. Anyone could leave the ship at any time in any place and as long as they left with a clean disciplinary record they could return at any time. As for discipline, punishment for misconduct would be administered by the chief executive committee. A member of the crew committing a serious offence or a series of repeat offences would be locked up and sent ashore at the very next land fall – with only personal effects a la pirate lore.

This was the premise for his proposal and it was met with approval. Actual details would be formalized moving forward but for now, their first destination had to be decided, his proposal was Bermuda. However, he stressed that he had made a commitment to the departed seaman that they would remain in port until March 1st so they would be unable to leave until that date. By midday a draft had been distributed to the two crews. The proposal stated the company vision and basic rules of conduct. At 2:00 PM a meeting was held on the dock with all the men in attendance. Some stood, some sat on the decks of the subs and others brought collapsible chairs to hear what the Admiral had to say. An air of excitement was obvious as a sense of purpose was now apparent and when the first destination, Bermuda, was put to the vote, it was unanimous. The Admiral proposed the executive committee that included six crew members three from each sub with himself as a tie breaker. A whoop of delight went up from the entire company when it was announced that Giles, the only non-commissioned officer, would be one of the six. Other announcements were made. The resulting resource balancing between the skill sets of the two subs meant a transfer of a few personnel but this was met with approval and only added to the excitement of the venture. It was agreed that dress code would be informal, as long as it was clean, appropriate and could not be considered lewd. It was at this point that the Admiral revealed to the crew of the USS Connecticut that there were two women on board the Augusta that were victims of former Connecticut crewman.

This news caught the latest crew members by complete surprise, full credit to the Augusta crew, as per the Admiral's instructions, complete secrecy had been maintained and even Giles had not been made aware of their presence let alone the circumstances in which they had become victims. Obviously, it wasn't rocket science to determine what had happened, they had also seen their former crewmen in action and knew what they were capable of. But the Admiral went on to explain their current condition and that when they were well enough they would be extended the same voting privileges and options as the rest of the crew. On that note, the Admiral felt it was time to bring the meeting to a close, he asked if there was any other business, which of course there wasn't as the talking point for the next couple of days would be about the events leading up to the rescue of the women and now that the embargo had been lifted both crews could swap stories. Moral had suddenly skyrocketed and preparations for departure were carried out with gusto. Communications with other subs continued but mutinies were a common theme and the Admiral chose not to encourage a rendezvous with other subs while the women remained on board. Furthermore, it was stressed by the Admiral that during these communications with other subs it was absolutely imperative that the presence of the women was never mentioned. By now Mary had made sufficient recovery to make tentative appearances on deck, always accompanied by Hargreaves, but Janet was still in a coma even though her vital signs were improving.

The men, dressed for the most part in their working blue fatigues, enthusiastically stepped up to the task and after a few weeks of gathering supplies and carrying out necessary maintenance they were ready to depart. During this period some of the men even took off for a few days to check out the surrounding area and the results of the devastation. Eventually they were ready to set sail and the Admiral added a day's grace to the timeline of March 1st before departing but no subs or personnel had shown up. A schedule had been agreed so that at least one of the submarines would regularly return to both Norfolk and Wilmington for any wayward survivors who would like to join them. Posters were printed, framed and placed in strategic locations beyond the dock gates. They indicated the dates a sub would dock and in case all sense of time had been lost by would be survivors, the signs showed graphics of the cycle of the moon and how it corresponded to a scheduled arrival and departure.

It took four days, without mishap, before they arrived in Bermuda during which time Mary had ventured into the galley to assist with some of the meal preparations and Janet had come out of her coma but remained in a very distant state not responding to anyone and not speaking. On arrival in Bermuda they sailed into the Royal Naval Dockyard and selected a couple of vacant berths. Had this been normal times all the necessary paper work and pomp would have needed to have been completed. But these were not normal times and no one would be screaming about an infringement of sovereignty. Prior to the devastation they knew that British subs were on maneuvers in the area, specifically, HMS Dreadnaught and HMS York. Even though no communications had been heard they had half expected to meet up with their counterparts in the Royal Navy. Alas, both submarines were occupying berths in the dockyards and had suffered the same fate as the rest of the population. Crews from each sub were organized to clear the immediate vicinities of the now putrid bodies. They used heavy duty road construction machinery to clear the bodies, the vehicles were nearby to repair a local road. Other crew members found vehicles to make a tour of the island for anything of interest and they returned with fresh fruit and vegetables but reported they had seen no signs of life. This British owned jewel in the Atlantic boasted one of the finest climates in the world and the warm breeze beautiful beaches and turquoise sea was a wonderful reprieve from the cold Norfolk winter.

Once all the necessary tasks had been carried out and a staff rotation agreed upon the remaining members of the company went ashore to investigate. Those members of the crew who were diving enthusiasts set off to some of the more popular spots around the island. Others set off for the beaches while others looked for hiking trails and biking trips around the island. Inevitably, a few found bars where bottles of beer and liquor were still in abundance. By adding some ice brought in coolers from the subs they just got legless drunk. In the corner of one of the bars was a dance area with a disco unit in which was stored scores of CDs and cassettes of just about every song recorded form the rock 'n roll era to the present day. One of the sailors had procured a boom box and soon the younger ones were letting loose dancing and drinking while some of the older ones, with a memory for every song played, reminisced, talked of family and friends, wives and lovers lost forever. But, except for the hangovers the next morning, no harm was done and no trouble caused.

During this period, Mary returned to normal but the scars of those few days of capture would never heal, neither physically or in her mind. Although Hargreaves had been her constant escort, lovemaking was never given a thought. He was a very patient, compassionate man and perfect for Mary's needs. There was no question of their affection and love for each other and when Mary was ready to take the next step, he would know. Janet having emerged from her coma would occasionally join them on a trip, always accompanied by Doctor Moore, although for the most part she remained in an almost trance like state, never saying a word. She would sometimes inspect some of the more unusual fauna that was beginning to flourish on the now untended island, which in itself was an encouraging sign.

For a few months life went on this way with crews taking turns to return to their home docks in the event that some people had returned or seen the posters. This relieved a little of the mundane life but the Admiral realized things were beginning to get a little stale and it was time for another general meeting. He published the time and agenda for the next meeting with suggestions for the company's next destination. At the meeting, Brazil was suggested; a vote was taken and approved, however, this time, the vote was not unanimous. A few favored a return to the mainland but nevertheless, accepted the democratic decision without question. There were others, three to be exact, who did not wish to return to sea. They were content to take their chances and stay in Bermuda. The Admiral arranged to hold interviews with each of them in an effort to persuade them to take the trip but they were all adamant in their intention to remain. Arrangements were made to set sail and what provisions that could be garnered were brought to the sub. Those men who had been staying on the island moved back on board and for those who had decided to remain on Bermuda the Admiral made sure their share of the rations and some basic supplies were left with them. A radio schedule was arranged in the event of an emergency and the rest of the crew assisted in setting up a generator and assisted in gathering sufficient fuel from across the island. It was agreed that in keeping with the schedule the Augusta would return to Norfolk and the Connecticut would sail down to Wilmington and they would rendezvous in the Atlantic on their way to Rio de Janeiro.

The final evening before the subs set sail a barbeque was held on the beach. The whole crew was driven to the location by the senior officers using some of the finest vehicles found in Bermuda. A Rolls Royce, fit for the queen, brought the two women and their escorts to shore. Mary was accompanied by Jason Hargreaves and she clung to him like a limpet. Doctor Moore escorted Janet ashore, although she now looked healthy and normal, she still hadn't spoken a word. An entertainment committee had been formed and they had begun to build a barbeque pit on the beach. By the time the guests had arrived, candle lit tables, adorned with the finest crockery and silverware, purloined from nearby hotels, had been set. Coloured lights had been erected powered by a generator that was far enough away for the smell and sound to be inconspicuous and elaborate ice sculptures had been created by the subs' catering staff. There was even a rotating ball hanging in the center of the eating area reflecting beams of light from strategically placed spot lights. Not to be out done, the chefs had gone to town, cooking stuffed marlin, shrimp, lobster, all freshly caught by various members of the crews, all accompanied by the finest wines selected from local establishments. Choices of deserts included crepes containing fresh fruit, cheese cakes and various pies were in abundance. In fact, the chefs appeared to be enjoying the feast more than the rest of them as they watched the fruits of their labours being devoured avariciously by all and sunder. Normally, military chefs have to cater for the masses and produce food by the vat full, but their training and experience would have allowed them to work in most of the best hotels in the world. The ambience, food and entertainment would have done a luxurious cruise line proud, it was as if the submarines' crews were passengers enjoying a shore excursion.

At the end of the evening the Admiral gave a little speech and a toast to the 'new pioneers', the three men setting up a base in Bermuda. The crew that were leaving formed a line and paraded past the three that were remaining, shaking hands, wishing each other well amidst hugs, tears and the usual crew bantering. Mary, with Dutch courage obtained from a couple of glasses of wine felt comfortable enough to let go of Hargreaves and gave each of the three men a hug. Janet, managed a wave before Mary assisted her into the Rolls that was to take them back to the sub. She could still not bear to be touched by anyone except Mary and Doctor Moore. A few minutes later the skeleton crews for the next morning's watch were transported back to their respective subs. It had been agreed that the subs would embark at 0800 the next morning and those scheduled to be on the first watch had agreed to leave the party early and remain relatively sober. The remainder of the departing crew would be transported by a volunteer from the USS Connecticut who would be at their disposal until just after midnight when he would ensure all the remaining passengers were to be escorted to their respective subs.

At promptly 0800 the next morning the armada of two submarines noiselessly left for the open sea, apart of course from sounding their sirens for the benefit of Bermuda's new residents. All the crew members made a ceremonious line on the decks and waved to the three lonely souls standing at the gates of the dockyards – all crew members that is, except those that were down below who were essential to the running of the subs or those that were totally incapacitated from the previous evening. Within minutes they were out of sight of each other and the subs prepared to submerge and position themselves for their respective trips.

It didn't take long for the crews to revert to the daily pattern of undersea life. Their years of training kicked in and even those who spent the first few hours praying to the porcelain god as a result of the previous evening's celebrations didn't take long to adapt. Neither submarine picked up any survivors nor was there any evidence that anyone had been around the dock areas. So they merely updated the posters for the next scheduled visit and rendezvoused as planned. Their course to Brazil would take them along normal shipping lanes and avoid the infamous Bermuda Triangle, not because of any folklore or superstition, the sophisticated technology and professionalism of the subs and their crew were above that, no, it was simply the most direct route. They would be bypassing the Puerto Rica trench, one of the deepest parts of the Atlantic and the islands of the Caribbean and heading straight for Brazil. Many of the crew felt a stop in the West Indies would have been interesting and would break up the trip. However, the decision had come about democratically and it was agreed to stand by it. It was on the second day out that Sparks, working the sonar, picked up a faint but distinct sound of diesel engines. Instantly, he alerted the officer of the bridge, which in this case was, *quelle surprise*, the Admiral. It seemed that since the devastation, the Admiral was on duty 24 hours a day. The Admiral knew that Sparks was an experienced operator and did not question the news, he merely asked for the position and gave the order to change course towards the source of the sound. As reluctant as he was to venture into the archipelago of the Caribbean with its reefs and shallows he knew that if there were others who had survived then he had a duty to offer whatever support he could. It was approaching dusk and he gave the order to surface. It was normal procedure to have one radio tuned into the marine emergency channel and within a few seconds of surfacing the radio crackled with the sound of a conversation occurring between two men. The Admiral gestured to Sparks for a headset and Sparks passed one to him.

"This is Admiral Stanford of the US Submarine Augusta over." There was silence for a few seconds and then a tired voice replied.

"Er, this is John. John Hamax. Oh my God, what a relief to hear there are others." The radio reception was very poor, not because of the equipment on the sub but because of the limitations of the yacht's radio. On a good day it would be limited but the powerful receivers on the sub amplified the signal. Even so, it was very faint.

"Same here John. What's your position?"

"Well, sir, we're just approaching Cockburn Harbour in the Turks and Caicos islands. The GPS is reading, er hang on a second." There was a pause as John had to leave the radio at the navigation desk to go on deck in the cockpit to retrieve the portable GPS handheld. "That's 21 45 North and 71 55 W, if that helps. Boy is it good to hear from you. I'd given up on meeting anyone other than the four people on St Santia. Then we met Danny, now you.

"You said we?"

"Yes me and my wife and two young babies we happened to come by. We were in hospital breathing oxygen when whatever it was hit. Then we woke up and found everyone dead. It was like a bad dream and then the phone rang and it was these young kids phoning from St. Santia. Their story was that they had surfaced from a dive and found everyone dead. Well we traveled from Maine down to Florida and we met Danny. Now we're on our way to St. Santia to meet up with the kids. We estimate another couple of days before we get there. They don't know we're coming, hell I don't know if they are even still alive. So it will be a big surprise for everyone if we meet up. If they are alive I'm sure they could use your help too. How far away are you?"

"Well John, we are approximately 1,000 miles south east of you and approximately 700 miles from St. Santia. I say we, there are two subs, ourselves, the USS Augusta and the other is the USS Connecticut. It will take us a couple of days to get there. We will probably travel submerged so radio contact with you will not always be possible. So, as the song goes, we will see you in St Santia."

"Look forward to it Admiral – over."

The conversation between the Admiral and Hamax had been monitored by Drexel, the radio operator on the Connecticut. "What a coincidence," he thought idly "one of the mutineers was called Danny."

Chapter 29

St. Santia

Turks and Caicos Islands - Caribbean

The radio encounter with the Augusta had bolstered the spirits of both John and Joan no end and they couldn't wait to meet the kids on St. Santia where they would be joined by the crew of two submarines and all the technology and expertise that accompanies it. Their energy levels were piqued and after a good night's sleep they were awake with the crack of dawn and after an uneventful couple of days they arrived at St. Santia. Of course, not knowing where the folks were living they had agreed with Danny to circumnavigate the island looking for signs of life. They arrived at mid-day on the Atlantic side of the island, which was the opposite side to where the four men and women had set up their home. By the time they reached the bay where the young folks lived it was dusk and their location was given away by the light emanating from the two houses which were the only illuminations on the island. They cruised in as close as they could to shore and were about to weigh anchor when Danny, using his powerful searchlight, located two long jetties not far from the houses. One of the jetties was empty and the other was filled with boats of various shapes and sizes. Danny indicated to John that he would motor in first to the nearest jetty, which was void of boats, and very gingerly he maneuvered his boat forwards, closely monitoring his depth finder as he did so. Once he reached the end of the jetty he moved forward a boat's length to ensure it would be safe to dock without his keel hitting bottom. He then reversed back and repeated the process on the other side of the dock to verify that both sides of the jetty had similar depths. Satisfied, he secured his boat then directed John in using his hand held radio and was on the jetty to help him tie up. Within a few minutes the three of them, with Joan and Danny carrying a baby each and John a powerful flashlight, were on the beach walking towards the source of the lights. They approached the first house and knocked on the door. Receiving no reply they walked around to the rear of the house and there they heard some shouting coming from the other lit house. They crossed the road, amazed to see chickens which were the first animals they had seen since the devastation. As they approached the rear of the house they saw an open door to what appeared to be the kitchen. They neared the door and took a quick look through the window, it didn't require much gumption to realize what was going on. John, knocked quietly on the door and above the mayhem occurring inside he asked, "could you folk use a little help?" Before the occupants could utter any surprised response Joan handed John the baby she had been carrying and was instantly barking orders to the astounded two men and woman in the room. Joan thought the woman standing there did not look too far off giving birth herself.

"You -," shouted Joan pointing to Bob, "mattress, pillows, blankets and towels, *NOW!*" Bob, without a thought, leapt up and was gone before Joan had time to turn her head to Tony, "you - boil water, as much as you can." Tony ran to the sink and stated filling electric kettles, plugging them in and turning them on before turning his attention to filling pots to go on the stove. Neither of them stopped to question who these people were, what they were doing there or where they came from. They were just grateful that someone had taken charge and they were now contributing instead of panicking and feeling useless. Joan took hold of Maria's hands and smiled at her, "you're going to be fine dear. How far apart are the contractions?" Marlene answered for her "about 30 minutes apart but a couple of hours ago she wasn't even in labour."

"Well that's good dear," Joan replied soothingly, "it will all be over before you know it."

"But, my baby. It isn't due yet." Maria spurted out between breaths, "my baby."

"She's not yet 8 months." Marlene offered putting an arm around Maria's shoulders. Before Joan could reply Bob had returned with the bedding and they proceeded to prepare a makeshift bed there on the kitchen floor. Everyone helped to move Maria onto the mattress before Joan ordered all the men out of the kitchen but not before a final order to them, "she will need a couple of nightdresses too." When the men had left Joan and Marlene were able to strip off Maria's clothes put her in the bed and made her comfortable. As they were doing so, Joan inspected the opening of the vagina and assured them that everything looked fine and it wouldn't be long at all. There was a knock on the door and Bob returned with the nightdresses. He had wanted to be present for the birth and was coming in to insist on that. But just as he was passing the nightdresses to Marlene, another contraction hit and Maria let out such a blood curdling scream he just turned and joined the other *men* in the dining room. John just smiled, assured him that she was in good hands and took him over to the drinks cabinet.

Danny had already started. After a grueling sail and now this excitement the Irish in him needed a stiff drink and he found it in a bottle of malt whiskey. He poured a shot for all of them and gave a toast,

"To the new bairn."

"To the new bairn" they all replied in unison and gulped down their drink.

"My name is Danny" and he held out his hand to the two strangers.

"Tony, Tony Dilenti."

"Then you must be Bob," John interjected, turning to face the other ashen faced man, "my name is John Hamax, out there is my wife Joan. We spoke on the phone a few months ago." The sudden realization of who these people were suddenly dawned on Bob and he reacted by bursting into tears and hugging this wizened, old, salt encrusted stranger whom he had never met before. Then catching sight of the babies sitting in their carry-seats that they had brought with them Bob and Tony were dumbfounded.

"We had found them in the hospital the day of our last phone call but I was so absorbed with my own problems I forgot to tell you about them." John offered in way of an explanation. But, a couple of nips later and a brief history of each of their adventures they had almost forgotten why they were standing there drinking in the dining room of a once rich recording artist when the crying sound of a baby emanated from the kitchen. Bob rushed through the swing door connecting the dining room to the kitchen and looked over the food preparation island to see a heavily perspiring Maria smiling up at him holding a small bundle.

"It's a boy. A little boy" Maria managed to whisper.

"Six pounds three ounces of little boy." Marlene added, pointing to the baking scales they had used to measure the new born.

"And a healthy looking one at that." Added a beaming Joan.

Joan was now tidying up as the others returned to the kitchen. They all said 'hi' to the mother and baby before being ushered away so that Maria could start feeding the baby, in private. It was at that point they all realized they hadn't eaten, the sea-fearers had been too busy looking for this place and none too soon. The others were about to have dinner before Maria decided to go into labour. Now, everyone was famished. Marlene helped Joan prepare a supper consisting of soup, out of cans, followed by fresh fish and chips, in between cooing and aahing with the young toddlers that appeared to be huge compared to the recently born baby. While that was being prepared the men snacked on potato chips, still relatively fresh, and assorted canned nuts washed down with the same bottle of malt whiskey. So by the time dinner was served, unaccustomed as they have been to drinking of late, the men were in a happy euphoric state. Everyone was seated, all except for

Maria who was quietly sleeping in her makeshift bed with her new charge. Marlene had laid the table with all the best china and crockery she could find, together with an antique white lace tablecloth that had slightly greyed with time. They had just started eating when John suddenly looked up as though in pain.

"Bless me," he said, looking directly at Danny, "I really must be getting old. In all the excitement I completely forgot about it."

"Forgot about what?" Danny asked curiously.

"The other night, while you were, shall we say, incommunicado we were contacted by a crew, a submarine crew, the USS Augusta. Actually there were two subs but we only talked to one of them. The other was the Connecticut. I'm disappointed we didn't bump into them as we circumnavigated the island, they said they would be here. I didn't tell you because I thought it would be a helluva surprise for you when we arrived.

Judging by the pallor of Danny's face, which would have been easily camouflaged by the once white tablecloth, it certainly was one helluva surprise.

Chapter 30

COLLISION

Below the Caribbean Sea

Admiral Stanford broadcast the change in direction to the crews of both subs simultaneously and of course, his reason for doing so. He had made that decision to change course, instantly and without consulting anyone, which was a full 360 degrees on the 'company vision' and majority vote approach, yet not one person protested and in fact they were delighted with the possibility of meeting other survivors. So, once more they submerged and altered course for the islands of the Lesser Antilles. The excitement on board was mounting at the prospect of meeting real people. Not that they didn't consider themselves real people but these were civilians, people who would be in need of help and assistance, something they had been trained for. More importantly, it would give the crew an even greater sense of purpose.

Stanford's only concern was the experience of his counterpart on the Connecticut, Sheldrake. He had been a junior officer up until the mutiny but he became senior officer after the departure or demise of all his superiors. He was in command by default. It had been suggested that the Admiral should transfer Hargreaves to be commander of the sister ship but this was waved away without a thought. In fairness, Sheldrake had carried out all his orders precisely and there appeared to be no dissention from his crew, mind you, he also had Giles to assist in that regard. But there would be periods during the trip to St. Santia that the skeleton crew would be even further depleted as some slept. They would no longer be travelling through deep trenches of ocean but through shallow waters littered with reefs and the remnants of sunken ships. The Admiral immediately gave the order to reduce speed which would automatically be relayed to the Connecticut. This was intended to provide more lead time against any unforeseen obstacles. Unfortunately, this had the opposite effect. The crew of the Connecticut did not compensate quickly enough to the reduction in speed and it lost a few feet of depth which was sufficient enough to lead to a collision that not only seriously damaged the Connecticut but endangered the lives of the crews of both vessels.

Chapter 31

REPAIRS UNDER
THE SEA

Below the Caribbean Sea

Admiral Stanford, as technically he was the Commander in Chief of the fleet, bore the brunt of the blame but with skeleton crews on both vessels there was only so much experience that could be split between the two subs. The Connecticut was cruising approximately 750 yards and 45 degrees astern of the Augusta, both subs were approximately 60 feet below the surface. For the most part, the depth of the water around this area was relatively shallow, which made it excellent for diving but precarious for nuclear submarines. To make matters worse, a large container ship had drifted west during the devastation, hit a reef and turned turtle before sinking and of course would not be visible on any chart. As the ship lay lifeless, air that was providing support to the vessel escaped through the many orifices in the sides and hull of the ship to be replaced by the indefatigable water that was slowly taking the ship to Davy Jones locker. Uncannily, as the ship finally sank the containers that had been on the deck of the vessel had fallen to the bottom of the ocean and formed a cradle so that when the ship finally settled the bow was protruding upwards at an angle of 60 degrees. If the sinking had occurred on the reef the Augusta was cruising over it would have clearly been seen but unfortunately the sinking had occurred in a gorge beside the reef so the only thing that was visible was the bow. It was this protrusion that the Connecticut collided with at a speed of 20 knots. Had they have been going at full speed the damage would have been critical, however, had they had been travelling at full speed they may have avoided the collision. Not only did it wrench a major hole in the sub the force of impact dislodged the ship from its supporting plinth and as the bow slowly fell from its platform of containers to level its length on the sea floor its superstructure married with the sub forcing both vessels to sink to the bottom. From the time of the collision to finally resting on the sea bed only took a few seconds but to the crew on board it was a terrifying experience that seemed to last forever. Although relatively inexperienced, the crew of the Connecticut had been superbly trained and immediately emergency procedures were put into action by the crew. The bulkheads were secured to reduce flooding and all crew members were called to station to report damage control. Captain Sheldrake on the Connecticut immediately contacted the Augusta to inform them that a collision had occurred but they didn't know what with and they certainly didn't know why they had drifted down and were now stationary. The Admiral immediately was on the radio.

"Has the nuclear source been compromised in any way?" The Admiral demanded to know in a tone that expected an instant response.

"All indications are that the nuclear source is NOT compromised sir." Sheldrake replied in naval vernacular reflective of the emergency they were experiencing. "All instruments are showing normal but despite applying power we have somehow been dragged down to the sea bottom sir." The Admiral was visibly relieved as a problem with the reactor could spell disaster for all of them. Under the circumstances he admired his subordinate's coolness in the wake of the collision and informed him that they were on their way back and would have a diving team in the water once they had surveyed the damage from the outside. However, this was merely brash talk as all they had on board were some recreational divers. Neither were there any professional Navy divers on board the Connecticut that could assess damage and make emergency repairs at sea. They had all deserted in Norfolk, with the exception of one who had remained in Bermuda. So now, with all but essential systems shut down and laying immobile on the sea floor an eerie silence enveloped the sub. It was reminiscent of all those World War II movies when a submarine was at the mercy of the accuracy of the depth charges being dispatched from warships above them as the submarine lay defenceless. Only this time there was no one to blow them out of the water but the harrowing thing was that they were stuck there 100 feet below the surface. To their credit there was no panic amongst the crew as they waited patiently for the Augusta to return. Giles the wizened old boson barked out a couple of orders to keep everyone focused but inwardly even he was feeling a little trepidation.

It didn't take long for the Augusta to return and from their videocam they could see the source of the problem. The sub had just clipped the tip of the bow of the sunken ship but in doing so it had torn through the steel and wrenched apart a lance-like protrusion of metal. As this was one of the strongest points of the structure it reciprocated by thrusting its point into the belly of the sub. The speed of the collision was enough to knock the ship from its precarious perch and send it down to the sea bed dragging the submarine with it. During the trip back Hargreaves had polled the crew for personnel with diving experience. Of the certified recreational divers on board the two subs, all of whom volunteered their services, only one of them, Wayne Oliver, had experience with underwater welding tools. Another was a young seaman who had been transferred from the Connecticut, Dave Lester, who spent most of his free time diving and was considered one of the fittest men on board.

Admiral Sanford considered the options and discussed them with Hargreaves.

"We could surface and augment emergency exit procedures on the Connecticut and pick up the crew on the surface," suggested the Admiral.

"It's almost dark we could easily miss someone," replied Hargreaves, "and leaving the sub in this position until daylight is an added risk. Furthermore, emergency exits are risky under the best conditions." He called over the two men selected as potential working divers.

Able Seaman Dave Lester had been brought up in Hawaii and had been snorkeling and diving since he could walk. His love of the sea and the historical connections of the US Navy to his place of birth acted like a magnet to sign up. Unfortunately, his scholarly abilities had taken a back seat to his outdoor activities and although he was a very intelligent individual he had nothing to show for it. So at eighteen years of age, a mere year ago, he joined the navy and promised his parents he would follow a secondary education, which he had been doing, until the devastation. Wayne Oliver or Ollie as he was known had been a recreational diver which had helped him secure an apprenticeship in the shipyards of Pittsburgh. After a couple of years of doing this he felt he needed something more, so he joined the navy believing that his experience would be a shoe in. It was, but in their wisdom the navy decided he would be best suited as a Radar Operator.

Hargreaves pointed to the screen to let the two volunteers digest the gravity of the situation. They talked amongst themselves for a couple of minutes continually zooming in on specific areas and determined nonchalantly that they could do it. The Admiral thanked them and announced to the rest of the crew that the two men were going to carry out the dangerous task of removing the protrusion and sealing the holes, while the remainder of both crews were on full alert in the case of an emergency. They repeatedly went over the procedures and steps to minimize any cause for error. Even so, it took a full two days for the two divers to make the necessary rudimentary repairs. First they had to cut away the part of the ship that had entered the sub. This required special underwater oxyacetylene equipment that had to be negotiated in a restricted area between the two vessels. Once this was accomplished, the serrated parts of the sub were cut away before new plates were welded over the gaping hole. It was extremely taxing work for the two divers and Admiral Stanford insisted on adding safety parameters to the compression tables extending their time between trips. Now that the problem had been identified and the damage assessed they were in no immediate danger so it didn't really matter if the repairs took two hours or two days, the safety of the two divers was paramount. He also refused to endanger the lives of the other recreational divers who had offered their assistance, except in the case of an emergency where assistance was feasible. They felt that just helping transport equipment and carrying out some of the more laborious tasks would alleviate a substantial part of the strenuous effort. But the Admiral was adamant, they had not been trained, one slip and the working divers would become underwater medics and would have to return to the sub encountering further delays. However, he compromised by allowing them to be dressed and ready in the event of an emergency to the two working divers.

With the Admiral calling the shots they were back in military mode. Yet, there was no talk of mutiny, nobody questioning the soundness of the commands, just everybody doing their job. There was an emergency and mixed messages would only create confusion and bring possible danger to both subs. The main reason of course was that the personnel wanted to be there and were quite happy to be doing what they were told, albeit, at times, with mutterings under their breath regarding their superior's ancestry. But what soldier, seaman or airman had never done that at some point in their career?

Once the outside repairs were completed, the water was expunged from the flooded area and a crew was assembled to make good the inside, as best they could with the limited expertise and resources available. Additional plates and welds were applied to the inside of the damaged compartment as a further insurance. The sub was serviceable again but it was decided that until they could get to a dry dock and make more permanent repairs the remainder of the trip would be at sea level alleviating any undue pressure to the temporary welds. This was a sound approach until they surfaced, right into the leading edge of what had all the makings of a major hurricane.

Chapter 32

HURRICANE
APPROACHING

St. Santia - Caribbean

"Danny, are you alright? You look a little pale." Joan said with a concerned look as she gently touched his arm.

"No. Yes, I mean yes. I think everything has just caught up with me I guess and I shouldn't have drunk as much as I did on an empty stomach. I'll be fine, really." Danny replied and then tucked into some of his fish and chips. Joan still looked at him a bit concerned but accepted his explanation. They finished supper and everyone helped clear away the dinner things. The men insisted on having one more for the road and then another to 'wet the baby's head' so by the time they were ready to hit the sack they were feeling no pain. Joan insisted on sleeping downstairs with her now extended, extended family while everyone else retired to bed. Marlene and Tony returned to their own house and Bob showed John and Danny to their guestrooms.

Next morning Bob was up bright and early, albeit with a hangover and after a quick trip to the washroom he went to the kitchen for a large glass of water and to check on Maria and their new born. Maria was awake and breastfeeding Anthony John, forever to be called AJ who was tucking in for all he was worth. Bob went over to them and gave Maria a loving kiss but she immediately remonstrated him to get away if she didn't want to harm his son with poisonous fumes. The alcohol content of his breath was still enough to peel paint. Joan, meanwhile, was fussing around like a clucking hen preparing baby food and gathering all the necessary paraphernalia to raise the only child that had been born, anywhere in the world during the last eight months. She was now in her element and with a half a dozen adult mouths to feed and three children in her charge her next task was to prepare a full English breakfast for all of them, as was her custom. Bob, stumbled outside to tend to the chickens and to do some chores and by the time he returned the smell of bacon sizzling in the pan was overwhelming. During the previous few months most of their meals had been a weight watchers dream consisting of fruit, vegetables, eggs, fish and only occasional meat from their cache. He had forgotten what a good cooked breakfast tasted like but Joan, bless her heart, had found all the ingredients she needed buried deep in the freezer. By this time John was up, slightly the worse for wear, and sitting at the kitchen table with his head buried in his hands, a cup of black coffee in front of him and his wife cajoling him. Bob went over to the barometer in the kitchen and gave the glass a light tap.

"Bad news," he said soberly, "I think we have a hurricane on the way. The wind and waves got up during the night and the mercury is dropping like a stone. Once we've had breakfast we should prepare to batten down." Joan turned and looked with concern at her charges.

"Oh, don't worry Joan," Bob consoled her, "there's a safe room in the house. We have practiced this a few times we'll be fine."

"Yes, but you now have five more extra mouths to feed." Joan retorted, "will there be enough provisions for two extra adults and three extra children?"

"Food and water yes, but baby food and diapers we might need to stock up on." Tony replied. "As soon as the others get here we can start making the preparations. Not that there is a lot to prepare everything is set up. By the way, where are the others? I would have thought at least Marlene would have been here by now." Before anyone could answer Tony burst through the door.

"They've gone. Danny and Marlene, they've gone."

Chapter 33

RESCUE AT SEA

St. Santia - Caribbean

Bob had shown Danny to his room and after a few celebratory, drunken exchanges across the hallway between his host and John, Danny closed the bedroom door to take in his surroundings. No sooner had he done that he heard voices. Looking out the window he saw a very pregnant Marlene attempting to support a very drunken Tony negotiate a path across the lawn to her house. Danny thought for a few seconds and decided on a plan. He quietly opened his bedroom door and listened for a few seconds for any movement in the hallway. Deciding that the coast was clear he crept down the stairs and quietly opened the front door. Fortunately, the door wasn't locked, after all, who was around to break in? He silently closed the door behind him and walked quickly to catch up with the couple struggling to their home. As he came within a few yards he called out softly, trying not to alarm Marlene.

"Hi, do you need a hand there?" Danny asked as he caught up to them. He grabbed the arm that Marlene was supporting, "he looks a little worse for wear."

"Well, he's not used to drinking." Marlene replied, now relieved of the burden she was carrying, "during the last few months all he's had is the occasional glass of wine or a beer. Certainly not hard liquor. Boy is he going to feel it in the morning. Anyway, how come you're not drunk?" She asked surprisingly.

"I didn't drink that much. I was just pretending to go with the flow but in actual fact it was ginger ale I was drinking." Danny replied without any slurring of his words.

"Wow, you fooled me. I thought you were all two sheets to the wind." Marlene laughed.

"Hold it." Tony interrupted, "I think I'm gonna throw up." Danny stopped and supported him and sure enough Tony puked, most of which went on the lawn but his legs and feet caught a good splattering.

"Oh God, Tony." An exasperated Marlene sighed, "you can't go home like this!"

"It's O.K. Marlene," Danny said, "let's get him to the beach, let him paddle awhile to clean himself up. Maybe even a good dunk in the sea will sober him up a bit." It was a hundred or so yards away from the house but it seemed to Marlene to be a good idea, especially with Danny assisting.

Tony was dressed in t-shirt and shorts which had become normal dress code in the clement climate and after paddling in the sea it had the desired effect. But Tony was beginning to get belligerent and insisted he couldn't walk another step and he was going to sleep right there on the beach. By now they were only a few yards from the jetty where Danny and

John had moored their boats. Danny gently lay Tony on the beach out of reach of the tide and asked Marlene if she could go to one of the boats and grab some cushions from the cockpit. Marlene obliged and walked towards the jetty. She then stepped onto the first boat she came to, which happened to be the one Danny had arrived in. Danny was watching her and once she was on the boat he covered the distance to the jetty with lightning speed. Marlene climbed down the steps leading to the cabin and in the poor light she managed to locate some cushions, she bent down to pick them up and as she did so Danny was on the boat locking the cabin door behind her. At first she was a little befuddled, there she was in the dark and Danny appeared to have locked her down there in the cabin. Danny wasted no time untying the lines and raising the mainsail. There was a reasonably strong wind and it was conducive for sailing away from the jetty and the island. It meant that he wouldn't have to use the engines ensuring they would not bring any undue attention from the house. Down below Marlene could feel the momentum of the boat and she realized that Danny was taking her away from the island but she still couldn't understand why.

There was no moon and in the cabin the only light that made its way through the cracks in the cabin door was being emitted from the deck instruments and a low voltage deck lamp. In the near darkness it took a little time for Marlene to get her bearings and once she did she could feel the boat heeling over as it cut through the waves. She waited a while to find her balance then she attempted to climb up the steep steps to the deck. There was no handle or anything to grab on the cabin door and it was locked fast from the outside.

She banged on the door and shouted out to Danny to let her out but she knew it was futile. She had no idea where the light switches were so she needed to locate a flashlight, there had to be a flashlight somewhere in the cabin. She started to rummage blindly through the drawers and cupboards and it wasn't long before she felt what she was looking for. She ran her hands down the shaft of the flashlight and found the on switch. Now that she had a flashlight she took the time to survey the cabin. After a couple of minutes she found the main switch panel by the chart table. She flicked on all of the switches that not only provided full light to the cabin but lit up the deck like a Christmas tree. On deck, Danny didn't feel threatened, by now, they were out of sight of the houses on the island and he was putting further distance between them at a good speed of knots. By morning they would be so far away neither John nor the other men would be able to track him down.

For an hour or so as Danny sailed through the night all was quiet down below, or so he thought. During that time Marlene had been searching through the cabin for some type of weapon and a tool that would be capable of breaking down the door. In a cupboard beneath the mattress in the forward cabin she found both, a knife and a small anchor. The knife was a seven inch fish scaling knife that would suffice as a weapon. It was in a leather sheaf that she slipped in the back of her maternity pants. The anchor was a small Danforth type attached to a light chain. The anchor was obviously designed for a small porter and was left there by a previous owner. But the length of chain was sufficient to swing the anchor against the door. Marlene figured a couple of accurate swings and the wood would splinter enough for her to wrench open the door. She grabbed the anchor by the shaft and with all her strength she crashed the end of the steel anchor into the centre of the teak door. Unfortunately, her precarious footing on the steps leading up to the deck became only too obvious as the momentum of her swing made her fall unceremoniously back into the cabin. Undaunted, she picked herself up reached once more for the anchor and proceeded to climb back up the steps. Her first attempt had in deed splintered the door but as she began to prepare for a second swing Danny interceded.

"Alright, alright," she heard Danny say then there was the sound of the door being unlocked, "no need to ruin the boat."

Danny heard the first crash of the anchor hitting the door and despite the kidnapping, he was genuinely concerned for her welfare, more for his long term plans rather than for Marlene. He had no reason to believe that their departure had yet been detected and even if it had, they were so far from land without anyone on the island capable of catching them. So, he relented and unlocked the cabin door to allow Marlene to come on deck. After all that exertion she was hot and sweaty and the cool breeze made her shiver. Danny passed her a warm sweater and a blanket and she sat as far away from him as possible while she gathered her thoughts and regained her breath. Finally, when she did speak, her voice was calm as was her demeanor.

"Why Danny?" Marlene was all she asked as she glared directly at Danny.

"Very simple Marlene. I would have been quite content to stay on the island with you forever. Sure, my natural testosteronal needs would have been difficult to overcome with two such beautiful women as yourself and Maria but I would have managed. But I want something more."

"So you did have too much to drink. Danny. Look, we're all in a difficult position, we need people like you to help with the upbringing of my baby, Maria's baby and the future of the human race. What you are doing now is so, so selfish. What you don't know is that Maria and I were lovers." Danny looked at her in amazement and she could tell that he had been taken by complete surprise.

"Yes, that's right lovers." Marlene sensed that he had been seriously taken aback by that statement, so she continued, "well, here's another big surprise. Tony and Bob were lovers too before the devastation but we had to sacrifice. Sacrifice our loves and everything else. Now I don't know what you are trying to gain here but it is totally selfish and is going to achieve absolutely nothing."

"Marlene, I agree." Danny said nonchalantly.

"So why don't you just turn back. I will say nothing of this to any of them, I promise. I need to have my baby, which is the most important thing right now." Marlene pleaded.

"Sorry Marlene. I have to get away. The submarine that is on its way?" Danny said.

"What about it?" Marlene asked.

"Well, I had been on another sub. A group of us left and one of the officers was a pilot so we flew from the coast until we hit bad weather in Georgia. The pilot was forced to make an emergency landing in a shopping mall. Coincidently, two women had found their way there, driving a RV. Well, I don't need to go into details but it wasn't pretty. I might add, I had nothing to do with what went on, I tried to prevent it but it was pointless. The other men were like animals." Danny explained. He was lying profusely, in fact, he had been the first one to abuse Janet. Her aloofness and '*you can't touch me attitude*' just made him want to do all types of monstrous atrocities to the woman. He was just fortunate that when the rescue team came for her he happened to be in the washroom. As the shooting started he stood petrified on one of the toilets in case whoever it was out there made a random search. None came, but nevertheless, he waited until well after the receding sound of the helicopter's rotors had gone before he cautiously left the washroom. He saw the carnage that remained, Linmore's body was still twitching in its death throes. There had been so much death and violence in the days leading up to this confrontation that the deaths of men he hardly knew meant nothing to him. He was alone and the only place he would feel comfortable on his own would be in Florida. He calmly, walked out of the mall into the RV and headed south.

"But, I don't understand. What does this have to do with the sub?" Marlene inquired.

"The rescue team was from the Augusta, the very sub that John said will be rendezvousing with us shortly." Danny explained.

"How do you know that?" Marlene asked trying to digest all this new information.

"I heard one of the men shout out to another man to get the helicopter over so they could get back to the Augusta." Danny replied.

"But if you tried to prevent it then surely the women could verify your story, in fact you could be a hero and – wait a minute," Marlene stopped, even in her disheveled state, still shivering from her efforts, all the tumblers were beginning to fall into place. "You lying bastard. You participated in the attack didn't you? You know that if those women turn up with the sub, they would recognize you and you would be dead meat." A malicious grin appeared on Danny's face, altering it so that in the glow of the instrument lights it resembled an evil, malevolent, human being. The realization that Marlene's fate was to be a sex slave to this piece of crap spurred her into action, it was now or never. She reached behind her and felt for the fishing knife tucked in her pants. Still holding the blanket around her she brought the knife to her side, and extracted the knife from its sheaf. She rose with a pronounced effort then she covered the short distance to where Danny was piloting the boat with a speed not common for a woman in her final weeks of pregnancy. In one movement, she flung off the blanket and lunged at Danny with the knife through the spokes of the steering wheel and into Danny's chest. He staggered back but did not fall. Marlene negotiated her bulk round the steering wheel and with a banshee like scream she used her full weight to push Danny backwards to the railing and with him leaning backwards into the sea with one last effort she grabbed his legs and he fell into the ocean.

She sat down on the bench seat and totally spent, cried hysterically. She really hadn't thought this plan through, she had no idea how to sail a boat, she was a farm girl and here she was in the middle of the ocean with no land in sight. To make matters worse the wind was beginning to blow with some ferocity and it was only then as a wave broke over the side of the boat that she noticed the sea was beginning to look really menacing. The only thing she could think of was to get the engine going, that she did understand. She hauled herself up and looked at the instrument panel. There was a key in the ignition and she turned it. Feeling the vibration under her feet of the big diesel engine coming to life she gently moved the throttle forward. The frothing of the water as the propeller began to turn gave her great comfort. Marlene was just about to provide some power when a hand reached over and turned off the ignition. Terrified, she looked up to see Danny before her, barely able to stand, with the knife still protruding from his chest. During the time it took between Danny falling overboard and Marlene grabbing the wheel the boat, without anyone at the helm, had begun to circle and Danny had grabbed hold of the stern as it came round to where he was drifting. An opportune wave helped him climb onto the transom and he had lain there regaining some strength before climbing on deck while Marlene was absorbed with getting the engine to function.

Marlene let out a scream that was drowned by the wind and she fell back onto the port bench in complete surprise. Danny stumbled towards her, still with that malicious grin. He lifted his arms above his head and joined his hands together by interlocking his fingers. It looked to Marlene as if he was going to bring his hands down on her head and beat her to death. Which is exactly what he would have done but the boat, still circling, now had the stern turning into the wind into what sailors call an accidental jibe. A jibe would only be performed during a race by experienced sailors or in gentle breezes by day sailors. Certainly not something you would entertain in winds approaching hurricane strength. As the stern turned through the wind the wind caught the sails and flung the boom to the port side of the ship with such ferocity that it struck Danny's head and knocked him over the rail and into the sea for the final time. The boat heeled well beyond the safety point but the wind was now so strong that rigging came loose and the sails were ripped to shreds. With the sails gone, the boat righted itself somewhat but it was far from safe, it was bobbing up and down like a cork in a whirlpool. To make matters worse Marlene began to feel sharp pains in her abdomen but her survival instincts forced her back to the instrument panel and she attempted to '*drive*' the boat again. Once more the engine started first time, her only inkling of piloting a boat was to steer into the oncoming waves. She managed to turn the boat into what she thought was the oncoming waves and as the waves approached she gunned the engine to ride through the crest. The pain in her abdomen was getting worse and spasms of additional pain were becoming more frequent. To add to her dilemma, the waves seemed to be in sympathy with her pain and were also becoming higher and more frequent. Her strength was fading and her pain was excruciating, she knew the baby was coming. After a particularly high crest, that took all her remaining effort she dropped to her knees yet still managing to keep the wheel head on to the oncoming sea. She had nothing left, and just before she finally passed out she happened to look out to the side of the boat where she saw an angel standing on the water, reaching out to her. The head of the angel was surrounded in a bright light and he was beckoning her to come to him. She was not a god-fearing individual and after all the devastation that had occurred she knew that this must be just her imagination playing tricks. She knew this was the end, she had done her best but she had no more to give. Marlene, now resigned to her death and that of her unborn baby, she just hoped it would be quick and to assist with the inevitable she found the strength for one further Herculean effort. With the help of the wheel she pulled herself to her feet and threw herself into the arms of the waiting angel.

Chapter 34

BIRTH UNDER
THE SEA

Below the Caribbean Sea

Sanford's original decision for the submarines to travel on the surface had been trumped by the approaching hurricane. However, the two subs were now making good progress just beneath the cauldron of waves that was beginning to churn up the surface. The repairs on the Connecticut were standing up well but rather than take chances a 24 hour watch had been arranged on board to detect any seepage through the welds. Their original ETA at St Santia was to be the early hours of the morning but due to the hurricane they were forced to remain submerged until the storm had passed. They felt there would be less of a risk to the damaged submarine if they stayed under the surface than being battered around by the waves that were currently being driven by the hurricane. According to the charts there was no suitable dock and they would prefer daylight and calm seas to arrange tenders to shore. Everyone was going about their business and Sparks was at his usual station, communicating with the Connecticut as well as monitoring sonars and listening devices. Suddenly he distinctly heard the sound of a diesel engine, faint but definitely a diesel engine. He summoned over the officer of the watch, no guesses needed there, it was the Admiral, who happened to be in charge of a skeleton crew.

"Sir, I'm hearing an engine approximately 10 knots east of us."

"An engine, in this weather. Are you sure?"

"Yes sir." He slipped off his head phones and handed them to the Admiral. The Admiral first held one of the speakers to his ear and not hearing anything he placed the headset on his head to get the benefit of both ears.

"Dammit Sparks, I don't hear anything but static, you must be imagining things. But because we have nothing better to do we can meander in that direction." With that he tossed the head phones back to Sparks who immediately placed them on his head and was bewildered to find that all he could hear was static. While the Admiral gave orders to change direction and increase speed Sparks played around with a few dials and squelch buttons but still all he could hear was static then suddenly the unmistakable sound of a diesel engine was back on line.

"Sir, noise is back, 9.5 knots east of us." The Admiral barked further orders to full speed and had Sparks radio the Connecticut to maintain their speed and course while they investigated the source of the noise.

As they approached the vessel, they ascended to come within periscope depth of the surface. By now the entire ship's crew was on station and Hargreaves ordered the raising of the periscope, the Admiral quite happy to let him. Dawn was still a few hours off but breaking through the thick sheets of windswept rain Hargreaves quickly located a sail boat and zoomed in on the only occupant he could see.

"I can only see one person on board. Female and very pregnant. She doesn't appear to be too competent at steering the vessel and she appears to be struggling badly. Sir we have to surface and rescue her."

"There's a hurricane beginning to blow out there, surfacing would put the entire crew at risk."

Mary and Janet had been awakened by the activity and were standing on the bridge with the Admiral and Hargreaves.

"Admiral, the entire human race is at risk. If we don't save that baby there is no point us being here." Everyone turned and looked at Janet. Not only was it a profound statement, they were the first words she had spoken since her rescue. She was also the only person who would dare stand up to the Admiral in front of other crew members. The Admiral calmly gave the order, "prepare to surface." As the rest of the crew prepared to surface and carry out rescue procedures Dr. Moore leant over and whispered quietly into the Admiral's ear, "I think the bitch is back."

Dressed in full bad weather gear and safety lines tethered around their waists a group of seamen stood on the deck of the Augusta as Hargreaves gave instructions to bring the sub directly alongside the boat. Because of various technical difficulties they had not managed to turn on the powerful search lights until the very last minute. Two of the seamen had successfully secured grappling hooks onto the stricken vessel and had drawn the boat towards the sub. Grover had climbed down a boarding ladder nearest to the boat and leaned over as far as he dared and held out his hands to the occupant of the boat. It was obvious she was in serious difficulties and for a minute he feared he would have to board the vessel to attempt the rescue. But suddenly, totally unexpectedly she leapt and her arms were holding his. For a few terrifying seconds she was dangling precariously between the boat and the sub. Grover managed to hold onto her and with a strength that materialized through sheer will power he managed to bring her safely on board. While Grover was carrying the stricken woman to the open hatchway Hargreaves shone the searchlights down the boat's open cabin door. As best as he could tell there were no other occupants on board and as the main mast of the boat came crashing down on the bow of the sub, barely missing the seaman securing the front of the boat, he ordered the men to let loose and return inside.

Down below, Dr. Moore was treating his new patient and it didn't need a degree from Hopkins to realize the woman was in her final stages of labour. By now Marlene was unconscious, Mary and Janet were both on hand to assist as they stripped off Marlene's sodden clothes. Between them they dried her and wrapped her torso in warm blankets. While this was going on the birth was imminent and Dr. Moore had hold of the baby's head and was gently pulling its tiny body from the comatose Marlene.

"It's very small, it desperately needs incubation and stabilizing." Dr. Moore said matter of factly to no one in particular. "We're just not equipped for this and with the trauma, well, I don't hold out much hope." After these words from the doctor Janet left the surgery. Mary looked up at the doctor and she started to leave but realized right now he needed her help a lot more than Janet did. Gently he continued pulling the baby from the womb until it and the afterbirth were on the table. He cut the placenta cord, cleared the airways, cleaned the baby and wrapped the tiny girl in towels as it kicked and flung its arms as if it was enjoying freedom for the first time. Dr. Moore passed the baby to Mary who looked down at it as though it was her baby and a small tear ran down her cheek, knowing that it had little chance of survival. It made a gurgling sound and Mary did that cooing thing that all women seem to do when they hold babies. Just then, Janet returned to the surgery and after a brief smile asked if she could hold the baby. Mary gently passed her to Janet who promptly turned around and left the surgery. For a few seconds the doctor and Mary looked at each other, then at the empty doorway, then again at each other before Mary took off in pursuit of her former boss. Hearing the footsteps running after her Janet barely turned her head and whispered, "it's alright Mary, I know what I'm doing." At that moment Mary realized that she did and slowed her pace to match Janet's and like she had been doing for the last few years, just followed her.

She didn't have to follow her far. They were in the galley and so it seemed were the rest of the crew. It didn't take long to realize why. As soon as the doctor had mentioned incubator Janet realized that the kitchen had everything they needed. She had gone immediately to DeVersa who had disinfected one of the Perspex covered warming trays that kept the crew's food warm during meal times. Clean drying cloths had been meticulously placed in the tray and the heating set to 98 degrees, the perfect incubator. Like a small village, nothing could be kept a secret on a submarine and in short order word had got around and the whole crew had become instant god fathers. As Janet approached, DeVersa slid open the curved Perspex lid and Janet gently placed the baby in the tray and closed the lid. On the side of the incubator one of the crew had even made a label similar to the type you see in the maternity wards, it said 'Baby Augusta'. Janet looked at Dr. Moore and gave the slightest nod of her head, he reciprocated. It was a sign of mutual respect, their efforts had provided this little girl with the chance of life which was a rare commodity given the circumstances.

The next few hours were critical for both mother and baby. Above them, the hurricane approached, raging throughout the morning, churning the surface of the sea into an angry maelstrom. In the sick room, Marlene drifted in and out of consciousness and in the mess room, Baby Augusta was visited by everyone on board. During breakfast, as they filed past, they each kissed the tips of their fingers and held it briefly against the Perspex lid and each one whispered a private greeting to their baby girl. Not one of them had any doubt she was going to survive and they were each planning the types of dolls houses and swing sets they were going to build for her. The same ritual was repeated during the lunch session and even the Admiral participated in the ceremony. Based on the doctor's requirements Janet and Mary concocted a drink for the baby consisting of dried milk and various vitamins which were administered with the use of eye droppers, closely monitored by the wary eyes of the numerous god fathers. By mid-morning, Marlene was awake and she was wheeled into the galley on a gurney. The sight of her baby surrounded by the crew like anxious fathers was overwhelming and when they burst into applause, albeit quietly so as not to alarm their god daughter, she began to cry again. A couple of the crew had made her a bunch of paper flowers and on the accompanying card it said 'To Baby Augusta's mommy'.

Chapter 35

HUNKERING DOWN

St. Santia - Caribbean

"Gone? What do you mean gone?" Bob asked incredulously.

"One of the boats has gone and Marlene didn't sleep in our bed last night." Tony replied his panic obvious to everyone.

"Well you were so drunk maybe you hadn't noticed she slept in another room and maybe Danny just went out for a sail." Bob offered.

"I always thought there was something not right about that Danny. Like he had a secret." Joan said quietly to no one in particular.

"You didn't say anything when he decided to come sailing with us!" John remarked.

"Who cares," an exasperated Tony shouted. "The question is, where are they right now? He's taken her I tell you. I'm going to get her." Tony made a move to the door but even as he spoke their hurricane early warning bells were beginning to chime with some ferocity and Bob walked over to look at the barometer, it was under 28.5 and falling rapidly. Dawn was breaking and the sea was surging to the shore powered by gusts of winds accompanied by dark and ugly thunder clouds. Tony reached the door before Bob and grabbed him.

"You are going nowhere." He ordered desperately, "Danny is not stupid, even if he has kidnapped her he wouldn't risk their lives he will be holed up somewhere, waiting out the storm. There's a hurricane out there and you are not a good enough sailor to weather it. You will be killed. Then if this is all a misunderstanding Marlene would have lost you, we would have lost you" Bob was holding him, almost in a lover's embrace, whispering in his ear. It was at that point Maria entered the room and saw the couple, Tony crying and Bob talking softly to him. At first she thought it had all been too good to be true. The relationship, baby, family and an almost idyllic lifestyle all reverting back to their old ways. Until John calmly spoke, "he will be headed back to Florida, we know where he will be. Just be patient son. Wait for the storm to pass. We will find them." John was trying to offer some wisdom and comfort.

"What's going on? Where's Marlene?" Maria managed to stutter.

"Marlene and Danny aren't at the house and one of the boats has gone." Bob replied and realizing he was still embracing Tony he slowly let go.

"Oh my God," was the best Maria could reply as she sat down on one of the breakfast bar stools in the kitchen, dutifully assisted by Joan. Joan held her tight as Maria cried silently into Joan's bosom, unsure whether she was crying because of Marlene's fate or the poignant moment that had just occurred between Tony and Bob. The moment had not been lost on Tony and for a brief period he was cast back eight months into the arms of his lover. But another gust of wind brought him back to reality as it caught the emergency bells and Bob began to take charge and the moment was lost, never to return again.

"We must head for the emergency shelter. The edge of the main storm is nearly on us. Joan, John, get your children together, Tony, you carry the baby I will help Maria."

"What about supplies, batteries and stuff, shall I bring some?" John inquired.

"Everything is in the shelter. We don't need to take anything, just follow us."

For the rest of that day the storm raged, although inside the former recording studio you would never have known it. Periodically, John or Tony would venture out of the room to monitor the weather and to deposit some of the used diapers into the garbage. Ventilation was not the best in the confined space and with the concentration of sweaty, nervous people together with a porta toilet, removal of the diapers was a must. The original planning was based on four adults, now it was five with three pooping, pissing babies. The newly born and the toddlers were not happy in this claustrophobic environment either and they made sure everyone was aware of it. To add further to their woes, Tony was beside himself and had to constantly be consoled and prevented from leaving the room. Bob thought that it had all seemed so simple during their previous dry runs.

Late evening, after a quick check on the weather, Bob reported that they appeared to be in the eye of the storm and felt this was a good time to get out of the room and grab some badly needed fresh air. It also gave him an opportunity to empty the porta toilet and spray some air freshener around. The children and Maria appeared to be holding up well but they still made sure John or Bob was between Tony and the outside world. The skies still looked violent but there was an unusual kind of calm in the air. The waves were penetrating further up the beach than they had ever seen since taking occupancy of the house. In fact, they were hitting the scrub land beyond the beach. Flotsam was being left with every recession of a wave, should be some interesting beach combing there Bob thought. After about half an hour they could see the other side of the hurricane approaching like a brick wall and they could feel the breeze beginning to increase in velocity. Bob shooed everyone back to the shelter and made sure they were all comfortable. During that night, John and Bob actually got a good night's sleep, as an extra precaution Bob slept by the door just in case Tony decided he wanted to do a runner. But Tony slept, albeit fitfully, while Joan kept Maria comfortable and assisted her in the feeding of the island's brood. Edward and Amilia had gotten to the age where they could sleep until the early morning so they were reasonably low maintenance. Eventually, Joan settled down and was soon fast asleep, although by then it was the early hours of the morning.

Inevitably, early morning arrived at one of those few junctures where everyone in the shelter was asleep, except for Edward and Amilia who were actually talking to each other, in their wonderful baby talk. Consequently, they were the only ones who saw someone attempting to open the door of the recording studio.

Chapter 36

COME TOGETHER

Below the Caribbean

The USS Augusta continued to maintain underwater orders until the early hours of the morning at which time they felt it was safe to surface. Unlike Danny and the Hamaxs on their trip to the island, the crew of the Augusta had Marlene on board to direct them to the correct side of the island. Just before dawn they felt it was safe to surface and they were positioned directly opposite the homes a few hundred metres from shore. The waves had subsided enough to tender to one of the jetties and a small crew put to sea to reconnoiter. Marlene had provided instructions as to where everyone would be in the house if they couldn't be seen. Led by Hargreaves, the crew landed without incident and they made their way up to the houses brushing aside branches and loose shrubbery that was in their way that had been deposited there by the hurricane. Hargreaves, was the first to arrive at the house and not seeing any sign of life, knocked on the door and after receiving no reply, attempted to open the door and called out, "Hello, anyone at home?" Again, hearing no reply, he proceeded down the stairs using the directions Marlene had given him. Close behind Hargreaves were Grover and Graneski. Once at the door of the shelter, he attempted to open the door. The door opened but there appeared to be something preventing the smooth opening of the door. Grover assisted Hargreaves to gently push the door until there was enough of an opening for Hargreaves to enter the shelter. A small battery night light was on and together with the light from the stairway there was enough illumination to see Edward and Amilia, smiling and jabbering away at each other without any cares in the world. The submariners slowly entered the shelter and it was as if an alarm was turned on as every one of the adults began to stir and awaken. Bob reacted first with a start but Hargreaves had anticipated this and calmed him and explained who they were, as if they could possibly be anyone else.

"Tony? Which one of you is Tony?" Hargreaves asked as he looked from Tony to Bob.

"I'm Tony," said a disconsolate Tony, still in that land between being awake and asleep.

"Come with me, we have a surprise for you." Hargreaves replied and turned to go back up the stairs. Tony looked around at the others but dutifully followed not having any idea why. As he reached the front door and looked out to the beach, in the early dawn he vaguely saw images of a line of men, two of whom were carrying what appeared to be a stretcher with a bundle on it. Suddenly, he realized who it was and took off like an Olympic sprinter. When he met up with Marlene he bent over to give her a hug but he stepped back in amazement as she pulled back the corner of the blanket that was covering her and baby Augusta. For the second time within the last forty eight hours he fell to the beach and felt that he couldn't get up. Two of the foster fathers from the Augusta, grinning from ear to ear, helped him to his feet and carried him alongside his new family towards the house.

They reached the house just as the others made it upstairs from the shelter. They helped Marlene into a comfortable chair and she was able to show off the latest member of the recent population explosion. Dr. Moore had felt that the baby was healthy enough to be taken ashore providing it was kept warm. Everyone was asking questions at once so it was Hargreaves who quieted everyone done and provided a quick summary of the events of the previous night, he concluded by saying,

"I'm sure at the appropriate time Marlene will fill you in with the details, but for now, we have brought some fresh coffee, juice, bacon sandwiches and pastries from the submarine, courtesy of our chefs. Admiral Stanford will be joining us as soon as the submarine is properly secured. Enjoy," he gestured to the food that had been laid out in front of them while he had been explaining events. The residents did not need a second invitation, realizing their hunger after a long night in the shelter.

After breakfast and still caressing his cup of coffee Tony emerged from the house to survey the aftermath of the hurricane. Submariners were already clearing away debris blown in by the wind and placing them in piles. Introductions were made and conversations ensued centred mainly about the existence of the chickens. The chickens appeared to be enjoying new tidbits uncovered by the hurricane and were going about their business as if nothing had happened. On seeing the birds pecking away at the scraps the crew of the submarine was astonished and was impressed with the stories of the effort taken to raise them, under the difficult circumstances. The remaining inhabitants were beginning to emerge from the house and began to look around. Further introductions were made and jovial conversations were being had by all until Admiral Stanford was seen to be arriving at the jetty. Although the seamen were no longer bound by navy rules they immediately returned to work, such was the respect for their captain. Only now they were not putting out the effort because they had to but because they wanted to.

Not long after breakfast the Connecticut made an appearance and began ferrying crew to the jetty to assist in the clean up on shore. John Hamax's boat had miraculously survived the hurricane, even the porter that was being towed was still attached. This was quickly detached and used as an additional boat to assist in the ferrying of goods and men from the submarines to shore.

The Admiral surveyed the scene and after exchanging names and pleasantries quickly got down to business. He spoke briefly with the residents regarding the implementation of plans, both short and long term to stabilize the habitat. They now had two nuclear submarines at their disposal with additional expertise and resources. They had doctors, biologists, engineers and the know how to accomplish just about anything. There was no reason why a thriving community could not rise from the tragedies of the last few months. A few of the seamen had already decided they would like to stay here on the island and become part of the 'village' life. Mary was even flirting with the idea of setting up house with Hargreaves and dropping subtle hints to that end. As if to condone this, the houses appeared to have weathered the storm, a few tiles were missing from the roof, some of which were later to be found buried deep in the ground and embedded in trees, such was the force of the winds. But all in all the shutters and structure of the house were as they were prior to the storm. A few plants and trees had been torn from the ground but there was nothing that couldn't be re-sowed. In fact, as St Santia was in the direct path of the hurricane, the tidal surge caused by the winds had reached over the sea walls of the island. The rotting carcasses and vegetable matter that had remained in areas not visited since the devastation had now been taken by the sea and nature had continued its cleansing process.

For the rest of the day everyone spent their time cleaning up and being introduced to each other, submariners to submariners and submariners to islanders. Origins were exchanged and as always a few coincidences were unearthed as mutual acquaintances, places and events were discussed. After all the depression created by the devastation these introductions provided a new lease of life for everyone. Approximately mid-morning Janet and Mary came ashore and there was no question that Janet was emerging from the funk caused by her frightening ordeal. She had been provided with a new purpose in life. A new worthwhile, lifelong project ahead of her to ensure the welfare of the next generation and she couldn't wait to get started. Helped by Mary she met the Hamaxes and the other families. Joan was to provide the life experience and Janet was to be the medical matriarch.

Small clusters of men were discussing short term plans and suggestions were being traded back and forth. During all of this there was no stoppage in work and the cooks set up a tent with food being available all day. Dinner was a festive occasion, not too much alcohol but excellent food and drink concocted by the catering staff of the two submarines, who were determined to outdo each other. It reminded everyone of the cook-off programs they watched prior to the devastation on television. They even voted on the fare and it was declared a resounding draw with everyone the winner.

After dinner, fatigue quickly caught up with them all. They all said their thanks and their good nights. The sailors assisted the caterers by carrying their pots and utensils back to the porters for the respective submarines. Mary and Janet helped with the wrapping of the leftover food and the islanders returned wearily to their houses.

Epilogue

The next morning the sun rose on their island for not only a new dawning, but a new beginning in a new world. It was a beautiful sunrise quite common for this part of the world, one that would be witnessed by the island's residents for many years to come. However, this morning was very different. This morning the only witness to the glorious sight was a solitary bird foraging for food along the deserted beach.

Printed in the United States
By Bookmasters